J. F. DANSKIN

The Twisted Forest

Contents

People of Ystrad Clud

AD 869, summer

A ragged line of riders was silhouetted against the sinking sun. As the great island mountains turned to shadows against the late afternoon glow and sunlight reflected off the waves, Donnell held up one hand to shield his eyes from the glare. There was still no sign of movement from their Norse foes on the shoreside road below where he stood, though he was unable to see the occupied village of Weir from this far inland.

He turned and gestured, and the half dozen novice troops picked up their spears again and swung their horses around, each turning at a slightly different angle and forming into a careless-looking line. Donnell sighed, and spurred Beira closer, then passed in front of the small line of troops.

"Your spear has slipped from your stirrup," he said to the first, pointing. The boy Óengus was a promising horseman and strong of arm, although still too young to head a household of his own. The lad nodded, and adjusted the unfamiliar weapon.

The next pair were older, experienced in the saddle but no soldiers, nor would they ever be. They did the minimum required at each training session, then returned to their crofts and families as early as possible. Donnell nodded slightly and passed them by.

The next figure was a real soldier, broad and steady in the saddle. Erik was a former Norse warrior who had stayed in Cardhu after being injured at the battle months before. While most of his surviving fellows had been exchanged with the Norse for the food and metalware that the outsiders seemed to have in abundance, Erik had sworn allegiance to the village and to the Laird, and promised to fight for them if called upon. A muscular man with a short blonde beard and cropped hair, he had no family across on the islands, he said, and no love for the Norse leader Iohric or his henchmen. Donnell wasn't certain about the young man's loyalty over the long-term, but for now he was easy company, and a helpful example for the others to mimic.

"Good work, Erik," Donnell remarked, before turning and giving a few pointers to the older pair. The riders charged once more against their imaginary targets, and then Donnell had them dismount and dismissed the group for the evening.

Turning, he spurred Beira forward, but Erik came alongside him. "Touring the defences, chief?" said the man. "I'll come with you if want the company."

Donnell nodded. It hadn't escaped the men of the fledgling cavalry troop that he preferred his own company, but he appreciated their occasional efforts to bond with him.

"I would be happy for it. I'm going along the forest edge first, then down to check on the new wall. Do your best to keep up."

Donnell spurred the great chestnut mare towards the tops of the village, where there were larger outfields of sheep and cattle, on poorer, hilly terrain. Here, a long line of trees on the higher ground marked the extent of the crofters' lands.

With Erik riding just behind, he then followed a newly constructed path that ran between the drystane wall and the trees. After a couple of boggle attacks in which livestock and tools had been stolen, defences had been improved here too, even although it was in the opposite direction to the new Norse camp. On the orders of Niamh, the Laird's new Luftenand, the walls had been raised to chest height, and had been reinforced with a wooden tower every couple of hundred paces, three in all. People had come to refer to this new structure as the East Wall. It was clear to see where numerous trees had been felled to build these and other areas of the improved defences of the small community, leaving a broad cleared area between the East Wall and Holm's Wood itself.

As Donnell rode, he glanced down and patted Beira's flank with a smile. Whether or not the young nobleman Mac Rath had interceded on his behalf after the Battle of Cardhu, he did not know. But one way or another, the farmer Tarin had received word from the Laird's household that Donnell's debt had been cancelled, and that the former woodsman should be released to help Niamh to prepare Cardhu's defences.

Tarin had been furious, of course, and his anger had deepened when Donnell had then advised Niamh to requisition all of the farmer's horses to help with the defence of the village, and she had agreed. In a rage, Tarin had turned Donnell out of his previous lodging behind the stables – despite outrage from some of the other villagers at this treatment – and had also refused to allow the horses to be stabled there any more.

Now each horse was being looked after by its own rider, and Donnell was living in one of the outbuildings behind the blacksmith's shop, sharing this makeshift accommodation with Malcolm. It was little more than a shed, but he and Malcolm had taken the time to fix it up, repairing holes in the roof and walls. Malcolm in particular had a lot of skills with stone and woodwork, and together they had done an efficient job.

Donnell and Erik now continued to ride past the East Wall until the path turned down towards the ancient earthworks that marked older defences at the north of the village. These had now been reinforced with spiked branches along their length to make it near-impossible for troops or horses to approach from the shore.

"How are your fellows getting on?" Donnell asked, slowing Beira's pace to a walk as they approached the end of this part of their route.

Erik wasn't alone in having changed sides – another three Norseman had been badly wounded in the springtime battle, and had been nursed back to health by the druidess Fenella. They said they wanted to show their gratitude; they would leave back to the islands the following summer, but for now they were among the volunteer foot soldiers who were being trained and guided by Malcolm. As with the mounted troops, these troops were a mixed bunch, mostly farmers and youths, but were gradually learning the skills that they might need to defend the village. The sooner Cardhu could protect itself from attack, Donnell thought, the sooner he could relax.

"Those three are slow and stupid," said Erik, and he gave a short laugh. "That's why they got themselves injured."

"Maybe," said Donnell. "You think we shouldn't use them as mercenaries?"

Erik smiled again, and nodded. "Use them. Just make sure you send them in to battle first," he said. "Maybe their ugly faces will distract your enemies. Talking of which," Erik added, pointing downwards.

They had reached a vantage point on a rocky bluff above the burn, from where the settlements down at the shore could be easily seen. When Donnell and his companions had exchanged the remainder of the prisoners with the Norsemen who had settled there, Weir was little more than a fishing village. Iohric and his troops had retreated there and some of the local fishermen were now part of their horde, with Norsemen also reportedly marrying local women.

Now, there was a near-complete stone keep in a raised site at the top of the village, in the same place that a fortress had been abandoned by ancient people many generations before, and which had been little more than a set of stone ruins during Donnell's childhood. It was clearly a strategic position, and would allow Iohric and his men to watch for any vessels that travelled North or South, and perhaps prey on weaker targets, especially if they worked together with their kinsmen on the nearby islands.

One person in Cardhu was particularly suspicious about the uneasy truce with the Norse. The young woman Sahar – who Donnell had met and allied with when defending the village back in the springtime – had remained there, still hoping for an opportunity to exact her revenge on Iohric. Sahar had suggested that the only thing that had saved the locals from a bloodier conquest was that Iohric simply didn't have enough men after his losses from battle, in addition to losing two longships on the same day. However things had been relatively quiet after an initial exchange of prisoners, and there were now plans to trade with the Norsemen for much-needed supplies of fish and iron ore.

Donnell looked to where Erik was pointing. A dozen or so Norsemen, on foot, had emerged from the keep, and were gathered on the main Laird's road that ran up the coastline. Meanwhile, four mounted soldiers were closing in on them, riding north from Wherrycross, where the Laird of the area lived. Donnell was reminded of the band of soldiers led by Mac Rath who had ridden north and battled the Norse here in Cardhu a few months before.

Donnell dismounted, taking Beira by the reins and walking closer to the cliff edge; Erik did likewise. Donnell was generally considered to be tall, but the younger man stood a hand's breadth above than him as they looked down towards Weir.

The four mounted soldiers on the road had stopped, remaining on their horses. They cast long shadows in the evening light. The men were armoured and had shields, and for a moment Donnell wondered if battle would commence once more. However, instead, the two sides appeared to be talking. After a couple of minutes, the Laird's men turned their steeds and began to ride down the road, back towards Wherrycross.

* * *

"I wonder what that was…" Donnell began, but suddenly Erik's horse shied from something at its feet. It veered sideways towards where Donnell stood; he dodged out of the way, but overbalanced towards the cliff's edge. He felt a firm hand on his arm, and steadied, taking a step back from the edge. "I'm fine," he snapped, pulling his arm away, and then wondered why he hadn't just thanked the man.

Erik, however, was looking at the ground. He had pulled a knife from his belt. "Stand up, fiend!" he growled.

Donnell also looked down, grasping the pommel of the short sword which he now wore, and saw a familiar face crouching in the shadows. "Wait a moment, Erik," he said, putting one hand on the man's muscular arm. "This one is all right. I know him."

The mysterious little boggle who went by the name of Bib stood up in front of them and then bowed to the two men with a grin. "I see Cardhu is very much better defended these days. I can't shimmy up a hillside without having a knife pointed at me." His purple eyes gleamed with what could have been mirth or anger – it was difficult to say which.

"It's good to see you, Bib," said Donnell, not commenting on the creature's unconventional entry point, or how and why he had passed the other defences. The boggle, Donnell knew, couldn't always walk major paths without attracting unwelcome attention. "What news?"

"This little troll is with you?" Erik said, flipping his knife in one hand

and then neatly slipping it back into its sheath. "You are a witch-man, in truth."

"No, he's not with me, nor a servant of mine," Donnell said. "I know very little of the ways of these boggles. The others of his kind you should be very wary of. They mostly haunt the forest; a group of them captured and tormented me for sport not long ago. But I know that Bib, here, is one that can be trusted."

Bib bowed at the compliment, his blue travelling hood falling across his face as he did so. Then he walked past them to the grassy area behind the bluff, where a low wall marked the edge of a sheep pasture. He hopped up onto the wall, and sat. "Much news from the south," he said. "The Laird is mustering many troops".

"We just saw some. Will he move against the Norsemen? If so, we need to know his plans."

Bib inclined his head. "I believe that will happen eventually," he said.

"And Eochaid?"

Bib smiled slightly. "My master is much recovered from his ordeal in Cardhu."

"That's wonderful news," replied Donnell, walking forward towards the wall. "And in good health?"

The boggle hesitated. "Eochaid was very ill when he returned from here back in the springtime. After that, he slept for many days, pale and sickly looking, sweating and filled with dark visions. When he woke, he seemed to be back to his normal self, but I was too optimistic at first. Normally he… Well, let us just say that he has recovered. But it was a slow process. The events took their toll."

The little creature seemed much less sure of himself than Donnell remembered from their previous meetings. He nodded and said, "Please, pass on my wishes. I know I said I will visit, and I certainly still intend to."

Bib cocked his head and narrowed his eyes slightly. "I was actually sent to see the apothecary today, but when I saw you, I thought I would remind you about this visit." He shrugged. "Yes, come to Wherrycross. There is much to discuss. After another week or two, I am hopeful, he will be well enough to receive you."

"Agreed. And can I help with anything?"

The boggle sniffed and looked towards the village. "You can tell me where I might find the red-haired druidess."

When Bib had gone on his way, Donnell completed his circuit of the defences, still accompanied by Erik. Two new stone watchtowers were under construction by the main route between Weir village and Cardhu, though progress was slow, and the mason was arguing with a group of youths who had been helping. Erik and Donnell agreed to meet there the next day in the mid-morning to lend a hand; Erik was due to patrol first thing, while Donnell was required to meet with the village council. The two men then went their separate ways. Donnell had to make his way back towards the wooden watchtowers where he was due to take his turn on guard duty, but first he needed to leave Beira safe and secure overnight.

As he rode, he started to feel the fatigue of the training session course through his body. At least there had been no further wyvern sightings, he thought to himself. Perhaps the great flying beast was truly dead by Eochaid's hand, or had somehow been compelled to return to its home in the north for a generation.

But more sightings of these creatures of dread seemed all too possible in the current times.

The Young Guards

The evening sky was turning pink. Donnell patted Beira's flank firmly as he tied her in the small paddock that ran alongside the blacksmith's workshop, nearby their lodgings – an arrangement which was another outcome of the uneasy truce with Malcolm's father, Willem the blacksmith. On these mild nights he felt reasonably happy to secure her outdoors, especially as it was so close to the village square. It wouldn't be long before he would need to find her a more permanent stable with straw for her to bed down upon.

Donnell paused near the Celtic Rock, the huge and ancient obelisk that sat above the village square and most of the houses of Cardhu, and which was the focus of the druid gathering every Samhain. It was the first really warm evening of the summer so far, and as such the village was still busy despite the relatively late hour. Smells of roasted mutton drifted across the square. He was tempted to find the cook and ask for a bowl, but the time was getting on – he would have to content himself with the dried meat that he had in his pouch.

He noticed a small gathering in front of the tiny roundhouse on the other side of the square where Niamh and her children lived, and started to walk in that direction. The widow was a crofter, and looked after her three children – the toddler Siamaidh, and two older girls, Kit and Rana. After taking up her post, Niamh had established a council on which he was included, and hosted its meetings at her modest home.

Malcolm had later joined the informal leadership group too, due to his taking responsibility for training the foot soldier levies.

The druidess Fenella was also a member of the village council. Out of the three druids who had survived the recent series of events, only she remained in Cardhu. She had also been using the Greathouse which had previously been occupied by Ogledd, the disgraced Luftenand of the village, both to live in and as a place of healing for the sick and wounded, and had also taught Malcolm some of the basics of healing and medicine.

As Donnell crossed the square, he saw that Niamh was directing the loading of a large wagon with farm produce, a job which was being impeded by three of the more prominent crofters of the village. He knew that it was due to be taken down to Weir. The Norse appeared to have an appetite for the summer farm produce from Cardhu and were willing to trade it for fish and metal. Towards the back of the wagon there was also a wooden chest with ropes looped through it; this contained a Norse artefact, Donnell knew – an item that the invaders appeared to greatly value.

Sahar was standing nearby, playing around with Niamh's children. It had been agreed that she would live under Niamh's roof for the time being. The children were in awe of her. In particular, Niamh's twelve-year-old daughter Kit begged to join Sahar's crossbow shooting practice, and tagged along with the young woman whenever she got the chance.

Two elderly men were deep in conversation, leaning on rustic staves just ahead of Donnell as he approached the scene. "No, it was the huge Norse warrior with the white hair that killed the old druid," one was saying. "He pulled out his axe and thumped it into the man's back – typical Norse coward."

The other shook his head. "You didn't see it right, Lan. The druid was slain by a hooded boggle that sneaked out of the woods, just after the Laird had arrived and they were making a truce. That's what got the whole fight started again. Achair told me that, and she was standing right over there". He nodded across the square.

The first man stroked his beard, and looked in the same direction. "Well, all of this happened just as that there Moorish girl arrives in Cardhu. I'm not saying it was her fault, but you know…"

"Aye. Smoke comes from fire," said the other.

Donnell grunted, and pushed past the pair, unwilling to take the time necessary to correct their misconceptions, and greeted Sahar warmly. "I'm heading to the East Wall, my friend," he said, "are you on watch duty, too?"

"Not tonight, Donnell," she said with a wave, smiling and putting one arm around the shoulders of young Kit as she spoke. "I promised to tell this one some of the tales of my homeland."

He nodded; he hadn't said so to her, but he was pleased to see how well his young friend had taken to spending time with the local family. "I'll see you on the morrow, then."

He considered stopping to speak to Niamh about the plans for the following day, but was wary of interrupting her when she obviously had her hands full with tricky village affairs. It was an endless task, he knew. Instead, it was time to head towards his watch.

Walking uphill towards the eastern side of Cardhu, he passed by several houses and crofts. He was headed towards the East Wall with its wooden watchtowers, and the dark shape of Holm's Wood loomed up ahead of him in the dusky light. These days it always felt like much slower progress to be moving on foot, but it made it easier to eat; he munched on a couple of slices of dried mutton as he walked, and washed them down with a drink from the waterskin that hung from his belt.

The darkness was closing in, and a crescent moon glimmered almost directly above, though the dark blue of the sky still provided enough light to walk by, and the remnants of a warm pink glow could still be seen above the jagged mountaintops to his left. A bat flitted past at the edge of his vision, but was instantly out of sight.

* * *

Crossing the low style into the field, he headed towards the centremost and largest of the wooden watchtowers, where those on night watch would always meet initially before dividing themselves among the three towers come nightfall. The centre tower stood several times the height of a man, with a lookout platform at the top and a rail around, open to the elements but with a rawhide canopy immediately above to protect from rain. There were simple rungs rather than proper steps up the side of the structure, with a long stripped-pine branch as a handrail to help people climb up.

Donnell ascended to reach the platform. The other two watchmen were already there waiting for him. It had been agreed some months ago that three people would keep watch for the whole night through, cutting down on the number of watches that each villager needed to do, and eliminating any need for a further shift to wake midway through the night. At dawn, the three would be relieved.

His two fellow guards were among the levies that Malcolm had been training as foot soldiers, and he knew without needing to ask that both were more familiar with a plough than with a bow or sword. Donnell nodded at the pair, saying nothing as he sat on one of the log rounds that served as stools atop the tower. Both men were younger than him – barely twenty summers – and both were short, though one was very skinny and the other quite large. He didn't know them well, nor did he feel inclined to get to know them. In his years of working the horses and riding out to carry messages he had come to prefer the solid company of his horse, Beira, to that of his fellow villagers.

The pair spoke quietly to one another, nodding a greeting but otherwise paying little attention to Donnell. They looked like they had recently filled up on a hearty meal, and perhaps a number of ales as well. The skinnier man even had some grease across his face and through his beard. They looked overly fed and drowsy, and sure enough, it wasn't long before the thinner of the pair had drifted off. The other had crouched down in the corner, and his eyelids were drooping, too.

With a sigh, Donnell stood and lifted one of the bows that had been left here, and nocked an arrow, looking around from the vantage point. Although the sun had disappeared, there was still enough lingering light in the sky to see the ground around them and to see along the wall to either side, though the forest itself was a dark mass. He could take watch by himself for now, and let his fellows sleep off their meal, waking them and sending them to the other two towers when required.

He scanned the forest's edge several times, taking care to look as far as he could in both directions, not just in the flat area immediately in front of him. Even in the gloom it would be easy enough to spot any movement, Donnell knew, and for a long time there was nothing to see. He glanced around occasionally – both of his companions were now sleeping soundly. He was tempted to give them a kick to wake them up, but then considered that it could be for the best if he let them get some sleep in the first few hours. He knew from many years of walking forest paths that the worst of the dangers came later into the night.

Bonfires had been readied along the perimeter of the wall at ground level, one near each tower and roughly halfway between the towers and the tree line, but these were not yet lit. The intention had been to allowing the guards in the watchtower a clearer view of anything that passed by after the sun went down, while keeping their own location in shadow. The fires might also serve to deter predators. Shouldering the bow, Donnell climbed down the rungs to the foot of the tower, and walked over to the nearest one.

Hot coals had been buried there earlier. He nodded to himself; she had her faults, but Niamh was scrupulously organised, and made sure that things got done according to plan. He lifted these between two flattened sticks, and placed them onto the pile of twigs and dry grass which had been set on top of some larger branches and logs. He blew, enjoying the magical orange glow as the coals came dancing into life. Before long, the bonfire was blazing vigorously.

He looked off in both directions. According to the plan, the other fires would be lit by the other pair standing watch, but at this point there seemed little point in his climbing up and rousing the useless crofters who had been stationed to the night's watch with him. Besides, he wanted to stretch his legs. He turned to his left, and set out on the short walk towards the north-western watchtower.

* * *

As he walked, he heard the sheep bleating in the outfield. Some had lambs, and they were clearly gathered together at the far side of the field as if sheltering from the wind, despite the relatively mild conditions. Or instinctively sheltering from the dangers of the forest, he reflected.

Staring at the firelight had momentarily dulled his night vision, but he forced himself to keep looking in every direction. Glancing towards the forest, he stopped, heart suddenly thumping furiously. Did he imagine it, or did something move in there?

Donnell stood completely still for at least as long as he had been at the fire, eyes gradually accustoming again to the darkness. He was a trained woodsman and hunter, and knew how to stay perfectly still when necessary. After he was satisfied that there was no further movement – at least nothing that he could see now beyond the gentlest swaying of the treetops – he moved on, quietly unsheathing his short sword.

Perhaps it was just a deer bolting, or another bat, he told himself. Or perhaps not.

He continued, moving more slowly now, and glancing over his shoulder every few paces. Soon he reached the second bonfire, placed his sword down beside him, and lit it in the same manner. Feeling uncommonly jumpy, he glanced over his shoulder every few moments. But he saw no further signs of movement from among the trees.

Now he had to backtrack, walking past the middle tower and its now-lit fire to reach the third one, off to the southeast around a dogleg in the wall. As he approached the central tower again, moving carefully and quietly, he appreciated how much more he could see. The fire illuminated the ground from near the base of the tower right the way to the forest, including an area of stumps where trees had not long since been felled. He could make out the bottom of the tower, but little of the upper area.

As he walked forward again, there was a twang and a spark, as an arrow shot out from the dark and hit the drystane wall that ran between the watchtowers. He cursed – he should have listened to his instincts when he first saw movement. There was only one thing that could be firing at him now – they were under attack from boggles, intelligent but malevolent creatures that dwelt in areas away from human habitation and were known for attacking lone travellers.

Forgetting about the third fire for the moment, he vaulted the nearest section of wall and began to climb back up to the central tower. Several more arrows pinged past him as he did so, and he yelled, "Boggles – get your bows. And keep down!"

The two guards were quickly wide awake, and didn't need to be told twice. As Donnell reached the platform, one was already clutching his bow and had nocked an arrow to the string, but it was pointing much too high, and he looked tense enough to fire it off at any moment – if it didn't simply drop from his shaking hand. Donnell reached over and put his fingertips gently on the tip of the arrow, guiding the man to change his aim in case he accidentally shot his comrades the next time something made him jump.

The other recruit was in the corner, pale and shaking, and appeared to have dropped his own bow in his hurry. Donnell picked the man's bow up and handed it to him; the man clutched at the string and tried to turn it in his hand, whereupon he dropped the weapon again.

Stepping past the incompetent pair, Donnell moved forward and looked down towards the forest's edge. There was nothing immediately visible; he loosed an arrow into the trees despite not having a mark, in the hope that this might make their attackers more wary.

He then looked back at the two young guards. Despite their sloth and ineptitude, Donnell was starting to feel a bit sorry for the pair. "What are your names?" he asked.

"C… Calin," said the fatter man; "Rian," said the one with food on his mouth, who was unable to keep hold of his bow successfully.

"First time you've been posted on guard duty?" said Donnell softly. They nodded. "Look, there are some strange things in the woods, there is no denying it – boggles and worse. These creatures can frighten us, and I'll fully admit to you, they are dangerous. But we can take care of them. If we don't, it will be the villagers sleeping in their beds who need to worry."

Calin was still holding an arrow to his bow and looking out, making him marginally the more competent of the pair. "All right," said Donnell. "You can stay here by yourself for a moment, Calin. Rian, you grab a spear and come with me – there is still one fire needing lit."

Arrows From The Forest

One by one, Donnell and Rian descended to ground level, and clambered over the nearest section of wall.

Rian looked more frightened than ever as they passed the central fire, but Donnell nevertheless felt glad to have the clumsy man close – or rather, glad that he wasn't attempting to get to grips with the fundamentals of archery while Donnell was walking around below. "Stay close, and keep your spear raised and pointed towards the forest," said Donnell, walking immediately behind the younger man.

They lit the third fire without incident and stood back. Just at that moment, though, there was another pinging noise, and an arrow banged as it struck the watchtower which stood behind them, embedding itself into the wood. Two others followed; one clattered on the stone, and Donnell felt the third pass very close past his face. "To the field, quick," he called, and again crossed over the drystane wall, ducking down behind it.

Rian was slower to react, but the skinny young guard also managed to clamber over and get himself behind the wall without being hit, and had even thought to throw his spear ahead of him. There must be more than one shooter, Donnell then realised, because several other arrows flew out in short succession, some hitting the watchtower with a thudding noise against the wooden surface, and others striking the wall with a sharper, rattling sound.

Keeping almost perfectly quiet, Donnell moved along below the level of the wall, past the tower, and peeked up from the other side. He couldn't see anything at the edge of the trees, but he was still fairly certain that they were dealing with boggles – what else could it be?

He peered more closely, looking for any sign of them, and then noticed a slight movement of leaves. He unslung his bow and let fly an arrow that crossed the open area in a neat arc, and then disappeared into the undergrowth. He then sent a second and third after it; on the third attempt, he heard a strangled yelp from among the trees, and he smiled.

Donnell knew that he was carrying only two more shots in reserve, and it would be difficult to retrieve any of the enemy arrows without exposing himself to their return fire, as most of the fallen arrows were on the other side of the wall. He glanced up at the nearest tower – the unoccupied south-eastern tower near the end of the wall. "We need to climb up there," he called to Rian in a low voice, "I'm low on arrows." He then crept over to the rungs, staying below the line of the wall all the time, and began to climb. Rian followed after him.

On reaching the canopy of the smaller watchtower, Donnell peered down at the forest, then glanced back towards the larger central watchtower where Calin was still stationed. And then he froze. Something was climbing up the outside of the central tower, where Calin remained alone – a large, dark, and hairy shape, clinging onto the wooden structure with its claws.

"Stay here!" he called to Rian. He dropped his bow and then let himself back down from the tower faster than was advisable, clinging to the guide rail and jumping the last half a dozen feet. Abandoning any stealth and only keeping his head bowed slightly, he charged towards the foot of the central tower at top speed and began to climb. As he did so, there was a scream from above him.

* * *

Cursing, Donnell reached the top of the rungs and put his hands up onto the platform, pulling himself up. He saw a large, hairy, humanlike figure immediately ahead of him, and it was bending over the young guard. The man was scrabbling towards the corner to get further away, a look of terror written across his face. He had one hand held up in front of him, shielding himself, and seemed to be nursing a wound.

At first Donnell thought that the creature was perhaps a wolf, which had somehow managed to scramble up and was now rearing up on its hind legs. But then he recognised it as a creature that the wood folk sometimes talked about but which he had never before seen – a wulver. Its head was very like that of a wolf, but its hairy body was more like a man's. It had a small muzzle and jaws but enormous hands with straight, spike-like claws. There was a rotten smell to the beast, too.

Fully raising himself up onto the platform, Donnell unsheathed his short sword, and then moved around towards the creature, holding on to the edge of the balustrade to steady himself. He lowered his sword towards the wulver's side, ready to strike if necessary, but the creature must have sensed his movement for it ceased clawing at the man on the ground, and turned towards Donnell with a snarl.

Instinctively he pulled back slightly, raising his sword, but the creature did not attack him. It looked briefly at the figure of the guard on the ground again, and then turned and dived downwards, head first, from the raised platform. Donnell heard the clattering of its claws – apparently sharp and strong enough to let it cling securely to the outside of the wooden tower as it clambered down. He peered over the edge, sword raised, and by the firelight was able to make out the creature dashing on all fours towards the forest.

He turned back and knelt down to check on Calin. The young

man seemed dazed, and Donnell quickly established that he had been knocked to the ground and had taken a blow to his face, but was not seriously injured. He did, however, have a nasty set of parallel gashes on the arm which he had raised to shield himself from the wulver's claws.

It took a few moments to persuade the terrified man to get up out of the corner, and when he did so, Donnell took a look at the wounds in the moonlight. "Here, let me bind those scratches, Calin. You must have had quite a fright, but I don't think that creature will be back any time soon."

Even in the relative darkness, the wounds on Calin's arms didn't look right. They were puffy, like the flesh around an adder bite. Donnell covered them with the cloth that was used to wrap around the arrows stored on the canopy, but knew straight away that there was only one thing for it – he had to take Calin to see the druidess. And that would mean leaving Rian alone – and, frankly, unable to defend himself. Never mind the whole village.

Calin sat, and started to slump down. Donnell shook his shoulders and the young man sat straighter, but was shuddering, muscles tense and breathing fast. Then, suddenly, he began to cry.

Unfortunately, it didn't seem that Donnell had any choice but to move him. He knelt and put an arm on Calin's back, helping the man up again by lifting under his armpits. With this help, Calin managed to get himself seated at the side where the rungs led downwards. Slowly he turned himself and climbed down to ground level, miraculously not falling as he did so.

Donnell quickly followed his younger companion to the ground, and together they walked a dozen paces towards the village, before Calin slumped down again.

It was going to be a long way back to the Greathouse and to the care of the druidess.

* * *

When Donnell finally awoke the next day, it was late in the morning. Having deposited Calin with the druidess Fenella, he had returned to the wall and sent Rian back to the village as well, then kept watch alone for the rest of the night. Malcolm had obviously decided to let him catch up with sleep, and now their lodgings were unusually still, with no sounds of movement within or outside.

He dressed quickly, and walked out into the village square. The morning was dark and cloudy, threatening rain, but many people were around, with several small groups huddled in deep conversation. But he didn't see Malcolm, or any of the trainee warriors.

Having slept so late, he knew he had already missed the day's village council, as well as his arrangement to meet with Erik at the new stone defences. However, he would see the young Norseman later in the day for training. It was more urgent for him to go and check on the defences. Soon Beira was saddled up, and he was riding hard towards the East Wall.

Before he reached the great outfield, however, he heard the sound of cantering hooves from his right, on the path that led up from the shore to the village along the base of a line of cliffs. He pulled Beira to a halt, not far from the farm where he used to live, and waited.

The approaching figure was unmistakable – ring mail, knotted and braided dark hair, and an enormous black war horse. It was Mac Rath, the knight who had helped to save Cardhu from the Norse incursion back in the spring.

"Well met, woodsman," called out the warrior as he approached. "Are you well?" Donnell had learned that Mac Rath had a reputation as a violent scoundrel among some, but he had so far found the man to be brave and honourable. Of course, their interactions had been brief. From what little he knew of the politics of the Laird's Hall, he was aware that as a bastard son – the Laird being otherwise childless – the man was potentially in conflict over succession with the Laird's brother. The brother, Tudorr ab Owain of Inverkip and Greenock, lived in a broch further up the coast to the north.

"I am well, thank you, though tired – we have been experiencing many incursions from the forest. Boggles, and worse."

"Really?" Mac Rath's dark blue eyes tracked the vista from left to right. "I see that the towers on the wall are complete. Is that where the attacks took place?"

Donnell nodded.

"Then let's take a look, shall we?"

They rode around below the low hills on the approach to Holm's Wood, and paused at the first of the three watchtowers. "These are very impressive," said Mac Rath, "though the walls in-between need to be higher."

"I know. For now, it is helpful to be able to pass to and fro. And they are high enough to impede boggles. But the plan in the coming weeks is to create a gateway in the base of the central tower, and to raise the wall itself."

Mac Rath nodded, and then looked up at the nearest tower. "You worked on these?"

"A little. My friend Sahar designed them. She is a young warrior who has spent time with the Norse, and knows their strategies."

"Indeed?" Mac Rath was at least as interested in this as in the towers themselves.

Donnell nodded. "She has created some brilliant designs that we are still working on. And Malcolm, the blacksmith's son, has used his knowledge and skills in the construction, too."

After riding the length of the wall to inspect all three towers, Mac Rath led the way through the outfield and back towards the village. Local people stood back in wonder as the knight upon his huge warhorse came cantering through the village square, with Donnell just behind mounted on Beira.

Soon the pair stopped again, this time between the two stone-built towers that marked the main path down towards Weir.

"These are less complete," remarked Mac Rath, dismounting and handing his reins to Donnell, and then walking forward for a closer look.

"Yes," replied Donnell, also dismounting. "Our Luftenand, Niamh, felt that as they face towards the Norse's stronghold, their new keep, we should build them of stone. However, it's a slower process without the ready availability of stone from the beach."

The nobleman looked to both sides. "These would also be better if they connected to the walls along those fields."

"Thank you – I will say so to the others. Please be in no doubt – we are very mindful that the Norse could attack again at any point. We have been training a defence force, both foot soldiers and riders."

Mac Rath walked back over to take his horse's reins from Donnell. "Good. And you have been at liberty to do so? The farmer hasn't maintained his claim on your time?"

"No. The Laird's household has freed me from my bond to Tarin, I'm very relieved to say."

The young nobleman nodded with a slight smile on his face, and Donnell wondered if it had perhaps been him after all – rather than the Laird – who had interceded with the farmer. It made him feel very uncomfortable to think that he might be in the nobleman's debt without knowing how things had transpired.

But despite his unease, he felt unsure how to raise the matter, or offer thanks. And before he could say anything more about it, Mac Rath surprised him again.

"In any case," said the nobleman, "you shouldn't expect a Norse attack any time soon. Just yesterday, my father the Laird struck a deal with the Norsemen at Longfort Keep. We can hope that the uneasy truce may develop into a lasting peace."

"A deal?" Donnell frowned, looking down towards the coast, and recalling the riders that he had seen. "But they attacked us, and still occupy Weir. People have been forced from their homes, or subjugated into virtual slavery."

Mac Rath nodded, his eyes shining as he looked at Donnell. "Believe me, I feel the same way. I'd like nothing more than to dislodge them from here. But my father... well. He thinks often of his brother's ambitions, and fears that a war here would weaken our side, leaving us open to an attack. And so the Laird would rather neutralise this threat for now, and take time to build up his forces."

Donnell sighed slightly, and looked back at the two half-completed watchtowers. "Are you saying we should stop work on our defences?"

"Far from it, my friend. We both know that another attack could come as soon as the peace breaks down. We see what others do not. So use the time that this gives you. Work hard, and ensure that when it happens, Cardhu is ready."

Donnell nodded. "We will."

"I will return when I can."

With that, the young knight mounted his stallion and began to make his way back down the main path from Cardhu leading down to the coast and to the Laird's Road.

Treasures

As Donnell returned to the village square and saw the Greathouse up ahead of him, the events of the previous evening flashed across his mind, and he decided to check on the wounded man before moving on to his daily cavalry training drills. The Greathouse was one of the oldest buildings in the village, and the traditional home of the Laird's representative, the Luftenand, but since Ogledd's betrayal and the battle with Iohric's Norsemen it had instead been used as a place of healing. Unlike many of the smaller dwellings in Cardhu it was oblong rather than round, with two straight walls and two smaller rounded ones, one of which contained the entrance – a wooden double door, carefully crafted, and inlaid with multiple carvings of scenes of the Celtic gods battling their foes.

As expected, Calin was inside, being tended to by Fenella. The man was sleeping, and as Donnell approached, he could see that the young recruit was still unwell – perhaps worse than before. One eye was puffy and swollen and his colour was unusual, but he looked otherwise comfortable, and the swelling on his arm had reduced. He was sound asleep.

Fenella turned and came over. "Good day, woodsman. You did the right thing, bringing the lad in to me."

"He looks poisoned."

"To an extent. There is something in the wounds that I haven't seen before. I'm applying a tincture of sorrel, though, and that seems to be calming it, and starting to reduce the swelling. He has passed the worst, and for now it's best that he sleep."

"I sometimes see that herb in Holm's Wood. Shall I get you more?"

"If you see it when you are out, then yes, please".

"I hope to get out to the woods more soon, but the attacks from the boggles have thrown things into uncertainty. Talking of which, did you receive a visitor from one of our small brethren, the one we call Bib?"

"Mmm." She nodded slowly, then swept her long red hair back from her face, gazing towards the doorway with narrowed eyes for a moment. "He wanted some supplies of dried rowan berries from me, but I have a limited amount and cannot get more until the autumn, and so I was unable to help him."

"I see." Donnell walked over to look at Calin's wounds again, and then crossed the floor to check upon another injured soul, a young woman called Avelina who had taken a boggle arrow to the arm while on watch a couple of nights before. This patient seemed to be recovering without any complications.

"You must be very busy," he said to Fenella.

"Yes. But your friend Malcolm has offered to help more – he has a certain knack for healing."

"That's good." He paused, and glanced around the interior of the Greathouse again. "I'm concerned about how aggressive the boggles have been, Fenella," he said. "I mean, they've always been unpleasant, dangerous even, but not in such an…active way. And they are using bows – that's new to me, too."

"It is strange, right enough," the druidess replied, looking at him. "Though they have always been cunning, and able to set traps of various kinds." She walked over to the door, apparently lost in thought, and stood there for a moment, then sighed and walked back over towards

Donnell. "There must be something causing their unusual behaviour. And if this was indeed a wulver that attacked Calin, well…they are dangerous, powerful creatures, but normally gentle – harmless as long as not provoked. I would like to speak to my fellow druid Loarn about this. Although he represents the god Lir, he also pays dues to Cernunnos, the forest god, and knows the ways of such creatures better than anyone."

Donnell made a slight bow and touched his forehead. Although those days were long gone, he had been trained by Macswain in his youth, and like other hunters she paid particular reverence to the ancient god Cernunnos, and so Donnell had come to do so as well. The horned and bearded forest god was a figure that was otherwise little spoken of among village folk, and even regarded with suspicion and distrust.

"Loarn would have a better idea of why the boggles are behaving so unusually," she continued. "He rarely leaves the forest himself. Perhaps I will need to go to Druid's Hame myself soon to seek him out, rather than wait until he next passes through here."

"It's dangerous at the moment, as you can see. I would recommend not going alone. For that matter, I wouldn't travel in the woods alone myself at the present time. We were actively under attack by multiple boggle archers last night. I agree about Loarn but please, if you must go, allow me to accompany you with a couple of hand-picked guards."

She smiled at him. "Thank you. That would be most helpful."

Donnell wondered if perhaps she was mocking his concern slightly, and reminded himself that he was dealing with a powerful druidess, a woman of mysterious powers and who spent a great deal of time in the forest. He nodded in parting without further comment on the plan. "I'm going to check on the defences now, Fenella. Thank you for seeing to young Calin, and speak soon."

* * *

Later that afternoon, Donnell and the young horseman Óengus were tasked with escorting the trading mission down to Weir. The heavily-loaded wagon was driven by the old sheep farmer Wallace and was pulled by a pair of mules. The man's younger son sat on the back, resting against the wooden chest, while the two horsemen rode just behind as guards.

Donnell was uneasy. He called out to the others to be on watch for signs of treachery. Óengus nodded, and raised his spear in his hand, setting its base into the stirrup as he had been taught.

It had been a while since Donnell had come down to the shore. As a child he had frequently wandered down to while away the hours with his friends, diving off the rocks and swimming in the deep cold waters with the beautiful jagged blades of Arran's mountains as a backdrop, and then wandering back up the hill into the trees when it got late or they found themselves hungry. That was before his father's death, of course. After that, his family's debt had led his mother Wassa and young Donnell to scrape a living on Tarin's farm, paying nearly everything they earned back to the wealthy farmer in rent. Doing what he could to help his mother, Donnell had found much less time for carefree swimming and exploring.

The regular patrols from Cardhu typically stopped at the earthworks near Wallace's farm on the north side of the village, or at the rough forested area to the south, and on the main path they went no further than the new stone towers. Donnell glanced at these once again as they passed – each one round and sturdy, made of stone, but only one level high thus far. Although he heard the sound of stonework from inside, he didn't have the chance to stop and study the progress more closely.

Beyond this point the main path between the two villages showed signs of the recent lack of traffic; the route was also covered with weeds which were widespread at this time of year, but would normally have been trampled down by the feet and hooves of those passing this way. This caused the route to feel much wilder than he remembered. If he didn't know how close they were to Cardhu, they could have been making their way down a little-used forest track.

As they reached the Laird's Road that ran along the shore, however, the feel and look of his surroundings changed. Here, the terrain was flat, and the road that ran parallel with the shore and beach was paved and well used. It traversed the entire coastline, joining important centres of the kingdom such as Inverkip, Wherrycross and the Riverlands of Ayr.

The newly-constructed keep – some were now calling it Longfort Keep – sat right beside the old track between the Laird's Road and Weir itself. It was upon a slight rise, guarding the approach to the village houses which sat just behind it. It was simple and square-looking, made of stone and wood, and had no windows or even arrow slots on the lowest level, the entranceway being raised up to the first floor. In all, it looked to be three storeys high, with space on the roof for archers as well. It was undoubtedly a formidable defensive structure, and Donnell marvelled at the speed with which the Norse had established it – though he knew that much of the labour had been forced.

The wagon came to a stop just up ahead of the new fortification, and Donnell looked around at his companions. The horses were restless, and the men of Cardhu were staring with curious eyes around the area.

There was a single Norse guard stationed in front of the building, a man with a mean look in his eyes, and a curly red beard which covered most of his face. He gave a brief nod as they pulled up, and came over to look at the produce, which he did for just a few seconds and with little sign of real interest. He then walked back around the building and out of sight.

After waiting for a few moments, Donnell guided Beira past the wagon and rode a few paces away from the path. He moved past a ramshackle hut until he stood in a point from which he could easily see the comings and goings of the villagers beyond, without the new keep obscuring his view. He was still curious to know the whereabouts of Alna, a woman that Malcolm had expressed his love for earlier in the year, but who had apparently decided to stay in Weir with the Norse. Was she working with or for Iohric? Or worse?

However, something else quickly caught his attention. Among the small cluster of roundhouses, a single cart had been prepared – a much smaller vehicle than their own trading wagon and one with just two wheels, pulled by a small but sturdy ass. The cart was covered with canvas, making it hard to see what supplies were within, though it certainly wasn't piled high with goods. But even from a distance and with the local houses partially blocking his view, Donnell could clearly see the edge of a chainmail shirt among the cargo. Where were they heading, he wondered? Something was clearly afoot in Weir village.

Six Norse soldiers stood around the cart, each wearing helmets and travel cloaks. More mysteriously, there was a very short figure in a goatskin cape among the group. As Donnell looked on, this figure climbed aboard, helped up by one of the soldiers. This allowed Donnell a clearer view, and he saw that it was a very old and wizened man with a flattened nose and deeply wrinkled whiskery skin.

A thin, black-cloaked warrior then walked towards the group and spoke to the wizened old man. He had his back to Donnell, but his cloak marked him out as one of Iohric's closest henchmen, for there was a particular group who all wore black cloaks and appeared to serve as captains of the Norse leader's troops. Several of them had stood at his side when he had unsuccessfully invaded Cardhu back in the spring; Donnell had later learned from Erik that they were Iohric's most experienced warriors, and some were his cousins.

As Donnell continued to watch on, the black-cloaked warrior picked up an ancient-looking long-handled axe from beside the old man on the cart, looked carefully at it, turning the weapon in his hands several times, and then spat on it and polished the blade with his cloak.

He then turned and began to walk away from the group – and towards Donnell.

Mysterious Exchanges

Not wishing to be caught spying on the Norsemen, Donnell nudged Beira's sides and turned back up the path, rejoining at the point where his companions were waiting. He also loosened his short sword in its sheath. He didn't want to cause undue alarm among his companions, but something about the furtive behaviour of the cluster of Norsemen suggested that trouble or treachery were afoot. And if it came to it, his men were heavily outnumbered.

As he paused alongside the Cardhu trading wagon, he could still see the black-cloaked warrior approaching. The man spat again as he made his way towards their visiting convoy. The original red-bearded guard fell in behind him.

Back at the main path, young Óengus was staring up at the new keep as Donnell returned. The entrance to the building was a huge broad double doorway which stood at the top of a new wooden stairway. The door was inset into multiple layers of stone and had been decorated with runes above the threshold. The lower section of Longfort Keep was made entirely of stone, and was in part a reconstruction of the ruin which had stood there before. The uppermost floor and roof area were constructed mainly of wood.

As Donnell approached, Óengus pointed upwards. "The workmanship is superb, Donnell," he said. "My old grandfather would have loved to see this."

"Keep watchful," said Donnell, shaking his head slightly. "We always need to be careful around the Norse." He nodded towards the path along which the guard had recently departed. At times, Donnell felt, some of the villagers were a little too complacent, treating missions like this in the same way that they had always traded with nearby villages. The months since the Battle of Cardhu had been enough to reassure them that no further attacks were coming, it seemed. He considered reminding them that this was different, and they should be more cautious. Nevertheless, he didn't want to unduly alarm them either. The Norsemen and their local allies had been peaceable enough on their trade missions so far – each side had something to gain.

The black-cloaked warrior rounded the corner and approached them, with the guard falling in just behind him. Two further warriors approached not far behind, but they waited by the edge of the building.

While not as scarred as Iohric, the cloaked man was an ugly brute. He had carved teeth and blotchy pale burns across his forehead. His face was thin and skull like, and his arms were bare, showing them to be thick with hair like the limbs of a spider. He had apparently put down the axe that he had been examining with such interest, and Donnell was pleased to see that although he had an axe of his own, it remained strapped securely to his thick leather belt.

"Greetings, villagers," said the black-cloaked one coldly. "I see you have brought food to trade once again. But you know our demand. We want the Loki belt. Return it to us, or there will be no trading, none at all." He spoke very loudly, as if they were much further away than they actually were, and had a strong accent.

Donnell glanced down towards the wooden chest on the back of the wagon; he remembered that 'Loki's belt' was the name the Norse raiders gave to a huge silver disk which they had used as a focus when asking locals to swear allegiance. He dismounted, and strode up to the man. "So you still want that round chunk of metal?"

The man narrowed his eyes as he looked at Donnell, then gave the slightest of nods.

Donnell took another step forward and stared back into the warrior's dark eyes. There had been no sign or mention of Iohric so far, and Donnell decided not to ask after him – this man was in charge for now, that was clear. He was fractionally taller than Donnell, wiry but strong looking. He had thick, long, black hair braided into a knot at the back of his head, and terrible breath.

"How do we know you can be trusted to trade honestly after we return it?"

The man merely shrugged.

"What's your name," Donnell asked.

"Völundr."

The Norseman didn't ask for Donnell's name in return.

Donnell considered whether they should proceed with the return of the sacred object. On the one hand, the item could be useful to keep in reserve for any future bargains or trades that they needed to make. On the other hand, as Niamh had argued, it did belong to their foes. Returning it might build some goodwill, while if they refused to hand it over, the Norse may attempt to get it by force, while the Cardhu defences were unfinished.

And they were still much too weak.

"Very well," said Donnell at last. He gestured to Wallace, and the man and his son lifted the chest from the wagon and placed it on the ground. Two Norse warriors came forward to seize it, and then retreated with it towards the entrance to the keep.

"Now, where do you want the food – and where is our metal?"

The man continued to stare at him for a few seconds, cold and unmoving, and then he smiled, showing his disturbing teeth. Donnell had a feeling that this was someone who understood strategy, and had probably made the same calculations that Donnell had just made, and was at the same point in his thinking – if not a few steps ahead. "No," he said at last. "We don't need your turnips and greens. Take them away – find a different trade to make."

Donnell realised that his heart was thumping. So, they had just been used – tricked into making a delivery, when the Norse didn't need their goods after all. He glanced around once more at his lightly armed comrades. It looked like they would be returning to Cardhu without the supplies of metal they needed – and he could probably be grateful that the outcome wasn't even worse.

* * *

It was drizzling by the time the afternoon cavalry training session began, and thick grey clouds sat so low that the afternoon sun couldn't be seen at all. The sea and the islands were entirely hidden.

Sitting astride Beira at the lower outfield, Donnell watched as his troops arrived one by one. He noticed how poorly-cared for some of their steeds looked. Now that the animals were no longer being stabled on the local farms, the fledgling recruits were expected to see to their creatures themselves, finding space and food on their own crofts or by their dwellings. He would need to address this issue.

"How are you holding up, chief?" asked Erik with a grin as he rode up. "I heard you shot a dozen trolls and wrestled a werewolf."

Donnell shook his head with a half-smile. "Very nice, Erik. You've been making friends with storytellers. But you shouldn't believe everything you hear." He flapped his hand towards his face as a large fly bumbled past, and then struck it away again as it made for Beira's ears. "I didn't do much, and nor have I had any success when trying to complete the latest trade with your former comrades, as you may have heard. Niamh is furious."

Erik sighed and shook his head, but did not reply.

"How was the progress at our stone towers?" Donnell asked.

Erik narrowed his eyes, and looked off in that direction. "The work is good, but it's too slow. The lower level is constructed, and there is a platform inside for defenders, so people can already stand there and use it for bow or spear work. But there is no cover, and the doors are weak points. It would be better to build a pit before each door, with a drawbridge that could be pulled back".

"That's a good suggestion. I'll pass it on to Niamh – she has grand plans for the twin towers to eventually form the gatehouse of a keep, and from there, to connect a high wall that runs right along the front of the village."

The other horse troops had finished their long charge to the end of the field, and were returning to the starting point in a ragged line. Donnell waited until they had all assembled, hooves churning up the now-muddy ground.

"Right, spears down," he called, and waited again. "Now, listen all of you. I want more patrols around the outskirts of Cardhu in order to figure out what Iohric's men are up to," he said. "They have been moving weapons and armour around. I want to know where they are taking it…what new base or trading point they are using. This means that each of you will need to form into pairs. I want the routes varied, so you're going to need to help each other. Erik, you can go with Óengus. You two together, and you two. All right."

The men made eye contact and moved into their pairings without being asked, each one nodding at his partner.

Even as he spoke and began to detail their routes, Donnell realised that he was going to need more troops, and soon. A half day in the saddle was a lot for inexperienced horsemen, and they would need breaks. He resolved to speak to Malcolm straight away about releasing some of the foot soldiers to take turns riding patrols. Perhaps Niamh's sister Branwen could join them, too – she had recently returned from Eas Mòr village after the cruel slaying of her husband in one of the early Norse raids, and Donnell knew that the woman could ride well and was a skilled archer.

"We'll start tomorrow – meet at the village square at milking time. No – make it the day after. I want to get another pair of riders organised."

However when he returned and tied up Beira beside the blacksmith's, Malcolm was nowhere to be seen, and their shared billet was empty. The building was cold, too. Donnell sat down on his bunk, pulled his boots off, and gathered one of the woollen tartan blankets around his shoulders. He wanted to sleep early today, and would rise while Malcolm was still sleeping to take the dawn shift on the East Wall. However, he still felt tense after the failed trade as well as the previous day's attack by the forest, and having slept late in the morning he knew it would be difficult to get any rest now.

Sitting back against the building's wall, he reached into his coin pouch, ignoring the small number of silver groats, and removed the brooch with the amber stone which he had picked up during the battle a few months before. There was something very appealing about the object, and he found himself looking at it when he had quiet time to himself. He held it up in front of his face now, gazing at it closely. It was surprisingly undamaged – he couldn't see a scratch on the surface, although it was clearly very old.

It really was a beautiful object. It was roughly circular, with an arc of gold around the top of the yellowish gem, and a larger area below, decorated with carvings of deer. The areas in between these were filled with interlaced, knotted decorations, so carefully and skilfully done that Donnell couldn't see any ends or ridges on the looped Celtic patterns.

He turned it over in his hand several times. It felt slightly warm to the touch, which he supposed was due to it having been close to his skin, and it somehow calmed him to hold the thing. On a whim, he reached inside his tunic and pinned it securely onto his woollen undershirt. He then lay back, and pulled the blankets over him, turning over new plans for defences and patrols in his mind.

Despite his misgivings, he was soon asleep.

* * *

Donnell rode out early to the East Wall.

"What news?" he asked, as he arrived to relieve the last overnight guardsman. The light of dawn began to show over the hills and forest to the east. The information he received in return was welcome; the boggles were clearly at large, but their actions had been limited to a couple of arrows shooting out through the night and hammering ineffectually into the wooden towers. There had been no further sightings of the wulver.

The departing man certainly looked pleased to be hurrying off to his home, though, Donnell thought. He released Beira to graze in the field, and then climbed up the central tower and picked up a bow. At this time of day, only a single guard would be stationed, and they would stay at the larger middle tower. The watch fires were dying down, no longer needed as dawn broke.

As Donnell gazed from side to side in the early morning light, it occurred to him how cumbersome a standard hunting bow was in the close confines of the watchtower. He momentarily mulled over asking Sahar to join him for a bit of company, as her crossbow would work much better. Her shooting accuracy would be invaluable, too. But he also knew that Niamh would not approve; the older woman was acting almost like a mother to Sahar – something that the younger woman appeared surprisingly relaxed about – and was unwilling to let her stray far, especially with Donnell or any of the other men of the village. This was starting to prove an inconvenience in their plans for the defence of Cardhu, for Sahar's technical knowledge was unmatched.

He looked again in both directions. If he wasn't imagining it, he could see the watchtowers much more distinctly than he had been able to on previous early shifts, right down to the notches and grooves of the timber, and he wasn't in any way straining his eyes. It must be something about the light this morning, he mused. He then looked towards the forest itself. That way, too, seemed to be easier than usual to see. In fact, if he was not mistaken, he could also make out more within the forest, well inside its outer edge.

Then he leaned forward. There was a figure moving deep within the trees. And it wasn't a boggle, that was for sure. It looked to him like one of the wood folk – mysterious small individuals who in many ways were like his own people, but then, also, they were not. They were of a different sort, one who had an affinity with the forest, and they were nimbler and better climbers than any villager.

Some considered the wood folk magical or dangerous, and most didn't see them at all. As an experienced woodsman, Donnell had crossed paths with them many times, most recently when Caelia, a mischievous forest woman who he had known since childhood, had rescued him from capture by a group of boggles just a few months before.

Intrigued, Donnell shouldered the bow and climbed down from the tower, then crossed the few dozen paces to the edge of Holm's Wood.

It didn't take him long to find them. Just a few dozen paces into the forest there was a small clearing with the last dying leaves of wild garlic plants all around, and there he saw three of the wood folk, each in closely-fitting clothes of rough brown leather, and with short bows across their backs. The little people shied away from him at first, but did not flee.

Donnell crouched down and held out his hands in a gesture that he hoped would be taken as a sign of peaceful intent. "Do you know me? I am Donnell of Cardhu, and a friend of Caelia. I mean no harm to the forest folk."

"Caelia is not one of our tribe," said one, a male who stood less than five feet high. "But she is known to us."

"Can you tell me anything about changes in the forest?" asked Donnell.

The three small people looked at each other, but said nothing.

"Please. I know that something is going on. I have spent many long days walking the forest paths. The boggles have been aggressive, and it's only thanks to the druids that one of our young men is still alive. The place seems" – he looked at the trees all around him, breathing deeply of the forest air – "unsettled."

"The druids," echoed one, and they looked at each other again.

"Please," repeated Donnell. "Yes, we know the druids, and they are friendly with us too."

"Loarn will know," replied the forest man at last. "We listen to his wisdom, always. Yes, Loarn will know."

With that, the three wood folk turned away from him, and were soon lost among the trees.

It was a shame that Caelia hadn't been there, he reflected, as he made his way back to the watchtower. The forest folk in general might be flighty and hard to engage with, but he could always trust her – she looked out for him, and had saved his life in the past. It seemed it was going to take another approach to find out what was going on in Holm's Wood; as Fenella had said, it was time to venture in. For now, though, he had guard duties to return to.

An Attack

They were going to need more troops – and ones who could hold their own under the threat of attack.

The blacksmith's forge was already busy by the time Donnell arrived back at the square from his watch, its sweet smoke hung in the air and a painful clanging was coming from within. Tying the horse in the small paddock near the side of the building, he popped his head inside; a lad named Keir, the younger son of Wallace the sheep farmer, had been bonded there as an apprentice a few months back, and was now working hard on a bent-looking sword blade. He was a strong lad, and although his work was still rough and unreliable, he could be trusted to produce certain basic items such as arrowheads and nails. Gradually, the village was building up a stock of weapons, as seemed to be necessary in these dangerous times – as well as the skills required to fend for itself.

Turning, he circled the building. He needed to speak to Malcolm about recruiting a couple of foot soldiers to the cavalry troop, but there was no sign of his friend nearby, and so he walked over and entered their lodgings. Again, though, he drew a blank. Perhaps the man would return if he waited for a short time.

Inside, there was room for both of them to have a bunk, and they had placed a couple of split logs near the entrance on which to sit when they were eating. The door was wooden and Malcolm had affixed a simple bolt to hold it fast at night. They both had shelving for their belongings, too, and Donnell had taken his small chest from his previous lodgings – the one possession that he retained from his childhood in Cardhu.

Now he opened the chest. It mostly contained small items of clothing, but there was one item in there that he especially wanted to keep safe – the shimmering white travelling cloak which belonged to the spellcaster, Eochaid. He lifted it out and held it up. It was of no material that Donnell had ever seen before, and he had quickly come to recognise the special properties of the garment – it was almost entirely waterproof, and seemed to close in on him in windy conditions instead of blowing around like most hoods and cloaks did. He had never felt too cold in it, either, though of course he had not yet worn it through the winter. While thieves might not recognise these properties, they would surely notice the golden clasp that held it closed at the shoulders. For this reason, he buried the cloak below his other possessions when he wasn't wearing it.

He returned the cloak to the chest, and pulled out his spare woollen undershirt to change into. As he did so, something fluttered out of the chest from where it had rested inside a fold of clothing. At first he couldn't think what it was – he owned no books or parchments. But as he stooped and picked it up, he recognised a letter. The Laird's letter. It was the one he had been tasked to take to the Laird's brother at Inverkip some months before. He would have done so, too, had kidnapping by boggles and guardsmen, Norse invasions and a wyvern attack not got in his way.

The young nobleman Mac Rath had at the time informed him that the message pertained to the succession in his own noble house. Donnell had intended to give Mac Rath the letter, since he was much more likely to speak to the Laird than Donnell was, but had now twice forgotten to do so. Well, at least he could now carry it with him – perhaps he would see Mac Rath again, or else pass it to Macswain, the Laird's huntsmaster.

Donnell changed his undershirt, carefully transferring the amber brooch to the clean garment, then donned his jerkin and tucked the unopened note inside it. He then splashed his face with some water from a half barrel at the foot of his bed.

At first he had been wary about sharing his living quarters after so many years of living alone with just horses for company, but he had always found Malcolm very easy to get along with. And his old friend seemed in good spirits about it, too. Donnell had worried that with the new apprentice at work nearby, it would distress Malcolm to be reminded on a daily basis that he was no longer able to smith himself, after a combination of his injury – losing part of one arm – and his patchy relationship with his father Willem had ended any hopes of being taken on as a blacksmith's apprentice, back when the pair of friends were bonded to their trades almost ten years before.

* * *

Stepping outside, somewhat refreshed, Donnell looked around again. It was already a warm morning, with the summer sun high overhead to the south east. It promised to be a fine day, in contrast to the damp and gloom of the day before.

Sahar was playing with the children over by Niamh's croft, and he walked over to greet his former travelling companion. He noticed how much tidier she looked than when they had first met. Her travel clothes had been patched and washed, although her curly hair was as wild as ever.

As he approached the house, he finally saw Malcolm – far beyond the croft, near a cluster of mature hazel bushes. The levies were taking it in turns to circle the bushes while holding a spear; each time one finished, they passed the spear on to the next person. Donnell nodded with a slight smile. The task of training the village's levy foot soldiers seemed to have provided Malcolm with a welcome distraction, as he had rarely complained about the situation in the smithy, the downfall of his romance with Alna, or the threats that they were facing from the Norse invaders.

Donnell smiled to Sahar as he approached the house, but then remembered that he should first speak to Niamh – he already knew that he would have to miss yet another of her command meetings in order to run one of the longer patrols himself. With a brief wave to his young friend, he popped his head inside the door of the small croft house. There, Niamh was deep in conversation with another crofter, and she looked around as he entered.

"I'll be patrolling later," he said. "Is there anything you need from me before the next meeting? I will more than likely miss it."

"Thank you for asking, Donnell. I intend to speak about the number of guards we put on watch, and also have more patrolling within the village itself. But if there are any changes, I'll let you know later."

"Exactly what I was thinking," he replied, and then glanced briefly at the crofter with whom Niamh had been speaking. It was best not to delve into too much detail about defensive arrangements in front of other villagers, he had found, as the locals tended to panic easily. "I've been meaning to speak to Malcolm anyway. I'll try to catch up with him before I ride out."

"Very good," Niamh replied with a curt nod.

As he walked outside again, he noticed that Sahar was looking preoccupied.

"Everything all right with you, my friend?" he asked, as he reached her. He smiled down at the younger children as they peeked inquisitively at the sword hanging from his belt, and then began to walk with Sahar off to the side of the small croft house.

"Well, what can I say. Since your wulver attack, Niamh is re-thinking everything to do with the defences."

"Good," he nodded. "Yes – she said that she has plans to increase the number of patrols – I'm sure we can all agree with that. Is there anything else that I should know about?"

"A couple of things. The foot patrols will be going further out, and it has also been agreed that two people will be in every watchtower overnight from now on. Oh, and" – she caught his eye with a slight smile – "there will be strict rules and punishments for people falling asleep while on watch."

He chuckled slightly at the memory of the complacent pair of lads dozing before the recent attack. "Those things all sound like an improvement," he said.

"Very convenient for the Norsemen down at the shore, if you ask me," she replied loudly. "Now all these people are focusing their efforts in the wrong direction." She spat off to the side, and then looked over in the general direction of the road down to the coast, while absently pulling out one of her own knives and testing the keenness of its blade. Donnell noticed Niamh's youngest daughter, little Siamaidh, attempting to spit, too.

"'These people', Sahar?" he said gently. "They are your people now, unless you plan to return to the North Islands."

"There is nothing for me back there, you know that. And, well…" She looked at her feet. "I am quite liking having ordinary folk around me again. I was alone for too long. Not that this will last, in the end."

"I don't see why not."

She looked at him directly, the momentary uncertainty gone from her appearance. "In any case, I have yet to do what I came here for."

"Gaining revenge on Iohric? Yes, I haven't forgotten. Be patient – we are on the same side with that, and his time will come…" Donnell paused as he saw Malcolm approaching. The training session had been dismissed, and his friend was now coming towards the village square past the side of the croft, locked in stride with one of the Norse soldiers who had joined their side after being wounded fighting for Iohric.

"I don't trust those men," muttered Sahar.

"You should give them a chance. Erik has been a good recruit for me."

Little Siamaidh had now come over to stand with them; she tugged at Donnell's smock, and he patted the child on the head. "Niamh's looking after you well?" he asked, changing the subject.

"She is very good to me," Sahar smiled. Niamh had astounded all of them with her seemingly limitless energy since being appointed Luftenand. She had now emerged from her house, and was calling out commands to one of the local farmers. Sahar looked back at Donnell. "Look, there have been some real improvements. She listened to me about the towers, and I know you and Malcolm have been working hard with the recruits, but there just isn't a way with martial skill from an early age, like happens back home."

"What do you mean?" he asked.

"Everyone is a bit, I don't know… slow, in how they talk and act. They're careless, not like people who have actually grown up under a constant threat of attacks. The children hardly practise weapon skills at all. People are still wandering off with no heed to the dangers, unarmed, sometimes alone. No wonder most of the grown-ups can barely manage a spear."

He nodded and smiled slightly, looking down at Siamaidh and suddenly imagining how the villagers would react if all of their daughters took Sahar's approach to weapon skills and combat. "Right, yes. Fine. You know, if you wanted to teach some of the youngsters archery or knife throwing, I'm sure they would love it, and it might save their lives one day. You can set up an area of the village, maybe turn it into some kind of contest…?"

She nodded, thoughtfully, but before she could react with any objections, Donnell slapped her on the shoulder and began to walk away, hurrying in the same direction that Malcolm was headed. "Have fun," he called back, "and speak soon."

* * *

Donnell made his way away from the bustle of the village square on foot, and began to head downhill, near to where the path to the coast began. As he passed by, he saw Malcolm sitting on a wall off to one side, near where a tumbledown house had grown high with weeds. He was sitting below a spreading beech tree, but in a spot that was catching plenty of warm sunshine. Malcolm had his back towards him, and was looking down towards the shore, and so he didn't see Donnell as he approached.

"Good place for thinking."

Malcolm looked up with a start, then waved to his friend to join him. "You look tired, Donnell," he said.

Malcolm himself was covered in sweat and somewhat red in the face, but Donnell didn't point out the irony of the comment – he did feel exhausted after his early start.

"Yes. I've been up for many hours already, my friend."

"Why don't you head back to our lodgings and get some rest?"

Donnell glanced back in that direction. "I don't think so. You know as well as I do that it's hard to get any peace there during the day…" He was about to say *due to the noise of the smithy*, but decided to avoid that topic. "There would most likely be a stream of visitors asking about defences and troops," he finished.

"So you decided to take a walk instead, and clear your head?"

"Sort of," Donnell replied. "But also, I wanted to speak to you about the watchtowers."

"Why? How are the defences holding up?"

"Another raid overnight a day ago, but it was a lot calmer last night. There have been things coming out Holm's Wood that I didn't even know were in there. Most of our guardsmen are little more use than children, to be frank. They are easily scared. So we have no choice but to sit and watch, firing the occasional stray arrow at anything that moves near the trees. We need more troops."

"I'm doing my best, Donnell, but my newest levies are not up to much. They're certainly not ready for combat yet."

"I'm sorry, Malcolm. It was no criticism of you. You're doing well, but the people aren't used to this, as Sahar was just pointing out to me. You'll get them trained up soon, I'm sure. Honestly, you're so much better with people than I am."

Malcolm returned his gaze outwards, towards the shore. "Mmm," he said. "I don't know about that."

Donnell sat down on the wall beside his friend. "You've had some bad luck, old friend, but it doesn't change the fact that you are one of the finest people I know. I'm sure things will change. Perhaps the right woman is just around the corner."

"Thanks, Donnell. But really, who wants a one-armed man without a trade?" Malcolm pointed at his left arm, missing below the elbow, the muscles of his bare right arm rippling as he did so.

Donnell nodded for a moment, and said, "We all have our disadvantages. What about the druid, Fenella? She's very beautiful."

"For such a smart person, you're not very observant, are you? I don't think druids marry, and besides…well."

Donnell said nothing, but smiled to himself slightly at the prospect of Malcolm, of all people, objecting to a match on the basis that it was inappropriate. He had spent the last half year wooing the daughter of a family of fisherfolk in Weir, who were followers of a different religion, hated the people of Cardhu, and were now apparently allied with their Norse enemy.

Malcolm hopped up from the wall and began to pace back and forth. He looked about to say something a couple of times, and Donnell waited, rubbing at his temples to stay awake.

After a short while, Malcolm continued, "Talking of trades, there was something I've been meaning to tell you."

"Go on. I am listening."

"I'm thinking of studying again, you know – learning from old Eochaid. Seeing him again after all those years got me thinking, and then when you told me that he has recovered and is now in Wherrycross..." Malcolm paused again.

"So – what is it?"

"Donnell, I know that there is more that he could teach me. I miss reading...I am sure there is much that I could learn from him, even at my age. I want to ask for his advice. Perhaps get hold of one or two books to study from. That way, I could learn lore and come to help others like he does."

"Well, why don't we just ask him. I've been thinking of riding out there soon to pay a visit," said Donnell, standing. "We could travel by wagon," he added, knowing that Malcolm wasn't confident on horseback. "You know. If we can't trade with the Norse, then I assume we will be taking the goods to Wherrycross soon instead."

"I don't know if Niamh will be in favour of that," said Malcolm. "It's a time-consuming journey, and the last mission that went there was threatened by a group of raiders. She's concerned that the risks are only increasing."

Donnell nodded, and then sat back down in the sunshine, this time with his back against the wall. "She is, but it can't be helped. Trading with the Norse is more dangerous still – they've shown that we can't rely on them, and it's only a matter of time before they betray us fully and attack again. When Niamh looks at the supplies, I think she'll realise that we have no choice but to send out more of our goods to market. It's summer now, and the crofters need to sell. Besides, we desperately need more iron for the smithy, and at least two more horses." Donnell rubbed his eyes and looked around. "As for the danger, we'll think of something," he added. "It surely couldn't hurt to have more of us along on the trip."

"Well, I'll suggest it again," said Malcolm with a nod and a smile, and began to walk off.

Not far away, Donnell could see that people were again at work on the pair of stone towers near the road. He remembered his recent discussion with Erik, and resolved to go and help out with the construction later that day. Perhaps if he could just get a little bit of rest. Just for a moment – and then he would get moving again. His eyes began to close.

* * *

Donnell awoke to shouting. Blinking his eyes fully open, he saw several people running. He sniffed – there was an overpowering smell of woodsmoke, and he stood and turned towards Holm's Wood. Even from this distance, he could see that flames were rising from one of the wooden watchtowers, and a long wide plume of thick smoke was drifting right across the village.

He sprinted the few hundred paces to the village square, and grabbing the first villager that he saw on the way who was heading the other direction. "What news?" he shouted at the man.

"Boggles, they say," said the man in a shrill voice. "Hundreds of them. Hide!"

"Go and get your spear, then," replied Donnell with disgust, "you were given it for a reason". Releasing the man, he covered the remaining distance to his lodgings behind the blacksmith's. Following his own advice, he took his spear from where he had rested it behind the door, and then untied Beira and released her from the small paddock. He mounted up and broke into a canter, careful to avoid running down any of the other locals who were milling around on the road.

Sahar was at the top of the square, crossbow in hand; Niamh beside her shouting directions to several men and women nearby. Donnell pulled up beside them. "Jump on," he said to Sahar, "it sounds like there are some boggles we need to deal with. Let's hope it's nothing worse."

Sahar took hold of his hand and started to pull herself, but Niamh put her hands on the young woman's shoulders. "Absolutely not. You will not ride off with him, Sahar. You are an unmarried woman, and people will condemn it."

Donnell started to speak, but Niamh give him a determined glare, and he decided that it was not the time to argue. With the briefest of nods, he spurred the mighty chestnut mare again, and galloped the remaining distance to the wall and watchtowers, hoping that his friends would catch up with him soon.

He guided Beira up a track towards the outfield, and then to the low drystane wall on the village side, which she leapt easily. In the field itself there were sheep and some half-grown lambs, though several lay dead and bloodied, and were being dragged away by boggles. Others were still being chased around by boggles with knives. Some of the attackers were using slingshots or small recurved bows to target the animals.

Beyond this ugly scene, it was clear that that the defensive wall was damaged, and the nearest watchtower to him, one of the smaller ones to the eastern side – was in the later stages of being consumed by a flaming inferno. There would be nothing left of it.

At first there were no signs of local guards or patrols, but then he spotted a lone figure sprawled on the ground near the foot of the flaming tower. He thought he could see signs of movement, though the man clearly had broken a leg at the very least, and couldn't rise.

The boggles had spied Donnell, too. One took aim with a bow, and Donnell ducked down low to his horse and charged, raising his spear and holding it steady at shoulder height as he rode. On his approach the creatures scattered in every direction, only to regroup further off and begin to reload their weapons.

There were too many of them and in too many directions for him to go after them all at once. However, it occurred to him that rather like driving a school of fish into a net, they were likely to move towards Holm's Wood if he charged. Without hesitating he turned and made another pass with the horse, turned again, and then made yet another. The creatures were gradually being driven back towards the flames. But some of their sling stones were starting to hit their mark, and he heard Beira whinny in pain.

By now, he could see that at least half a dozen of the creatures had gone back through the broken section of wall and were heading for the forest, dragging the carcasses of slain animals, while a similar number remained in the field ahead of him. Two more had gone over to the stricken guard near the foot of the tower. As Donnell crossed the field once again, he saw their rusty daggers slashing at the man, and knew that there would be no saving the villager – the creatures appeared to be butchering him like they had done with the animals. And then a large flaming timber fell from the tower, hitting both boggles and guard alike.

Donnell was still moving, and instinctively ducked as another arrow was released in his direction – another near miss. Fortunately, they lacked much in the way of skill with their new weapons, he thought. But just then, he felt a searing pain in his thigh, and knew he had been hit.

Struggling to maintain his focus through the pain, Donnell paused, sat up in the saddle, took aim, and threw. His short spear glided through the air, taking the nearest boggle full in the chest and knocking it to the ground. Two of the others fled, through two with bows simply retreated further, stringing further arrows.

Suddenly he realised that his comrades were behind him. One of the boggle bowmen jerked and fell to the ground with a crossbow bolt in its neck, and the other suddenly dropped its bow with a terrified look on its face, turned, and ran. It hadn't got far before Erik charged it down, spearing the foul creature.

Donnell looked round to smile in Sahar's direction, then looked down. This was a mistake. There was a strange spinning sensation as he looked at his leg, which seemed to come closer to his face and then move away again before he realised that it was his whole body that was moving and he was, in fact, falling…

Defensive Plans

Donnell awoke. The ceiling above him was unfamiliar, steeply-pitched and dark with smoke. He sat, but the swimming sensation overtook him, and so he lay back again. He was in the Greathouse, he realised. Peering to the side, he could see another injury victim nearby – an old bearded crofter, perhaps also hurt in the recent boggle incursion.

A moment of panic overtook him as he remembered his injury. How bad was it? He looked down, lifting the blanket that was draped over him. His leg was strapped tightly across the left thigh. He flexed the muscle tentatively, and winced. It was very sore, that was for sure, but it didn't look like he was going to be permanently crippled.

"It was quite nasty, actually – deep. But you're healing well so far." He looked up, and saw the druidess Fenella across the room.

He had been badly wounded in the right thigh as a young man, and now it looked like he would have scars on both legs. On that occasion it had been a much more personal attack – a renegade druid shapeshifter by the name of Fáelán had taken the form of a boar, and had pursued and charged Donnell down. The attack had seen his leg gashed deeply by the boar's tusk – but not before he had struck the renegade a mortal blow with his hunting spear.

Fenella got up from a wooden bench and walked over to him, squinting slightly against the light that was flooding in from the building's entrance. "Here, drink this."

She proffered a small earthenware goblet with a murky liquid inside. Donnell hesitated, and then took it and drank. It tasted sweet, but after a moment his mouth felt as if it had filled with fire.

"Uch…that tastes disgusting," he said. "What are you trying to do to me, Fenella?"

She raised her eyebrows slightly, her green eyes fixed upon him. "Hmm. Well, I suppose your complaints are a good sign. You've got a bit of spirit left, and might even survive." She took back the goblet. "I'll bring you something to eat – I'm fairly sure you'll be able to keep it down."

She touched gently at the strapping on his leg; it hurt as she did so, but was more of a dull ache than the searing pain that might indicate a wound being badly inflamed. "Yes. It's looking a lot better now, Donnell. Just take it easy for a few days, all right?"

"Will I be able to ride?" It occurred to Donnell that his planned scouting missions to check upon the Norse activities were due to start.

Fenella took another long look at him, then gave a curt nod. "Give it one more day," she said. "Two for preference. And don't go too far."

"Thank you." He looked down at his strapped leg again. "You know, I don't know if you would remember, but…"

"Yes, I remember. I healed your other leg, too."

"You do?"

She moved away, and began to prepare the promised food – a cold porridge of oats with a dollop of honey. "You were carried back here unconscious and covered in blood," she said, "I remember it very well. Macswain was quite worried, you know. She's a good person, if not always a very warm one."

He sat up as the druidess brought the food over, and he began to eat. As he did so, he studied the woman, who had busied herself clearing up some supplies and the discarded goblet. Donnell had always admired her flaming hair, and the serene quality of her fair, freckled face. Right now, though, it was serious-looking, and her tiredness evident in the shadows and fine lines under her eyes. How long was she going to stay here and help the village, he wondered. Two of Fenella's fellow druids had died in the attack on Cardhu in the spring; one, the traitor Gabrán, had stabbed their leader Congal, only to be killed himself by the Norseman, Iohric. The other two, Loarn and Méabh, had left soon afterwards – perhaps to return to their base in Holm's Wood, while Fenella had remained in Cardhu to tend the wounded. She had also been meeting regularly with Niamh, Malcolm and Donnell to update them on the recovery of their warriors and other injured villagers, but her future plans had never really been discussed.

He decided to tackle the issue directly. "Are you able to stay here with us?"

She gave a single slow nod, accompanied by a slight smile. "Well here I am, as you can see. My healing powers are at their strongest in this place near the Rock, and recently people have begun to come here, rather than my travelling to them. But I still need to…well, I have some other places that I need to travel to. I belong to Ystrad Clud, not just to one village."

"And what about your brethren?"

She pondered the question for a moment. "The other Mor-druids are also stronger here," she said at last. "Our power was greater as a group. But now things are out of balance."

"I see." Donnell nodded silently. This wasn't what he had been asking – but it made sense. The circle had been broken, and only three of the great druids still survived.

She pulled her robes more tightly around her as she continued speaking. "I believe that this is the main reason why your village is being attacked by night. It's not a separate challenge – the threats are connected. You are now seeing the necessity of the work that we did to maintain peace between living things in this realm."

So, he thought to himself, it was no coincidence that the village was being attacked from multiple angles. Something was out of balance, and it was connected to the mysterious powers of the druids.

"Can I help at all?"

She looked away, and circled the room, thinking.

"I need to find a way to…" She paused again, and then looked at him, coming closer as she spoke. "When I mentioned travelling…the thing is, I have to find a way to restore the Mor-druids. And that will involve uniting the surviving members of our ancient clans."

"What does that mean, exactly?"

"You have seen the druids come here each year. As you know, each one of us is the representative of one of the gods. My bond is with Brighid, goddess of spirit and healing. When we came together, we five were able to channel the five greater gods, one of us connecting with each. Without this circle, the protection of the kingdom is weakened. If this isn't put right, the power will be lost entirely."

"So there are other, less advanced druids that you can bring into the group?"

She looked slightly amused. "You could put it that way. Others will eventually join the circle, yes, but prior to that they are already druids."

"And new druids come from these clans that you mentioned?"

"Each one of the Mor-druids takes over from a clan member. But the clans are small. I succeeded my father before me."

"And I suppose this needs to be done quickly, then, if we are to avoid further attacks?" he asked, starting to get up.

"If not before, then it must be done by Samhain of this year. That is when we renew the great protection ceremony."

He paused. "Can't we address it before that?"

"We will do what we can. But Samhain is when it is – we can't initiate the ceremony sooner. And please don't underestimate this – it is a task that will take some time, and will not be without its challenges. All the signs suggest that the druids are under attack, too."

He nodded again. "Fenella, I will help if I can."

"The circle has been broken," she said, echoing his earlier thought. "Perhaps if you help us now, we can restore the balance."

* * *

When Donnell left the Greathouse an hour later, limping as he did so, he realised with some relief that it was still very early despite the bright sunshine – a chill summer's morning. He checked on Beira, refreshed her water, and stroked the horse's face. The little paddock was too small, he realised, and he could tell that she was unsettled. But he must thank whoever had taken her back here after the boggle attack.

He then hurried on to the village square, thinking that his scouts would need further direction and perhaps a bit of clarification and encouragement before they set out on their long morning scouting missions. However, on his way he crossed paths with Erik and Óengus, who appeared almost ready to ride out on theirs, and were packing some food into their saddlebags before departing. He waved to catch their attention. "No further than the Eas Mòr waterfall," he said. "And back by midday. Be prepared to report everything you see. If there are any Norse soldiers at large, turn and get back here straight away."

"Got it, chief," replied Erik with a wink.

As the young Cardhu man and his Norse companion finished packing their supplies, Donnell turned and looked towards Niamh's house. Sahar was sitting on the bench outside the house, and he waved to her. She was stringing gut bowstring onto new short bows that she had recently carved from yew branches. Two youths, only a year or two younger than Sahar herself, were waiting eagerly, and he saw a cluster of others on the other side of the square who had already been equipped with similar bows and were starting to practise shooting.

"Are you well, Sahar?" he said, limping over.

"Oh, you're walking," she said, glancing up momentarily, then returning to her craft. "For a while there, I thought you would probably die."

"Very funny. I believe I owe you my thanks – and not for the first time."

She nodded with a half-smile, and then placed the bow she was working on carefully down on the bench. She rolled up the remaining bowstrings and tucked them into a pouch at her belt. "Those skinny little creatures make difficult targets, so it was a good challenge." She stood. "I don't want to get out of practice. Must say, you gave us all a fright when you fell off your horse. We didn't know how many times you'd been shot."

Together, the pair walked over to the centre of the street, where Óengus had just finished readying his horse. Sahar pulled a patch of long grass and fed it to the animal, then stroked its nose. "The Norse have more men here now. And do we know what they are planning?" she asked. "They will come for us. We need to be ready when they do."

He gave her a wry smile. "Working on it," he said grimly. "As are you, of course." Although Sahar had no official role among the village's leadership, she had already proven herself invaluable many times over in terms of identifying flaws in their defences and suggesting effective improvements. When she attended the leaders' council meetings that Niamh held, it was in part because she was living in the same house, but the others had started to draw upon her expertise with increasing frequency.

"Talking of which, I have something to show you," she replied. Crossing back to the house, she led him around towards the side. "Come on," she called to Niamh's girls, who were at the back of the house, and they both followed in her wake. Erik, who had been standing waiting for Óengus, passed the younger man his horse's reins and followed.

Donnell was by now feeling a lot of discomfort in his leg even from the small amount of walking he had undertaken so far, but this was soon forgotten when he reached the back of Niamh's property and saw the series of defensive mechanisms that Sahar had been working on.

"What is this?" he said, stopping to look around.

She smiled, and stepped over to a wooden post in the ground, to which she had rigged two of the recurved bows that the boggles had dropped back at the field. The bows were attached horizontally, and connected together by a pair of wooden beams. "Look," she said, reaching out to demonstrate her contraption. "The arrow drops down like so," she pointed, "and if you pull this wooden handle, it stretches back the bowstring. Then all you need to do is release." She demonstrated the effect; when the makeshift wooden handle was lowered, an arrow was released from each bow simultaneously, with both arrows arcing high towards a huge oak that stood twenty feet away. As each one thunked cleanly into this target, two more rolled down to take their place.

She smiled. "And I've nearly finished a larger version that can shoot spears."

"That's absolutely brilliant, Sahar," said Donnell, moving forward to gently run his hand over the mechanism.

"Works kind of like my crossbow, really," she said, with a satisfied smile.

"I like it," said Erik with a grin, just behind where Donnell was standing. "Can I try?"

Sahar regarded him with a cool expression. "Fine. But only if you go and pull the arrows out afterwards," she said. "And if you're lucky, we won't shoot you on your way back."

* * *

"It will really help if we get this fixed onto the East Wall soon," said Donnell, back in the village square. "And make more of the same if we can. Not least because half of the local guards don't know how to shoot a bow." He had helped Sahar to carefully disassemble the bow mechanism, and they had carried it together as far as the square.

"Hmm. I'm not sure you should let the local farmers use this," she replied. "Who knows what they might shoot with it."

"Well. We can just hope that the training brings them on as guards pretty quickly."

As they spoke, Erik and Óengus called out in farewell and rode off to begin their scouting mission.

"Where are those two headed?" asked Sahar, as the pair departed.

"Hopefully to find out as much as they can about Iohric's movements. The Norse are up to something, and we are not going to find out what it is unless we have reliable scouts going out every day and starting to piece the information together. Erik and Óengus will head past the wall, and then ride along the edge of Holm's Wood towards Eas Mòr in the north."

She nodded. "We are certainly getting more organised, but we also need to be faster. The stone towers by the road are just not good enough. They're not even close to full height yet."

"I know it's frustrating, but there has been work on them every day. I've also been thinking about scouting out Longfort Keep and the forest."

Sahar nodded noncommittally, but Donnell could tell she was interested. "Would you do that yourself?"

He winced as he patted his injured thigh again. "Perhaps. I suppose I need another day because of this wound. But one way or another, I'll be riding out tomorrow".

"Would you like me to come?"

He nodded. "For sure, but last time I suggested we ride up to the outfield together, Niamh looked like she was going to strangle me. And then I got shot."

Sahar scowled. "Niamh won't stop telling me that I am woman grown, and should get married before the year's end."

Donnell chuckled. "Good luck finding someone who's brave enough," he said.

Her scowl deepened. "Are you saying nobody would want me?" she asked.

"No, I just…" Donnell coughed, cursing himself silently over his poor choice of words. "On the contrary. I shouldn't…I just…I wouldn't want to contradict Niamh – she has your best interests at heart."

Her eyes continued to bore into his for a moment, and then she said, "Niamh seems to think it's less likely that I will be wooed by a suitable young man if I spend time with the likes of you and Malcolm, which is pretty stupid as you are both my friends. Plus of course, old enough to be my grandfather."

"Ow…hardly. Well, that was deserved, I suppose."

"So, what can I say?" She grinned at last. "I'll take this contraption on my own from here – I can't have you limping all the way to the wall and slowing me down. Perhaps I'll see you at the meeting."

Lifting the bow mechanism over her shoulder she turned and walked off, heading towards the East Wall.

"Until then," he called after her.

The Plot

That evening, standing by Niamh's house, Donnell found himself again looking over towards the small scrubby field which was currently serving as a paddock for Beira.

"Niamh, I know you have a lot to think about," he said, "but do you think you could arrange a better place for the horses? They need a proper stable – we've only been managing because it's the middle of summer. Most of the recruits have never cared for a horse before, and they don't have the skills or the space. And that," – he pointed – "is just too small for Beira."

She nodded slowly, eyes narrowing as she looked over. "Good thinking. I will get that done." She looked towards the doorway. "But first, there are a few other things that we need to talk about. It's the first time that all of us have been present since before the attacks on the East Wall began."

Donnell ducked inside the doorway for the meeting, and found Malcolm and Fenella already seated at the tiny wooden family table in front of the fireplace, each with a mug of ale in front of them. Together with Niamh and himself, they had emerged as the de facto leadership council of the village. Sahar crouched close by on a log seat with her back to the unlit hearth. The two older girls were playing a game with their younger sister by the other side of the small roundhouse, which had a small barn adjoining it via a door at the back.

"We've all agreed that we should place more watchmen on the forest's edge overnight," Malcolm was saying as Donnell entered. "We've been so focused on the Norse threat, but the reality is that it's the boggles and wulvers in the forest that have been causing us the most trouble of late. Just look at the injuries we've seen." He pointed at Donnell as he spoke.

Fenella nodded quietly, but Sahar walked over and leaned one hand on the table, shaking her head slightly. "I've told you a hundred times, Malcolm – you can't trust Iohric and his men. Things may have been quiet for a few weeks, but that is all the more reason to be worried. They're planning something, and when it comes, it will be a lot more deadly than a few boggles."

The young woman looked over at Donnell with a slight eye roll. "No offense," she added.

With that, she turned and walked over to the children, on whom she had made such an impression. Niamh's older girls, Kit and Rana, were each holding one of the short bows that Sahar had made, and were practicing the movements involved in rapidly turning and shooting.

Donnell walked up to the table and leaned upon it, looking around the group. "Sahar has a point. I saw something when I was on the doomed trade mission the other day. They were mustering troops, and had supplies loaded up. Armour included, I believe. They were being furtive about it. I mean, it could have been a trading mission, but it might also have been preparing an attack."

"If so, why take their supplies away from Weir? Why not attack directly from there?" asked Niamh.

"It could be that they are setting up a separate base inland from which to strike us," he replied. "There is a pattern to their actions – it all points to a building threat."

"Or they could be setting up a new colony, maybe?" said Niamh. "I don't trust Iohric either, but it is not the Norse way to move inland.

They are a people of the coast."

Donnell took his seat slowly, wincing at the pain in his leg, and then folded his arms on the table. "I keep saying it – we need help from the Laird," he said. "If Sahar's right that they are planning something, that's all the more reason to build our fighting capacity as rapidly as we can. We've already lost Weir – what next?"

"For certain," said Niamh, "But he won't want to send troops here, as it would risk undermining the truce that has been negotiated."

"Right," Sahar called over. "We are going to have to rely on ourselves. On all fronts if necessary." She had begun to adjust the young girls' posture as they aimed their weapons, giving them pointers on how to aim properly.

Fenella looked thoughtful. "It's true that we need to defend ourselves," she said.

"But we can't maintain this troop training forever," said Donnell. "You know what farming people are like. As soon as we get to autumn, they'll each leave their spear to rust at the back of a barn, and focus on the harvest."

Malcolm shrugged, but did not disagree.

"I could go and speak to Mac Rath," Donnell continued. "I think he trusts me, and understands the situation here. If he could be persuaded to move against the Norsemen at Weir, then we would have one less threat to worry about, and could focus on the problems in the forest."

"No. We need you here," said Niamh simply. "It sounds like our patrols will be more important than ever."

Malcolm cleared his throat, then took a sip of ale. "Well then, perhaps I could make the journey. We still need to trade, and Wherrycross is the natural place to take our farm goods. And if I were to lead such a mission, I don't, um…" He took a sip of ale, and made eye contact with Donnell. "Well, let's just say I didn't attract the same amount of unwanted attention on my last visit to Wherrycross as Donnell did."

Donnell glanced around, and noticed Sahar suppressing a grin at this; she knew very well how Donnell had spent a night in the gatehouse cell back in the springtime, and had only escaped by stealing a guard's cloak and helmet. He hadn't shared the embarrassing tale with Niamh or Fenella.

Niamh paused, looking around at their faces. "Very well. We can send a wagon under guard to Wherrycross with the farm produce. But we have already sent a message to the Laird. He has not sent any troops here so far, and I don't think we can just keep asking."

"I really think a message in person would help," said Donnell. As he spoke, he remembered the undelivered letter that he intended to give to the young knight Mac Rath, and reached inside his pocket. He pulled it out, and looked at it, and then glanced around the room.

"Is that..." began Malcolm.

"I did intend to give it back," he replied. "But yes. It's the Laird's message to his brother in Inverkip."

There was a moment's silence in the room. And then Sahar spoke: "Well, what does it say?"

"You can't open it," said Niamh, looking shocked.

Malcolm shrugged, smiling slightly.

"It's over now, like yesterday's cattle feed," said Donnell. "But I wonder..." He stared at the folded slip of parchment.

"What?" Malcolm asked.

"Well – we *thought* that it was a message from the Laird to his brother. But do you remember what Ogledd said to me, just before the battle? We didn't know until then that he had been working with the Norsemen. And it was him who gave me this parchment – not Macswain. How do we know that it was the original message?"

"Are you suggesting that Ogledd tampered with this?" asked Niamh.

"Or simply created an entirely false note. If he would ally himself with Iohric, then why not that? And he knows that I can't read."

"We'll never know unless we open it," said Sahar, raising her eyebrows. The young woman was clearly keen to uncover any possible evidence of Iohric's misdeeds.

Donnell paused, looking at the slip of parchment. "Then that's what I'll do," he said, starting to unfold the tiny object.

They gathered around the small table as Donnell spread it out.

"Mmm. Mmm! That's interesting," said Malcolm.

"What?" Donnell frowned up at his friend, trying to read the man's facial expressions. "What does it say?" His childhood friend was a good reader, but Donnell himself had never learned the art.

But it was Sahar who spoke up. "Cennaid is the Laird, right?"

"Yes," replied Donnell. The local Laird of Wherrycross and Cunninghame."

"Well then, it's about him. It says, *'at last the plan is in motion, our friends are established here and on the coast'*," she said. "And then it continues, *'when the base is secured, we can lure in Cennaid's main force and crush him. Be ready – it must happen by the summer'*. After that it is just signed with Ogledd's initials."

"That doesn't tell us much, my friend," said Donnell.

"It tells us enough," she replied, frowning.

"No. Sahar is right," said Niamh, getting to her feet. "This letter proves that Ogledd and the Norse conspired with the Laird of Inverkip – something that we already thought, but couldn't prove. And it also suggests that their association is ongoing. Their plan is old, but the endgame is to wipe out our Laird's forces – and to do it this summer. He needs to know about this."

* * *

Niamh circled the room, deep in thought. After a moment she stopped and looked out of the door where a group of youths were running past, also clutching bows which Sahar had made for them.

Moving over to the table, she sat back down. "Very well. Boggle raids are one thing, but it seems that the Norse are preparing for an attack, and the Laird needs to be persuaded of this threat. I will travel to Wherrycross myself, to speak to him. What we have just read about is treason – no less.

"Malcolm, you can come with me," she continued, "I'd very much appreciate your wisdom and your protection. But Donnell, you stay here." She paused for a moment, and then added, "If you could assign two of your riders to the mission as well, that would be ideal."

Donnell nodded. "As you wish. But in the meantime, it looks very likely that the Norse intend to provoke a conflict. The rest of us should place more of a focus on the stone guard towers, for if an attack comes from the Norsemen at Weir, as looks likely, we will need those defences to be ready. As soon as they are complete, we can feel a little safer, and our people will be able to rest more easily."

The druid Fenella leaned back, tying her long red hair with a simple leather band. "But again, that is only one side of the problem we face, my friend. We won't be safe until there is a balance in nature, and that begins with the forest. My brethren always worked to secure that, and their efforts need to be restored."

The others looked at each other. "It was terrible what happened to the other druids," said Niamh, diplomatically. "But what can we do to address that issue? We have other threats to think of, fending off any more attacks from the woods, and of course the danger of the Norsemen themselves. You have our deep gratitude, and are certainly welcome to stay as long as you like. If there are any other..." She tailed off.

"Niamh, what I am telling you will help with both of those things. You need to fight fire at its source."

Niamh took a sip of her ale. "Go on," she said.

"I know you're thinking about walls and defences, and you," – she nodded at Sahar – you've done some great work on those improvements. But the truth is that this place has been defended by the power of the druids for a generation. Every Samhain we come to the Celtic Rock, and make our enchantments. But what about the next one? We cannot do it without our brethren – and our objects of power."

Niamh nodded slowly, and said, "So what would you have us do?"

"We have to pursue Iohric, the Norseman that killed my companion."

"Yes – I've been saying so," said Sahar, looking up.

Niamh shook her head sharply. "We don't have the resources to run a direct revenge mission," she said. "The last thing we want to do is to poke the wasp's nest. If anyone has the power to attack Longfort Keep and Weir, it's the Laird."

Fenella stood. "No. I am not talking about marching troops to Weir – and it's not about revenge. At least, not for me." She gave a slight smile in Sahar's direction. "The power of our five brethren maintained the peace. If we don't restore the harmony of five druids, we disrespect the gods, and the attacks will just get worse."

"I hear what you are saying," said Donnell. "But why do we need to tackle Iohric?"

The druid Fenella leaned forward at this, reaching her hand out to his. "Donnell, you saw what happened before the great wyvern attacked. Iohric conspired to kill our leader Congal, and steal a ring that belongs to our circle of druids. It's a powerful object. With it, we can begin the work of restoring the circle of druids. Without it, we will face one threat after another. Indeed – the whole kingdom will."

"Fenella, this ring – I can't exactly sneak into Iohric's chambers in the dead of night and steal it."

"I could do it," said Sahar from across the room.

Donnell looked around, remembering how quick to shoot Sahar had been when previously facing the Norsemen and his men. "It's too risky, Sahar. You might get into a fight with no backup. It can't happen."

"I can do it, I tell you," she repeated crossly.

"Could you resist the temptation to cut his throat?"

"Enough," said Niamh, holding her hands out and glaring. She looked back at the druid. "Very well. We will work to do this. But first, we need to find out more about where Iohric is, and what his movements are. As soon as we track him down and isolate him, that will be the time for an attack – not while he sits in the keep. We will find a way, Fenella. We will return this ring to you."

Fenella nodded.

"And what about your fallen comrades. Are there others that we could gather to restore the power of the five? People who could join the druids, and rebuild the circle?"

"Well, there are…"

But before she could continue, there were yells outside, and the sound of horses' hooves, and the council rose and hurried to the door.

* * *

Donnell saw Sahar leap up and pull out her crossbow, and then move to the doorway of the house to look out. He rose and followed as quickly as his injured leg would allow, unsheathing his short sword.

A tall figure loomed up outside, partially silhouetted; after a second Donnell recognised Erik, the young Norseman from among his cavalry recruits. And stepping outside, he immediately saw that something was wrong. Erik had blood running down his face and neck, and was panting and covered in sweat.

Donnell took the younger man by the arm and helped him to take a seat on the low bench just in front of Niamh's house. Shortly, the others were outside too, and they clustered around.

Erik coughed and spat something dark and red, and then spoke. "I was with the young lad, Óengus. Our patrol went further than usual to the North, just short of the people that live near the waterfall."

"You mean the cattle farmers up at Eas Mòr?" asked Donnell.

"Yes, them. Well, not any more, perhaps. The houses were burning, and there was no sign of the people, or the cattle. There were bodies on the ground." The man wiped his brow, and muttered some words in his native tongue – Donnell didn't know if they were prayers or curses.

At the news of a possible slaughter at Eas Mòr, many people around began chattering anxiously, and Donnell heard some shocked wails from around the village square. He tried, nevertheless, to focus on what Erik was saying. Niamh's daughter Kit had brought out a cup of ale, and the warrior took a long draught, after which Fenella crouched by his side and began to staunch his wounds with a handful of dried herbs, chanting softly under her breath.

"Well, the Norsemen saw us," Erik continued. "We rode hard for home, but four of their warriors pursued us on horseback. They shot at us, and Óengus took a wound." He grimaced and paused for a moment, and then continued talking. "We kept riding and got away, but he…he has fallen bravely in battle, my friend. I'm sorry. The boy fell from his horse just outside of the Wall." The warrior shook his head once. "The body is at the outfield, by the style," he finished.

Donnell nodded slowly, thinking of the skinny young man's family. He himself had not long before persuaded them to let the lad train with the village troops.

"Did you see Iohric?" asked Sahar. Her face was cold, and she was still holding her crossbow. Donnell knew that she had little fondness for Erik or for any of the Norsemen who had joined their side, and wondered if she was doubting his story.

Erik broke into his native tongue again, speaking rapidly to the multilingual Sahar, until Niamh, putting a hand on his shoulder, asked him to repeat what he had said.

"I think he was nearby. I saw a very tall figure in the distance with his hood up. Anyway, this is his work, that is certain. One of the black-cloaks was Völundr, his closest companion." The warrior spat again.

"This Völundr – I think I met him. A thin, very hairy man? Long in the limbs?"

Erik nodded. "That's him. Nasty person, one of the first to execute prisoners if it comes to that. Takes a real pleasure in it."

The others around them broke off into smaller groups, chatting animatedly about the latest attack and what it would mean. Before long, most had dispersed, some of them helping the druidess take Erik to the Greathouse at the back of the square. Other people were asking questions of the man, and Donnell found himself making way. Sahar had moved off to the side of the square and was practicing with her crossbow, scoring fast, direct hits on one target after another.

Standing a few paces away, he turned to look around, and saw Niamh standing nearby, looking at him. He knew the implications of this would not be lost on her – it was obvious that Cardhu didn't have enough good men for the required scouting and defence.

"Weir is lost to us, and now Eas Mòr," said Niamh.

"Yes," said Donnell. "These are dark days for our people."

Words at Night

Donnell limped over to the Greathouse, where Erik had been taken by Fenella to check on his injuries.

He pushed the double doors open and stepped inside. Since Fenella had been using the Greathouse to heal the sick, it had been set up with simple wooden beds and blankets along one of the longer sides of the building. At the far end, away from the door, there were several tables covered with an array of mysterious supplies – mortar and pestle, woollen bandages, leather pouches containing animal bones, small knives, and many others. Further back were dozens of large stone pots, containing potions or fungi. On the wall above the tables hung herbs in various stages of drying.

Donnell saw Erik sitting upon a bunk, and was pleased to see that the blood from his wound had been cleaned up already, though the man's face was looking bruised. The warrior was grinning at the druidess, and the two looked up as Donnell entered.

"Donnell – are you all right? Has the leg started bleeding again?" asked Fenella, walking towards him.

"I'm doing well, thank you. And Erik – I'm so sorry. Clearly my idea of scouting further out put you in danger."

Erik stood up and shrugged, spreading his hands wide. "Perhaps. But now we know something more. It's such a big pity about the boy. I will go speak to his parents tonight."

"They would appreciate that. Can you tell me any more about what you saw?"

"They were lying in wait. I think…" He hesitated, and his eyes skipped between the two of them, and then he looked away with a shake of his head. "I think they must have identified this as a safe route away from the road, and decided to prey on anyone using it. It seemed like bandit behaviour. Or perhaps they simply realised that we were trying to check on them, and decided to cause problems along our scouting routes."

"Can you tell us where they were, and what they did?" said Donnell.

"They were not in the woods. No. They waited among some small trees and bushes near the path. The path is bad there, narrow and steep and stony, so we were on foot, guiding the horses along."

"And that's when they attacked?"

Erik nodded. "They surprised us. We pulled weapons and defended ourselves at first, but there were more of them than us. I told the boy to mount up and flee."

Erik paused for a moment, staring at the ground, and then continued. "We rode off, and I thought we had made an escape. But then I saw that the boy was bleeding heavily. I am not sure – I didn't see an arrow hit him, so he could have taken the wound either in the fight or when mounting his horse. He was pale in the face. We had far outpaced Völundr's men, but the boy stopped talking to me, and a moment later he fell from the saddle. I stopped to pick him up, but…" The warrior trailed off, shaking his head, a distant look in his eye.

Donnell sighed heavily, and patted Erik on the shoulder. "Thanks for what you have done. I'm going to ride up to do one last check on the East Wall, now – I'll speak to you tomorrow."

"I already told you, Donnell, you should definitely not be riding yet," put in Fenella, looking at him with a furrowed brow.

He patted gently at his injured leg, and winced. "Very well. So, I'll walk."

* * *

By the time Donnell was back in his own lodgings with Malcolm, it was dark and quiet outside. Both men had recently finished a light meal of onion and fish pottage with bread, the remnants of which were still in wooden bowls on the table. Donnell was lying upon his bunk to rest his leg. The light from the hearth was dimming, and Malcolm had just stood up to stoke it when a knock came at the door. He walked over, and, recognising the visitor, pulled the door wide. Fenella entered with a nod and a slight smile.

"Come in, take a seat, my friend," called Donnell, from where he was sitting. "And please accept my apologies for being such a disobedient patient. We all value your insights, and your dedication to helping and healing. It's just that there is so much needing done."

"Thank you, woodsman. I don't come seeking an apology – and after all, it was not so very long since you came asking my brethren for help, and came away with nothing. But it's time to speak fully and frankly, and that was difficult to do earlier in the meeting or with my patients in the Greathouse. This feels like a better time to talk."

"Take a seat, then," said Donnell, gesturing for the druidess to sit. "Will you drink some water or ale?"

"Ale would be fine, thank you." She seated herself on one of the long, rough benches, gathering her grey robes and swinging a small leather bag that contained some of her most valuable healing supplies into her lap. As she did so, Donnell caught a glimpse of an ornamental golden chain around her wrist. He had noticed it before, when she was ministering to the battle wounded. What he hadn't seen before was a clear red gemstone inset into the chain. It caught the light as she adjusted her robes, and then seemed to vanish as her sleeve fell down to cover it.

Malcolm had poured ale for the visitor, and the three of them sat in silence for a brief moment, sipping. Then Donnell said, "How is young Erik? He's a fine horseman – he may have originally come over here with the Norse raiders, but I'm very glad he made it back to us this afternoon."

Fenella smiled, inscrutably. "Badly bruised, but all right. He's a tough warrior. Amusing, too. He told me that he once successfully wooed the Queen of the Picts, only to be chased off naked by her army the next morning." She took another sip of her drink, eyes sparkling. "I treated his wounds with a compress of heather, and gave him a tea of bog myrtle to stave off fever. I think he's fine. You, on the other hand, need a few more days to rest."

Malcolm raised his eyebrows. "How did you gain your arts, Fenella? You can only be a few years my elder, yet you can do things that are entirely a mystery to me."

She laughed softly, looking down at her empty palms. "There is less of a secret than people commonly think. It is a matter of tradition and deep learning. I learned from my father, who was a master in the same arts, and he learned from others before him. It has passed down through our clan. Besides, what power I have is simply channelled through the great goddess Brighid, just as a stream carries water." She looked up at Malcolm, who was still gazing at her intently. "When you have helped with the injured at the Greathouse, I've seen enough to recognise that you are something of a scholar."

He blushed, and waved his arm as if chasing away a fly. "I learned a few ancient words and bits of lore from old Eochaid when I was a child. It's certainly nothing compared to what you and your brethren can do."

"Hmm. Well, one more foot down that path, and who knows where we might end up." She took another sip of her ale, and turned back to

Donnell. "No doubt you remember our conversation earlier?"

He nodded. "I know of the need to restore your druid circle, and Malcolm and I both understand what you do for us. It was he who asked me to seek your protection back in the springtime. But as you see, the village is under attack, and everyone perceives threats from two directions – the Norse, and also the forest. Rightly so. Even if I was sure that what you say is the priority…I mean, not that I doubt you…" he stumbled to a halt, and looked at his friend for help.

Malcolm, however, was deep in thought, his gaze slightly unfocused as he looked at the two of them, and didn't respond.

"What I mean is," Donnell continued, "there is going to be no persuading the rest of the villagers that we should prioritise looking for the lost ring or gathering together a new circle of druids, just at a time when they are fearing that their homes are going to be attacked any day or night."

Fenella inclined her head, accepting his point.

"And if that wasn't already the case," he went on, "with this attack on the community up at Eas Mòr, people are going to be more frightened than ever. There were already many more villagers coming to the forge this afternoon, looking to barter for swords or spears. And we simply don't have enough iron."

"Are you the Laird's Luftenand, Donnell? Is it your job to protect the village?"

"Well, no, but the Laird's bastard son Mac Rath told me I have to oversee the defences, and he would…" Donnell tailed off again. What exactly would Mac Rath do? What did the young nobleman know about what was going on right now? Did he even care? The man had only passed through Cardhu once since the battle back in the springtime.

Malcolm chimed in at last. "Donnell feels a responsibility. People look up to him."

"I don't know about that," Donnell said with a shrug. "I've always been an outsider here. The sooner I can move on and return to a life in the forest, the better."

"Malcolm's right, actually," replied Fenella. "I have seen it. I don't think you would really walk away from the people you have been helping while they are still under threat, much though you might prefer to roam the forests in peace. And if you want to see an end to this, you need to trust me. The attacks are not going to stop until the druidic balance is restored." Although the druidess still looked tired and careworn, she was precise and forceful when she spoke, and there could be no doubting the deep wisdom and conviction that she held.

"I suppose, then," said Donnell slowly, "we need to decide how to do that, while still protecting the village in the meantime."

They all sat quietly for a few moments, the fire crackling. Then Malcolm stood and topped up their ale mugs.

"Donnell," Fenella said, breaking the silence, "you know, you should move that leg. I know it's painful, but gentle exercise will help the healing process. Will you walk with me outside for a short while?"

* * *

Donnell nodded and stood, patting Malcolm on the shoulder on the way out. His friend seemed unusually distant, and Donnell wondered if Fenella's question about his learning with Eochaid, many years before, had again stirred some long-forgotten hopes – or fears.

They walked down the short rocky lane that ran past the blacksmith's, with its unique smell like burnt honey. Beyond was the village square, and the pair began to walk slowly around its edge. With the sun having set there was nobody else about, but the midsummer sky was still light enough to see by.

Despite having come to know her quite well over the past few months, Donnell felt strangely awkward to be walking alone with Fenella at night, so he was pleased when she spoke.

"You're a perceptive man, Donnell. You have seen much more than have most other folk of Cardhu, and have even been to our home in the woods. The place some call Druid's Hame."

Donnell nodded, unsure if this was a question.

"So, of course, you know about the druid stones." She stopped walking, and lifted her wrist, and he saw again the clear red gem at her wrist, glittering in its broad but delicate chain which looked like it had been fashioned out of pure gold.

"I… saw the ring," said Donnell, "the one that Gabrán stole. It had a white stone." He glanced to his right; although it was dark, their circuit round the village square had taken them very close to the raised rocks, at the top of which was the hulking black form of the Celtic Rock. He glanced up at Fenella, and saw that she, too, was looking that way.

"That's right," she said, sparing him the need to articulate his thoughts. "Five stones of power, one for each druid, one in service to each god. Our tradition tells that they fell from the sky at this very spot, centuries ago, in a great storm – a gift to humankind. Some say that this great Rock, too, fell at that time, as did three others further away, all of which are now holy places to us. But this one is the most powerful, and so it is to here that we come once a year to protect the kingdom, and from here that we summoned the féth fíada when the great beast attacked."

"I remember."

"But now, as I have said to you, everything is out of balance. And not least because two of the druid stones are lost. But in the case of one of them, the white stone of Lugh, the Great Craftsman, we know exactly where it is. That is what you saw in the stolen ring. I don't know exactly what Iohric plans to use it for, but we must find a way to get it back."

* * *

A chill wind suddenly raised, cutting through Donnell's smock, and he wished he had slung his travelling cloak around his shoulders before stepping outside, for he was only wearing a tunic and breeches. The wind swished through the treetops, and sent dust scattering across the open ground, forcing Donnell to turn his head away until it passed.

He then looked back at Fenella. "So Iohric still has it, we can presume. Do you know exactly what he intends to do with it? What powers does it have?"

"I do not know exactly. And it's mysterious to me that he sought out that gem in particular. I wonder, did he even know that each of us had one?" Fenella turned and began to walk again.

"And if so," she continued, "then why, when he had such a hold over Gabrán, did he not take the amber-stone in its brooch, the stone dedicated to Étaín? I can only assume that he didn't know about it, or what it could do. But regardless, both objects are missing. So, you see, Donnell, it is not just about replacing the druids – we need to locate both of those artefacts, or the power of the circle of Mor-druids cannot truly be restored. One stone we know is with the Norseman, and the other we believe may have been taken by the spellcaster Eochaid, or for him."

What it could do. As he walked, Donnell's hand automatically brushed against his breast, where the brooch had been secreted under his clothing since the previous day. Most people probably had no awareness of its role in the recent battle at all, but he now realised something that had not been clear to him before – the druids sought the brooch, and they assumed that when old Eochaid had used it to protect the village against the wyvern, it had remained in his possession. Perhaps they suspected Bib of securing it for his master.

But he had not. He, Donnell, had picked it up.

And since then, had kept it entirely to himself. He hadn't even told Malcolm, although he had told his friend everything else that he knew about Eochaid, including Bib's recent news.

"I got the impression that Iohric wants to use the ring to make a weapon of some kind," he said, keen to avoid further discussion of the brooch. "Willem said that when the Norse briefly took control of the town, they were asking him about how to forge a ring into an ancient Norse war axe."

"That makes a sort of sense," she replied. "Though it is…vile."

"Not what the stones are for?"

"Certainly not." She shook her head, frowning. "Well then, it is essential that we get it back before they have a chance to do so. If they damage it, its power could be lost to the kingdom forever."

As they walked they completed their circuit of the main square and began to make their way back up to the outbuilding where Donnell was staying, but Fenella paused outside. "There's another thing that I didn't want to tell the others about. To start rebuilding the circle, we need to free Gabrán's brother. The one they call the Dark Shadow," she said.

Donnell thought for a moment. Back in the spring, Gabrán had slain his own comrade and the leader of the group of druids as part of their plot to steal the mysterious ring. But the only brother he knew of was Fáelán, the evil renegade druid and shapeshifter long since expelled from the order after stealing artefacts from Gabrán, and who Donnell himself, as a young man, had faced and slain in self-defence.

"I'm surprised you'd trust anyone from that clan, after everything that's happened," he said.

"I trust this one. He's my childhood friend."

Donnell cast his mind back to the Battle of Cardhu, in the springtime. "There was a key," he said at last, as he pictured the scene. "Gabrán expected to be given it as payment for his crime, I think. Iohric, the

Norse leader had it."

Fenella looked at him and give a pained smiled. "Right," she said. "I cannot forgive Gabrán for what he did. He betrayed us and disgraced his role as druid of the sun goddess, lady Étaín. But I do think that when he conspired with the invaders, he did it due to a threat to his kin."

"And what makes you think that the Norse haven't simply executed this Dark Shadow? With Gabrán gone, he would be of no further use to them."

Fenella looked at the ground for a moment, and some of her long red hair clung to her face before she pushed it back and caught Donnell's gaze again. "It may indeed be the case that he has served up his usefulness, and that Iohric simply executed him after those events. But there is also good reason to think that he would be a skilled and useful prisoner to the Norsemen, especially if they plan to use the white druid stone. If he lives, then there may yet be a chance to rescue both him and the ring."

Donnell sighed. "I've told you already, Niamh will never agree to it," he said, as they went back inside. "But…"

"What?"

"Well, as she will be away over the next couple of days…" He left his statement unfinished.

Fenella narrowed her eyes, looking at him. "We should begin by finding out where Iohric is," she said. "He may be at Longfort Keep, but perhaps not. He will have the ring with him. And if we defeat or capture him, it will be easier to free the Dark Shadow."

Donnell nodded. "I'll begin by scouting out Eas Mòr, the village that they attacked today. If he is there, he will be much more vulnerable than at the keep. There could be a chance for an ambush. And if instead his right-hand man Völundr is still in control there, we could capture a valuable prisoner for trade."

Fenella shook her head. "It's too dangerous. And as I've said, you need to rest for another day or two."

"But now is the best time to do this unobserved, Fenella. And if we leave it longer, the Norse may fortify Eas Mòr, too, as they did with Weir. I have guard duty and also training to do tomorrow, but after that, I will set out."

She shook her head and looked at him, then blew out a long breath. "Very well," she said at last. "I'll give you something for the pain and swelling. But if you ride down there, I'm coming with you. That ring is dangerous."

"I think I know who else to bring with me, too," said Donnell, thinking of how angry Sahar would be to miss out on this chance to gain her revenge on Iohric.

"Please don't bring anyone else, unless you are sure they can be trusted."

Donnell thought for a moment. "I trust Sahar. Malcolm too, but he is due to travel to Wherrycross in the morn."

Fenella pursed her lips and looked to the side, her red ringlets covering her face for a moment. "I had considered going there, too, but…"

"What?"

"I can't do both, but we do need information on Eochaid. Is Malcolm up to that?"

Donnell thought for a moment. "He greatly admires Eochaid – has done since we were boys. I don't think he would spy for us. But I could at least ask him to visit. The old spellcaster is expecting us to make contact, anyhow."

"Very well then."

As Donnell stepped back inside, Fenella waved and began to walk away towards the Greathouse. "Tomorrow, then," she said.

Malcolm was already asleep in his bed, and soon Donnell was

likewise lying down and drifting off to sleep. And that night, for the first night in many, the defenders' bows stayed still, and Donnell slept soundly.

Departures

onnell was up at dawn again to relieve those who had been on watch overnight. He strode the length of the East Wall, checking on the wall itself, as well as on the guards. His leg wound was still tender to the touch but was giving him much less trouble with movement – the slight limp, he knew, was as much a habit as a necessity now, and he should try to move in as normal a way as possible.

There had clearly been good progress replacing the charred watch-tower since the recent boggle attack, and he nodded approvingly to himself as he checked the workmanship from the outfield side. The main section had been reconstructed, although it did not yet have a canopy or balustrade.

He carefully vaulted through the half-repaired gap in the stone wall to look from the other side, the area between the forest and the East Wall itself. Both the central and side towers now had turfs piled high around their bases. Touching them revealed that they were waterlogged – presumably to repel any future attacks that used fire. Nodding again, he returned to the central tower and picked up his bow.

When he returned from his watch in the mid-morning, archery lessons had begun. On the hillock at the top of the village square, not far from the Celtic Rock, a group of people, most of them children, were shooting at a set of makeshift wooden targets by the stump of a dead oak tree, with Sahar guiding them to the correct technique. She called out instructions periodically, setting a high level of expectations in terms of how exactly the learners should hold their bows, and not accepting any fooling around.

One young woman was doing much better than the rest, he noticed, and he suddenly recognised Branwen. The younger sister of Niamh had recently arrived back in the village, but he had not yet spoken to her. Her husband in Eas Mòr had been killed in a Norse raid upon the Laird's Road, and she had since moved back to live with Niamh's family. Niamh herself was also widowed, and as such their family had suffered the same trauma twice. But these were difficult times.

Donnell remembered well that Branwen had been a skilled archer in her youth. Now, one of her shots after another hit close to the centre of the nearest target. Sahar nodded approvingly, and moved on.

It suddenly occurred to Donnell that the cruel fortune which had taken Branwen's husband from her had also spared her life. Had it not been for his death, she would more likely than not have been in Eas Mòr village at the time of the most recent Norse massacre. He looked again at the young woman; she had barely changed since the last time they had spoken – slightly older, of course, for it was almost a decade ago. Her messy, wind-swept hair framed her pretty face in an unusual but appealing way, and he smiled to think how rude and difficult she had been as a youth when they had briefly trained together. As he looked on, he caught her eye and waved. She nodded slightly, staring at him for a moment, and then returned to her shooting.

Sahar had now moved on to stand beside Niamh's eldest daughter, Kit, and she reached out to steady the girl's shoulders, the muscles in her own arms standing out as she did so. With her posture corrected, Kit stood very still, concentrating on aiming and holding the arrow in place. Then she let fly, and the shot thunked into the edge of the target, a few inches from the centre.

"Good one," said Sahar simply, and moved on again.

As Donnell sat and watched the training session for a few more minutes, he mulled over what it would be like to be a sibling. Like Sahar he had grown up as an only child, living with his mother on Tarin's farm. He had been free to range far and wide when there was not too much farm work to be done, and although it was lonely at times, he had always enjoyed the sense of independence. But watching Sahar act as a mentor to the younger children gave him a curious sense of comradeship mingled with a strange, protective feeling.

He was distracted from his musings by the sound of a wagon being drawn into the square by two mules. There was a gathering of people and other horses around it, near the middle of the square, and he saw that Niamh and Malcolm were preparing to set out on the trading mission to Wherrycross. He hurried over to speak to them.

The pair were both seated at the front of a wagon, behind the mules, allowing either to take the role of driving the animals. Malcolm had put on some light armour – thick leather reinforced with iron plates at the shoulders. Donnell noticed that he had switched his usual maul for a full-sized warhammer; the head of this impressive-looking weapon was resting on the floor of the vehicle, its leather strap around his friend's wrist. These precautions were low key, but they added to a sense that this was a mission that would expose the people he cared about to real danger.

As he greeted them, two riders came over and took their places alongside the wagon, and a young lad of no more than eight summers brought over a bucket to give the horses and mules a last drink of water before the journey. Donnell looked up – he had already agreed that two of his mounted troops could be spared scout duty to travel with Niamh as guards, and now noticed that one of the pair was Erik, to all appearances fully recovered from his recent struggles, though his face was still showing some bruising around the eyes.

"Keep them safe, won't you," said Donnell to Erik, and then caught Malcolm's eye. "Malcolm – can I have a quick word with you please?"

Niamh gave a nod, and the blacksmith's son stepped down and joined his friend, with both walking a few paces away to confer.

"Are you planning to stay a night?"

"Probably two. We'll stay at The Mackerel's Eye, near the edge of town."

"Very well. And I don't know if you'd thought about our recent conversation about Bib, and, well, old Eochaid...?"

"I've not forgotten. In fact, I was giving it some thought last night when you were out speaking to the druidess."

"So you'll speak to him? And, erm..." He hesitated. Donnell found it uncomfortable to keep things from his friends, and now was doing so with two people that he respected. There didn't seem to be much point in following up with Fenella's request for information on Eochaid, as he himself had the very item she wanted to find out about. "Listen," he said after a pause, "can you just ask if he plans to come back here. And if he has any further wisdom about the wyvern. I don't want that creature returning – and we need to be able to tackle it if it does."

"I will," said Malcolm.

"And pass on my best regards, too," Donnell added.

"Sure. But I don't plan on telling the others that I am visiting the old spellcaster. I'll find a moment to do it subtly."

"Good, good."

"And Donnell...I am serious about learning from the old man. I may even make arrangements to stay in Wherrycross for a spell, if he's amenable to the idea."

Donnell looked towards the ground. "Eochaid has some remarkable powers, but I must say, we would miss you here."

"I know old friend, and thanks. And I would miss you terribly. I just think...my time here has nearly come."

"I see."

"Of course, the old spellcaster might have other things to do. He might just say 'no'. Who knows if he even plans to stay in Wherrycross, or has other designs of which we know nothing? Perhaps he doesn't just take in apprentices. And I am probably too old."

Donnell smiled, and clapped his friend on the back. "I hope he gives you a chance, Malcolm. You deserve it."

The pair returned to the wagon. The horses had finished drinking, and the last of the crates of goods for trade had been loaded on board.

"Ready?" asked Niamh, looking down at Malcolm, and he clambered back up.

"Niamh," said Donnell, "a little request."

"Go on, Donnell – but be quick."

He nodded. "With the numbers of available riders depleted by this and by all the scouting missions, I think I need some new additions to the cavalry training group. I'd suggest another four riders, if that is all right with you."

She sucked in her cheeks as she thought about this. "Take Calin and Rian," she said after a slight pause. "They seem to be somewhat in awe of you after your defence of them down at the watchtower the other night. So that's two."

"Thank you. Of course, they will be complete beginners, and it would be helpful to add someone with experience, too."

"Yes, well – I am not sure who else we have that can ride…I mean, there's my sister – I already said to her that she might need to help out, as it happens, and she's happy to do so. But I don't really want her going off by herself."

"Branwen would be a great choice, Niamh, as she has experience of tracking. And Sahar can ride, too. Perhaps they can train with the troop, with your permission, and that way the two women will be together, and safer." He smiled. "I mean, I'd feel a lot safer with Sahar by my side than either Calin or Rian, to be frank – or even both of them."

She studied his face for a moment. "Very well," she said at last. "But they are only to patrol within the village itself."

Donnell nodded and watched in silence as Niamh took the reins and shook them once to spur the mules into action. Erik smiled and raised his spear in a salute as they left, and Donnell saluted in response. Erik was the only one among the group who did not look tense, he thought. The small group moved through the square towards the road down to the coast on their way to Wherrycross. The new scouts would be very welcome, even with the restriction that Niamh had suggested – and he would work on getting that rule changed in due course.

* * *

As the departing wagon rounded the nearest buildings and moved out of sight, Sahar left her students to their archery practice and came over to Donnell, and together they walked over and sat in front of Niamh's house.

"I thought you might have persuaded them to take you along," she said.

Donnell nodded. "I thought about it. I am a little concerned for their safety, but we need to trust Malcolm and the guards," he said.

Sahar frowned, peering after them and then looking down towards her feet.

"I mean, they're very capable," he added, noticing the concern written across her face. "I am sure Niamh will be totally fine. Anyway, I have a different job for you, if you're not too busy training the children…"

She looked up at him. "Go on."

"Niamh agreed that I need to recruit and train a few more scouts. You can already ride a horse, right?"

She nodded, breaking into a smile "That's fantastic, Donnell! I can hardly believe she agreed to that. Scouting missions are just what I need…"

Donnell decided to leave mention of Niamh's rule about the female scouts staying in the village for another time. "And talking of which, I have another mission to go on, if you're interested – and I said to Fenella you'd be just the person we need."

"Well, I'm interested now – although I do need to finish this work with these young archers. They are trying hard, but most still have a lot to learn." She looked over in the direction of the Celtic Rock, where several children were still firing arrows towards the tree stump. Branwen had moved on.

"There is still a bit of time until we need to leave." Donnell was happy for Niamh's expedition to be well out of the way before he set out.

"So where are you headed?"

He smiled and glanced around; there was no-one else within earshot, but he moved slightly closer all the same and looked directly at her. "I'm following up on the attack on that poor lad yesterday," he said. "I need to see what the Norse are doing up at Eas Mòr. Erik told us of buildings burning, but we still don't know exactly what happened. I want to know whether Iohric has stationed troops there, and if any locals are helping them, as happened at Weir."

"The villagers are fools if they are," she said, rolling her eyes slightly.

"Right." He nodded. "But there's more. We are going to target Iohric directly. It might not be the village's top priority, but, well – let's just say there are other reasons."

"Finally." She stood and walked away slightly, kicked out at a rock which bounced away from her across the square, and then returned. "It keeps me awake at night, what he did to my father. He might have been a ferocious raider, but he was a good man, and fair-minded in both peace and war. Iohric, on the other hand, is a snake, a murderer, a liar."

"What exactly did he do?"

"I've told you some of this before," she said, looking down towards her feet again. "My father was a great warrior and hero – Hrólfr the Red was his name. Iohric the Ganger was a captain of his, one of his war leaders. But the black-hearted traitor was working both sides – helping the enemy. He always wanted power – not so much gold as powerful *things*. Great weapons."

"So they offered him something he wanted?"

She nodded. "A legendary axe, the weapon of Harald Wartooth, a king of Zealand from three generations back. I remember it well – it was a beautiful object, with the head of the King himself inlaid in iron and gold, and a curving spiked blade, gleaming and near-perfect despite its age. It was heavy, though – only the strongest of warriors could wield it. It had long been supposed lost in battle, but our rivals from Norðreyjar had the axe, and Iohric coveted it."

Sahar looked up and narrowed her eyes, scanning the high, feathery summer clouds in the morning sky, and then resumed. "The Ganger must have made some kind of deal. In any case, the axe came into his possession, and he changed sides. When my father tried to treat with the enemy, Iohric came to him like an old friend, promised to lead the negotiation, and invited my father and his closest shield brothers in to share meat and ale in his long house. There, after hours of talk and song, he murdered them. And so my people exiled Iohric."

"I'm sorry," said Donnell, and then stood up and began to pace from one side or another. "And the others, I suppose – some of them – were his warriors from that time?"

She stood likewise. "The blackcloaks, yes. They served him. They have been with him the longest."

"A coward and a liar. I can't understand why people would follow a leader like that."

"Right." Sahar was slowly shaking her head, and she aimed a firm kick at the bench where they had been sitting. "I hate them all. Iohric has a hold over them. And he still holds the axe – it has a mythic power that attracts followers."

The remaining children up at the top of the village square had stopped shooting, and were looking over at Sahar.

"All the more reason to track him down, then. In addition to everything that he has done to the people around here, this weapon makes it easier for him to rally more warriors to his cause and build his power. He has to be stopped."

"He will die a slow and painful death."

Far from unburdening her, the conversation seemed to have fired Sahar up with renewed hatred for her old enemy. "We will avenge your family," Donnell replied, looking at her with concern. Understandable though it was, he didn't like to think of the young woman being so consumed by her hatred. But perhaps defeating the Ganger would appease her rage and calm her mind. "So you'll join me?" he asked.

"Surely you are not going alone?"

"No – Fenella is coming." He shrugged.

Sahar glanced briefly towards the Greathouse, and then looked back at Donnell. "She's no fighter, and someone needs to watch your back. I'll come. Don't leave without me."

He hesitated. "It's dangerous, of course."

"All the same. The time has come. Destiny awaits."

"To be honest, I hoped you'd see it that way. You're a brilliant archer, and we work well together. And with Niamh away, well…it should be a bit easier to do things our way. But what about her children? Will they be all right if you are late back? We'll be travelling on foot."

"During the time that Niamh's in Wherrycross they are going to eat with their neighbours and with Branwen. They know where to go. So I can have a bit of freedom for once."

"Then I'll see you at the top of the East Wall, at the northern end. Gather your weapons, and I'll do the same. Don't take long."

Donnell checked on Beira in the new stables, a former barn which had belonged to one of the crofters slain in the springtime battle. By rights it was the property of the man's sister and her clan but they didn't need it, and had been persuaded to give it up for the needs of the whole village. The building was in a poor state but was clean, and was now well furnished with bedding and food. From Donnell's point of view it was ideal – large, and close to the main square.

He then returned to his lodgings. He put on his white travelling cloak and grabbed a leather satchel that could be worn across his shoulders when he was journeying on foot, into which he packed some dried chicken and oatcakes, plus a couple of silver groats. Finally, he took his favoured weapon, his spear, and strapped his long hunting knife to his belt. In addition, he took a much smaller knife in a tough leather holster from his wooden chest. This one he concealed in his left boot, tucked in on the instep, with a flap of leather from the boot covering its top.

Back outside, he nodded and smiled at Fenella, who emerged at almost exactly the same time, wearing her long travelling cloak.

"I'm ready," he said.

Thistles

The fastest way to Eas Mòr was to go northward on the coastal road and then directly up a rocky farm track, but Donnell was sure that that way would be patrolled by Iohric's warriors. After meeting with Sahar in the designated place, he instead led the way inland, following the scouting route along the edge of Holm's Wood. For the first mile or so he was able to keep to a clear and easily-walkable path, while looking for signs of where Erik and Óengus or their pursuers had ridden.

The forest naturally ended at a ridge that ran all along the coast up from Wherrycross, disappearing briefly in the hills behind Cardhu and emerging again beyond the village to the north. Ahead of them this ridge formed a line of low cliffs with trees atop them and enough space to walk between forest and cliff edge. The companions followed this narrow path for some time, and paused as the area in front of them widened and the path made its way towards lower ground by way of a crevasse in the cliffs.

"Which way now?" asked Sahar.

"Eas Mòr lies that way," said Donnell, pointing ahead. "From these cliffs come the falls that give the village its name, the 'great falls'. A river emerges from the forest there and drops suddenly, forming a mighty waterfall. But the village itself is down below the cliffs. After the falls, the water splits into several streams across a marshy grassland, and the settlement is beside the largest one."

"Then we should go down?"

"No, I don't think so. I'd rather keep off the main path."

"I agree," said Fenella. "We need to avoid notice for as long as possible."

"Very well then," said Donnell. "Then we leave the well-trodden path here as it diverges from the trees, and instead follow the edge of the forest as far as possible. I'm afraid it means there will not always be a good path to follow – more of a stony ground with heather and rocks."

"We'll manage," said Sahar, as they set off again.

Fenella turned out to be an entertaining travelling companion. "Keep away from there, my friends," she said, as they passed a pile of rocks near the cliff edge. "It's the home of the long-haired Gruagach."

Sahar and Donnell looked at each other. "The what?"

"You have surely heard of the Gruagach of Skipness? This is its kinsman. Or *kinswoman* – nobody has looked closely enough to find out which. Either way, that's what you hear making the whistling and wailing in the hills that can be heard at night."

"Interesting," said Sahar. "And why do we need to stay away?"

Fenella laughed quietly to herself for a moment. "I'm glad you asked. The creature's screams are unpleasant from a distance, but would drive a person out of their senses if they were heard up close. Disturbing the Gruagach would lead to insanity beyond my healing skills."

Donnell nodded slightly, making a doubtful face.

"They say it can be placated by the offer of a coat and a cap," she continued, "for it is a weak and sad creature, naked and ashamed of its lumpy earthen form. But I don't plan to test that theory."

They gave the rocks a wide berth.

Further on, with Donnell again walking ahead of the others to scout the route, he stopped to look more closely at the ground, lifting some damaged leaves and peering at the earth from a low angle. Then he stood up and turned to them.

"Can you see?" said Donnell, walking slightly ahead and pointing. "This way has been freshly trodden, and not by our scouts, who were on horseback. Someone or something has been regularly walking between here and Eas Mòr." He moved on further, not looking back to see whether his companions were following. "And look here – that mark was made by a cart or a wagon." He stopped, and pointed at a slight indentation in an earthy area below a protruding rock.

The other two caught up and gathered round to look. "Could be," said Sahar. "But it can't come from Cardhu. You'd never get a cart over the East Wall, for one thing. Nor has a cart arrived this way into our village. Which means someone has run a cart between Holm's Wood and Eas Mòr, at least once. But why?"

They both looked at Fenella, who looked puzzled. "The forest folk don't use carts, or even horses, to my knowledge," she said, "but clearly some things have changed in the forest. This is another thing that I must ask Loarn about."

Donnell continued to search around the area for a few minutes, but soon they needed to press on.

* * *

As they approached Eas Mòr, the route widened and became easier going underfoot. They were also further from the forest's edge. Now it was Sahar's turn to walk slightly ahead, on alert and with her crossbow readied, while Fenella and Donnell walked side by side further back. Donnell slowed his pace slightly and scanned the horizon. A few hundred feet further on, the clear area between the trees and the clifftops narrowed again, and the ground sloped steeply downward across bare rocks. It would be easy enough to walk down, Donnell thought, but surely a cart could not have been taken down this way.

Which would mean that whatever it transported was carried up to it, or down from it.

The only reason to do that, as far as he could think, would be to conduct trade between Holm's Wood and Eas Mòr without having to pass through Cardhu. As he mulled this over, he recalled the lightly-loaded cart he had seen down at the Norse fort, and regretted not getting a closer look at its contents.

The going got more difficult as they reached the rocky decline, with many loose stones underfoot making it likely that they would slip if they walked directly downwards. Instead they continued northwards, crossing the scree slope diagonally, and found themselves walking below cliff and tree again.

The sun was high over the sea by the time the great waterfall made itself heard, and not long after it came into sight up ahead. The white, foaming water seemed to tumble directly from among the roots of a line of enormous pine trees. It was channelled through a huge rent in the clifftop and then dropped for an improbably long distance into a large, round, dark lochan. The falls divided into three sections, one main cascade and a second, smaller section in two parts, which deflected off an enormous protruding rock halfway down. Everything around was lush and green, and tall purple flowers, thistles and lilies were in full bloom in every nook and cranny around the falls.

Near the edge of the falls a clear path emerged, indicating a route that farming folk from Eas Mòr village would frequent. It rose from the foot of the falls and climbed up towards the forest's edge where they stood. Following this route downwards, the companions reached the foot of the waterfall. There the roaring of the water was tremendous, and every surface around was wet with the spray. The afternoon sun sparkled upon clouds of droplets.

Looking ahead, Donnell thought he spied movement at the village; he peered ahead, hoping to ascertain whether someone was approaching, and – if so – if it was friend or foe. Looking downhill, Donnell could make out the familiar sight of a roughly circular cluster of homes built from stone and with turf roofs, a few hundred yards on. And sure enough, they showed clear signs of fire damage. Ahead and downhill their path continued to wind towards the houses, and he could also see where the major path between Eas Mòr and Cardhu, wide and muddy at this point, met the smaller path they were on near the edge of the village. But he could not make out any more movement.

He gestured his friends to follow, and then moved further down, following the narrow path, little more than a well-trodden area of long grass for the most part. The crashing of the falls receded as they went. After a few dozen yards, Donnell motioned for the group to stop. "Wait here a moment. I saw something back there," he said in a low voice.

They stood, listening and watching.

"I can't see anything, Donnell," said Sahar at last.

"I saw movement earlier, when we were at the foot of the falls," he insisted.

Fenella looked ahead, then shrugged.

"It could be the Norsemen," said Sahar in a low voice. "Let's move on."

"Just be careful now," he said, pointing. "Can you see, there? That's Eas Mòr. Erik and Óengus were attacked outside the village, so be on your guard."

* * *

They continued slowly, approaching the intersection with the larger path. Donnell stopped to peer at the ground every so often, and the other two stayed close behind him, Sahar holding her crossbow high and glancing from side to side.

After a few moments, Donnell thought he noticed movement again.

He stopped, and almost immediately he saw it for certain – two people had emerged from among the group of houses.

With a click of his fingers, he gestured to his companions to follow, then stepped off to the side of the path and crouched down. Manoeuvring himself slowly around behind a stand of tall flowering purple thistles he found a vantage point, and the other two followed close behind him without a word. As she crouched down beside him, Sahar winced as the jagged leaves of the spiked plants pricked into her arms. Frowning and swearing softly, she took a step back to give herself more room to keep her crossbow raised and at the ready.

As they watched from this hiding spot, the two men slowly walked towards them, together coming up the same path that the companions had been going down. Both were young warriors with braided beards and axes in their belts. Neither wore the black cloaks that marked out Iohric's most trusted captains. Thus far, there was no indication that the men had seen them, as they were walking quite slowly, chatting between themselves, and paying relatively little attention to their surroundings. One grabbed a handful of leaves from a young elm tree as he passed, shredded them as he walked, and then threw the debris off to one side.

Donnell touched Sahar's shoulder and with a downward motion of his hand, sternly indicated to her that she was not to shoot. And so, the three continued to watch in silence as the men passed right by the thistles and carried on walking up towards the falls. Unlike Donnell and the others, they then turned away from the waterfall path and began to walk along the foot of the treacherous rocky slope which the companions had traversed.

"What were they saying?" asked Donnell, when he was sure the men were out of earshot.

"Not much at all," Sahar replied. "Some stupid bragging stories of the past. And they mentioned a deal or risk of some kind – talking about gambling, maybe?"

"Hmm…right. So, we still don't know what they are up to." He narrowed his eyes, looking at the men as they receded into the distance. "Perhaps we should follow them."

"No," said Fenella. "We need to press on – Iohric is the target."

"True, but that pair could lead us to him. And if not, I certainly want to know why they are walking towards Cardhu."

"I think we have time to check the village first," said Sahar. "If those two really are going to Cardhu, they have a way to go still. We can catch them up – or follow with a clear distance behind."

"You're right," said Donnell. "And we can track them if necessary. We could even hurry through the trees and cut them off."

"Very well then," said Fenella. "Let's go and check the settlement, and then double back to follow that pair."

* * *

The path to the village led straight downwards at first, but before long it began to meander, taking them frustratingly away from the village and through more areas overgrown with thistles. Sahar walked slightly ahead, and unsheathed her dagger as she went. If she saw any thistles hanging over the rough path, she cut them down with neat, precise slashes with the weapon.

When the young woman was a few paces ahead of him, Donnell felt Fenella reach out and grip his arm. "I know about the brooch," she said in a low voice.

"What?" For a moment, Donnell felt a small, sharp piercing of fear, followed by something like embarrassment. Why had he not told the healer about the brooch before? There had certainly been plenty of opportunity. And she had a right to know.

"I don't blame you for keeping quiet. That is sensible. I mean, I wondered at first, but I wasn't entirely sure. The other druids don't suspect a thing. But you have it, don't you? You've had it ever since the battle."

Donnell closed his mouth. He didn't know quite what to say to the druidess.

"The brooch of Étaín," she continued. "I know you must. Someone close by has been using it. But listen, Donnell," she added, pinching his arm harder until he stopped walking and looked round at her, "I don't think you understand what it can do. It's just… it's not at all safe for you to use it. It has a raw, unconstrained power which could blast out unpredictably if used by someone who doesn't understand druid lore."

He gently pulled his arm away, and started walking again. Up ahead, Sahar had noticed that they had fallen slightly behind, and stopped to wait for them, looking back with a quizzical expression.

"All right," he muttered. "Yes, it's true. And honestly, I don't know why I didn't tell you the other night. I do trust you. And I'm not planning to keep it, either. It just seemed safer to hold my own council for just now." He looked up at her – the expression on the druidess's face was hard to read. "I haven't even told Malcolm," he added with a shake of his head.

As they got to within a few paces from where she stood, Sahar nodded once, and then turned and continued walking, just ahead of them.

"I'm really not using it," Donnell added in a hushed voice.

"Look, it's not about your right to the thing," said Fenella. "If Eochaid left it with you…?" – she looked at him again, raising one eyebrow – "then you were doing what you had to. But it has great power, more than you realise. Just… be careful, don't touch it, don't even wear it. And certainly don't show it to anyone else. All right?"

"That's a lot of things *not* to do," he said. "What would you have me do?"

"Keep it safe," she said simply.

* * *

They saw the bodies before they reached the cluster of buildings. A few had fallen at the entrance to houses, perhaps shot or speared on their way out, but most were in a large heap towards the midpoint of the settlement. Some of the bodies were tiny; all were scorched.

There were other signs of fires having been set, and a couple of the houses towards the rear of the settlement had been entirely burned out, their doors blackened and fallen. The great smithy, once the finest in the region, was a shell; it was uncanny to see the mighty iron anvil still standing in its accustomed location, while everything around it was charred and in ruins. There was no sign of Ambarsan the Smith, and also no sign of the famous Eas Mòr cattle, which had presumably either been taken as spoils of war or butchered at the same time as their owners. However, the Greathouse at the far side stood untouched, and most of the closer roundhouses were simply standing empty – a village of ghosts.

Fenella stood with her hands covering her mouth. Sahar gazed around with narrowed eyes, baring her teeth slightly as if she was about to growl.

Donnell felt sick. His eyes kept lingering on the burned-out smithy – the very place where Malcolm had apprenticed, so many years ago – and on the tiny burned bodies. "Come on," he muttered to Sahar. "We need to check for survivors."

The ground squelched under their feet as they walked closer. "Now I'm sorry I stopped you from shooting those rats," he said. "They deserve a bolt in the back of the head. To see them chatting and laughing, and now this…" He left his thought unfinished.

Sahar nodded slightly. Her expression had quickly calmed; she looked very much as she always did. He was reminded how much she had already been through despite her young age. This wasn't the first massacre that she had witnessed.

"You're a better person than them," said Fenella, walking up behind them. "You both are, which is why you didn't kill them in cold blood, without trial or defence. Those men don't share those values."

Sahar glanced thoughtfully at the druidess, but said nothing in response.

They walked in among the circle of buildings cautiously and in silence. As Fenella crouched and spoke some murmured rites, holding her staff over the fallen villagers' bodies, Donnell approached the Greathouse, spear held high, with Sahar close behind him. He thought he could see wisps of smoke rising from its chimney. Its door was open, and as he got close, he could hear a voice speaking in the Norse language. "This is it," Donnell mouthed, looking round. "They're inside."

Blood on their Hands

With the time for confrontation upon him, Donnell found doubts rushing through his head. Should they attack the Norsemen in the Greathouse? Was he putting Sahar in too much danger? He looked at the calm, determined face of his young friend – she was a skilled fighter, but so very young. What he wouldn't give to have some of Mac Rath's seasoned knights with them now. But no…he trusted Sahar's skill without question. And as she had said herself, her destiny awaited.

He glanced back towards the centre of the village for a moment. In any case, they couldn't just sneak off now, leaving the Eas Mòr victims to rot, unavenged…

With his determination restored, he moved alongside the building and edged towards the doorway, keeping his back against the wall. Sahar nodded in response, and pulled up against the other side of the doorway without going in, and then, leaning around, took the briefest of glances over the threshold. She nodded towards Donnell again and held up four fingers, then mouthed the word 'Iohric'.

Donnell moved to glance around the doorway too, spear raised, and found himself immediately having to duck as a spear was thrown full force towards his head. It passed just above his shoulder, and anchored itself into the doorway, quivering. Rising again, he rushed forward, holding his own spear high. Iohric was standing facing the door, the handle of his axe in both hands, while another warrior close by to him pulled out a dagger. Two other Norseman had been sitting with their backs to the door; slower to notice their foes, they were just starting to rise, each frantically clutching to pick up their axes.

Donnell stepped to one side, facing off against the dagger-wielding foe. As he readied his spear, he heard the ping of Sahar's crossbow, and his adversary dropped the dagger and fell to his knees, hands scrabbling at his stomach. Donnell took a couple of steps towards Iohric, but before he could close in, the two axe-wielding warriors were on him. He heard another crossbow bolt strike the wall, and out of the corner of his eye saw Sahar streak past towards Iohric, her own knife aloft.

His attackers swung their axes wildly at his head and Donnell had to step back again, thrusting with his spear repeatedly but without making contact. He was being backed against the wall at the side of the Greathouse, and he could feel the heat of its hearth behind his lower legs.

Twisting suddenly and dropping to the ground, he used the broad tip of his spear to sweep embers from the hearth up into the air and in the direction of his attackers. One pulled back easily, but the other was strewn with burning coals across his face and chest. The man staggered back, yelping, and dropped his axe.

The other Norseman took the opportunity to kick out at Donnell's spear and then stamped on its handle, causing Donnell to lose his grip on the weapon, his hand briefly crushed between spear handle and the ground. He recoiled as the Norseman raised his axe above him. But before a killer blow could fall, Donnell, from his crouched position, unsheathed the knife from his boot and forced it up into the man's chest. The blade made a crunching noise, and the warrior dropped backwards, the knife lodged firmly between his ribs.

Donnell reached down to retrieve his spear, then stood. Across the room, Sahar was facing off against Iohric, each slashing at the other rapidly, frantically. The young woman had managed to disarm the huge Norse leader of his axe and he was bleeding badly from several gashes in his lower arms, but he had likewise pulled a knife, and was starting to make use of his much longer reach. As Donnell watched, Sahar ducked, twisted, and hurled her weapon underhand towards Iohric's face, but at the last moment he dodged to the side to avoid it. Grinning, he charged towards his now unarmed rival.

Donnell stepped forward, spear raised, but before he could intervene, he was under attack again. The burned man had recovered his axe, and was approaching, swinging the weapon from side to side. Donnell didn't want to risk facing the man with just a knife, but there was no time to waste either; he threw his spear with full force, and it buried itself into the man's chest – a fatal wound.

Donnell ran across the room, pulling his long hunting knife from his belt as he went. Sahar was injured – her tunic sleeve was a mass of blood – and Iohric had pinned her to the ground. He was now pushing his knife towards her face and she was resisting as best she could; the iron blade was inching closer and closer as the great Norseman put his massive weight behind it. Donnell, in his hurry to intervene, aimed a kick as hard as he could at Iohric's head as he reached the pair, and the man rolled off, roaring in pain.

Iohric quickly regained his feet, and now Donnell faced off against him, both men holding knives, as the wounded Sahar began to rise to assist. Donnell could see that Sahar had wounded the Norse leader in multiple places around his arms; blood flowed freely but none of the wounds seemed to be inhibiting his movement. The horizontal scar that she had given him a few months ago was clearly visible across his face, and he now had several more reasons to hate the young Moor.

And then, perhaps uncertain about his chances in a two-versus-one combat, Iohric turned and fled. Donnell pursued him to the door.

Fenella was standing nearby, but Iohric ran without a backwards glance at her, heading downhill towards the coast. Donnell cursed his wounded leg, and turned, re-entering the building to check on Sahar.

Fenella was already at the door now, looking around at the carnage. "Please, you need to help her," said Donnell, pointing to Sahar's arm. "That looks really bad."

The druidess escorted the young woman outside, and Donnell turned back to the room, content to be alone. There was no need for others to bear witness as he finished the kills.

* * *

Donnell and Sahar washed the blood from their hands. Sahar's arm had been treated with one of Fenella's heather compresses and tightly bandaged, but she could still only move it slowly, wincing as she did so. Since the brief battle she had been pale and silent, a shadow of her normal self.

Leaving Sahar by the edge of the burn, Donnell stood up and walked over to Fenella, who was now standing by a mound where they had buried the villagers. The dead Norse warriors were lying outside the Greathouse where Donnell had laid their bodies and covered them, assuming that their own people would pass this way again soon enough to deal with them – if they respected their lost warriors enough to bother.

"She's still struggling a bit, I think," he said, looking back over at Sahar.

"It's affecting her movement, that's for sure," Fenella replied.

"Does the wound seem especially bad to you?"

She frowned. "There's something in it; the weapon may have been poisoned, or else perhaps enchanted by some evil charm of the Norse gods. I have treated it as best I can, but I need all of my supplies, not just what I carry with me. I have some lily extract back at the Greathouse in Cardhu…" She trailed off, looking once again in a pouch at her waist.

"Is there anything I can collect for you?" asked Donnell.

"Thistle helps to speed the healing – we can gather some on our way back," she said, "but she needs a charm against possession. Fox mushrooms, rabbit skin…"

"Right. Well, I'll help you gather what I can on our return," he said, glancing over at Sahar, who had risen and was walking unsteadily towards them.

"Let's focus on getting her back to Cardhu safely first," replied Fenella. "Iohric will have to wait, unfortunately."

They made a quick meal from Donnell's food supplies. There was plentiful fresh water from the burn that meandered downwards from the foot of the falls, a stream which eventually connected with the shore. None of them found themselves especially hungry after what they had witnessed, but Fenella insisted that they eat. There was also some ale that Donnell had found in the Greathouse – the only thing worth taking besides a few silver coins and a curious set of dice which the four men had been using to gamble. He had also retrieved their own weapons, including his boot knife. The slain Norsemen's weapons were of some value, too, but were heavy, so rather than carry them now, he had hidden them with the intention of returning on horseback.

They began their return journey, briefly stopping to gather a few thistles, which Fenella expertly stripped to reveal the fleshy heart section, stowing these in her pouch. Their sojourn in Eas Mòr had lasted much longer than anticipated, and when they reached the clifftop path, Donnell was unable to see any sign of the two Norsemen who had passed earlier, even though he could make out the route clearly for a great distance ahead. He was in no doubt that they had come this way, though, and the many signs underfoot showed to his tracker's eye that they had not taken any care to conceal their movements.

"I suppose you disapprove of what I did," said Donnell, walking beside Fenella again.

"Better than letting them die slowly from their wounds," she said.

"I mean taking them on at all. We could have sneaked away."

"Mmm."

"So, you disapprove?"

"Somewhat."

"Those men butchered the people of Eas Mòr. And they would have done the same to the villagers of Cardhu, or elsewhere."

"And what makes you any less of a butcher, after that?"

He sighed. "Perhaps nothing. But I would have had a chance of catching Iohric if he wasn't in the process of sticking a knife through Sahar's face. I had to act."

They walked on for a moment, and then Fenella said, "It wasn't all the people, you know."

"What?"

She swept her red curls back, and glanced round at him. "There were a few children's bodies, and some from older people. I didn't see many bodies of those of working age."

Donnell thought for a moment. "It's unlikely that all the adults would have fled without their dependents. So that means that they have been taken somewhere else. Most likely as slaves."

As they were talking, Sahar began to fall behind, and after a few moments she sat, and then slumped to the ground, rubbing at her arm.

Hurrying over, Fenella looked at the wound again, then stripped the bandages and redressed it. "Sahar needs to rest," she said simply.

"I'm all right," Sahar responded. "I just need a moment to regain my strength." She clenched her hands a few times, an angry look on her face, and then stood up.

They walked on, but Sahar was going more and more slowly. A few hundred paces further on she sat down again, closing her eyes and swaying. "That's it," said Donnell. "I'm carrying her."

Lifting the young woman in his arms was easy at first, but it wasn't too long before his shoulders and back were aching, much more so than they would even after a long day in the saddle. He rested briefly every so often, and tried his best to avoid bumping Sahar's injured arm as he walked. She initially protested, but it wasn't long before she had slumped against him, eyes firmly closed. Fenella agreed to carry their companion's crossbow, if only to give the group a semblance of a defence.

It felt like a long, long time had passed when at last they caught a glimpse of Cardhu and its surroundings again.

By this time the early evening darkness had closed in, but perhaps due to the power of the druid stone helping his vision in low light as well as at great distance, Donnell found himself able to see much further through the gloom than he would normally have expected. It was then that he spied the two Norsemen again, much further along the same route but still walking near the edge of Holm's Wood. "I think there is someone near the forest's edge up ahead," he muttered to Fenella. Not wanting to share the specifics of his newly enhanced vision – or that he was wearing the brooch – he left out the fact that he could now see clearly that it was the same two young warriors that they had encountered before.

Fenella peered in the direction that Donnell had indicated but shook her head, apparently unable to make out what Donnell had spotted. "Well, it must be them," she said. "The Norsemen haven't come back this way, and nor will any Cardhu folk be out at this time." She glanced at him, then narrowed her eyes and looked again, craning her neck forward slightly as she tried to peer through the gloom. "Which still leaves the question of what they are doing. We are almost at Cardhu, now."

"Yes. And whatever they are planning to do, it looks a lot like Iohric sent them."

The two warriors had rapidly progressed beyond some trees at Holm's Wood, obscuring them even from Donnell's vision. The companions carried on.

As they approached the wall and the edge of the outfield, Sahar stirred in Donnell's arms and asked to be put down, causing them to stop again briefly, but he was not willing to set her down until they were on safer ground. His shoulders and back might feel like they were burning from the prolonged exertion, but they were nearly home now. They had to press on.

When the familiar sight of the tall wooden towers of the East Wall came into view from behind the trees, the watchfires had already been lit. They continued cautiously and in silence, wary of a possible ambush from within the forest, and approached the home fortification.

Then, Donnell saw the two Norsemen again. The pair stood together at the edge of the woods, at the other end of the East Wall from where the companions had just arrived. Clearly, they had gone right beyond all three watchtowers without challenge, and had stopped; they were just visible to him in the shadows near the edge of Holm's Wood.

And they were talking to one of the forest folk – one of the kindred of Donnell's friend Caelia.

In the Shadows

As they stood near the edge of the East Wall, by the outside of one of its smaller watchtowers, they heard galloping hoofbeats approaching from the village side. Donnell looked up to see Branwen – Niamh's sister and his own newest recruit – racing across the outfield. He called to her, waving his arms above his head to attract the woman's attention, and Branwen checked her pace and then guided the horse over towards them at a trot.

Donnell carefully crossed the wall, and set Sahar down against the stone surface, helping her to sit up. Fenella crouched down beside the younger woman, placing Sahar's arm around her own shoulders, but Sahar simply slumped against her.

"Well met, Branwen," said Donnell, rubbing at his own arms and walking forward to meet her as she arrived. "I would greatly appreciate your help – my friend Sahar is wounded."

Branwen dismounted and led the horse over to the wall where Donnell's two companions were still seated. Fenella was mopping Sahar's brow with a scrap of cloth.

"Where have you three been?" asked Branwen. "Were you attacked? There was a report that Norsemen have been seen near the wall, so I came early for my watch."

"A pair, was it? If so, we have been following the same ones," Fenella replied.

Branwen scratched at her cheek for a moment before she responded. "Rian wasn't terribly specific as to the number," she said.

"First things first," said Donnell. "Sahar is badly wounded. We need to get her to the Greathouse, where Fenella will administer whatever treatments or potions are necessary. May we use your horse?"

Branwen nodded and held out the reins. Before long, Fenella was mounted on the steed with the younger woman in front of her, still slumped against her chest.

"Hurry on," said Donnell, patting the horse's rump. "I will follow up on these hostile warriors myself with Branwen and the other guards."

"Do not follow them into the forest," said Fenella, "Not at this hour. Let's meet at first light at the Greathouse and investigate in the light of day." With a nod, and holding Sahar firmly to keep the injured woman from sliding out of the saddle, Fenella spurred the horse and cantered back towards the village.

Donnell and Branwen watched after the departing horse, and then looked at each other in silence for a moment. Then, leaning on the low stone section of the wall, Donnell looked away towards the forest. "Thank you for investigating this," he said. "It was very brave of you, and you couldn't have arrived at a better time."

She tutted briefly, and leaned beside him. "You still haven't told me where you've been. It doesn't seem very safe to be out."

He looked back at her, wincing slightly as he thought about how best to respond. "I uh…thought it best to check on the route that Erik had taken yesterday. With poor Óengus. As your sister won't be back from Wherrycross until the day after tomorrow, there wasn't really time to discuss it with her."

She chuckled softly. "Donnell. You don't need to give me excuses," she said. "You always were up to something, as I recall – always bending the rules. If you want to investigate while Niamh is out of the way, that's up to you. Now – can I help?"

He smiled at her. When he had known Branwen in their youth, they had briefly trained together in the forest. He tended to find her difficult and frustrating – overly fond of following rules and listening to superiors – though on occasion she could be unsettlingly captivating. Her eyes looked almost black in the dark conditions but he remembered well that they were a dark golden colour.

"We need to increase the watch tonight," he replied, and then he sighed. "Branwen, it's just as bad as we thought, or worse – the Norsemen have killed many people at Eas Mòr. I don't know how many. Others have most likely been taken as slaves. None of the villagers were there."

She bowed her head, and he waited; it was hard to imagine how this news must feel for someone who had spent most of her adult life in the small village.

After a long moment, she looked up and sighed. "I already feared the worst after Erik's news. So, what now?"

"Things are dangerous. We have just killed three of their men, and that is likely to prompt a reaction." He looked off in the direction that Fenella had ridden, and then back at Branwen, feeling torn.

She put a hand on his shoulder; her face serious. "Go, Donnell. Check on your friend. We will keep watch here. I know how to use a bow, unlike some others. And if I see those Norse murderers, I won't miss – I promise."

"Thank you, Branwen – you're right, I would like to help with young Sahar. Please send for reinforcements the moment that you see anything further, though. In any case, I'll be back on Beira as soon as I can." He glanced back several times as he hurried away, and saw the young woman walk across to, and then climb, the central watchtower.

* * *

Back at the Greathouse, it was immediately clear that Sahar was still in deep trouble, despite Fenella's prodigious skill in healing. Donnell hovered near the doorway, popping in every few minutes for news, and then waiting outside in the dark in-between times.

The druidess was initially patient with his interruptions. Before long, though, it was clear that he was little more than a distraction. She looked up from her work and shouted over that she needed to focus. "You'll need to wait outside, Donnell – or else go get some rest. You need it."

Outside in the square, he lay his spear down on the ground in front of him, leaned back against a thin willow tree near the Greathouse entrance. But he had only been waiting for the time it takes water to boil when he heard a guard approaching – a bulky man with a short sword at his hip. The more frequent patrols around the village had been implemented, it was clear.

The guard walked on, clearly looking in Donnell's direction, but he appeared to be focused more on the spear on the ground than anything else. He stopped a pace or two away, and then unsheathed his sword and tentatively prodded at the spear with its tip, acting as if the thing might leap up and bite him at any moment.

Donnell began to rise, murmuring a greeting, whereupon the man gasped in shock, stood back, and pointed his sword directly at Donnell, who froze in the process of standing up. "It's me," he said, "Donnell, woodsman of Cardhu."

The man looked at him, wide-eyed, for another moment or two, and then lowered his spear. "What? All right! Oh, I am sorry. That was very strange indeed. I just didn't see you at all." He rubbed his eyes as if to emphasise this message.

"Well, what can I say. I'm good at keeping still," said Donnell, shrugging. "I suppose you just spotted my spear first and focused on that," he added, tapping the weapon with his foot.

The man shook his head. Peering at the face, Donnell recognised him as Kevan, a distant cousin of Malcolm's who lived on a farm at the southern edge of Cardhu and was rarely seen around the village square. "No, it was more than that," said Kevan. "Please, can you sit down again, and wrap your cloak around you? I am sure I didn't imagine it."

Donnell did as he was asked, pulling the hood up high around his face.

"Yes! I can see you all right, but when you do that, you look exactly like a rock. It's the colour of the cloak in the dark. That could be an incredible way to hide, Donnell." Donnell stood again, pulling his hood back down, leading to further gasps from Kevan.

Donnell put his finger to his lips and gestured to the man to calm down. "Very well – my thanks for the advice," he said quietly. "I'm going to stay here for a time, as I am waiting on news of my friend's injury. While I am here, you can take a break from your circuits, and go and grab a swig of ale somewhere." Donnell patted Kevan on the shoulder as a farewell. "But well done on your diligent guard duties," he added.

As Kevan moved off, Donnell settled back down again, considering the man's words. He already knew that Eochaid's cloak was an exceptional garment for travel, but did it have other, mystical properties?

Donnell watched on as Kevan moved away as he had suggested. With nobody around now to disturb him, he settled down and waited for another spell, keeping quite still as the sky darkened further and the moon rose above the hills to the left.

As his head had just begun to nod, he heard a distant noise from off behind where he was sitting, and realised that another guard had emerged and was beginning to patrol. Donnell was quietly delighted that the guards were doing as he and Niamh had instructed, but wished to avoid another distracting conversation.

Unable to contemplate returning home to sleep while Sahar was still battling for her life, Donnell instead took Beira from the stables, and set out for the East Wall once again. As he approached he looked ahead, but it was now pitch dark, and he could see no signs of any further enemy action. He rode for the central tower and ascended. As he topped the ladder, Branwen was there, an arrow to her bow pointing at him. Rian was just behind her, holding his own bow more steadily than in the past but fumbling to retrieve an arrow.

"Oh, you're back," said Branwen, relaxing. "How is she?"

"Still very unwell. But Fenella wants some peace to do her work."

"Fenella?"

"The druidess, I mean."

"I see." Branwen peered towards the village. "Well, we have enough people here, if you want to stay back at the Greathouse to check on Sahar."

"Thank you, but I think I'm just in the way back there. Also…" Donnell looked down, one hand on the pommel of the short sword which he now wore at his belt, then looked her in the eyes again. "Will you walk with me a moment?" he asked.

The two descended the rungs on the side of the tower and began to walk along inside of the wall. "I'm sorry about what happened," he said. "It must have been a terrible time for you."

She sighed again, and blew out her cheeks. "That's kind of you. I didn't have anyone there that I would count as a close friend, sadly. They never truly accepted me, and after Eanrig was killed I felt I had to give up the croft to his family, and come home. But of course, I am sorry about the innocents who have been slain. It is truly despicable."

"I know you must have a lot to think about, Branwen. Why don't you head back home now and get some rest?"

"No, no," she protested. "I don't need it. I was due to take an overnight watch, and the girls are being looked after. I promise. It's hard to sleep in such times, anyhow."

"Are you sure? I don't mind taking this watch for you."

She nodded. "Yes. I am sure."

"And I'm, erm…I'm sorry. Generally. I haven't been much of a friend. When you returned to the village, I should have made a point of coming to see you."

"It's all right. I know you've been busy – and injured." She stopped walking. "I'm glad you think of me as a friend," she added. "I was horrible to you, really."

He chuckled. "We were little more than children." He looked around again. "What a mess this all is. Do you think things will ever get back to normal?"

She frowned, unslinging the bow from her shoulder. "Only if we fight to sort it out."

They stood in an awkward silence for a moment, and then Donnell looked away, and pointed towards a spot in the forest. "Do you see that slight indentation, where there is an oak tree beside a pine sapling? It's the beginning of a path. That is where I last saw them. The chances are that they followed the path."

"So, they are waiting inside the forest?"

He nodded. "That's what I'm thinking, too."

"But what are they up to, do you think?"

"I intend to find out."

"You're not thinking of following them alone, are you?" she said.

He took a deep breath, and then sighed quietly. "No. Fenella was right – I can't go in at this hour. I just wish Malcolm was here. We could use another warrior at a time like this. Anyway – I'd better go and check on the other towers. Speak soon."

He set off towards the watchtower at the far end for the wall, nearest the spot that they had been looking at, rubbing his shoulders as he went. However, Branwen walked in the same direction, keeping pace with him. "Hey. What do you mean, Malcolm? Who was it that trained under Macswain with you?" She grabbed his shoulder roughly and prodded his chest with her finger.

He smiled. "That's the Branwen I remember."

She rolled her eyes but didn't respond to this. "Who was it that went into the forest there – was it the big Norseman? The one they call 'the Ganger'?"

"Iohric? No, but I think he might be close by. We saw him at Eas Mòr, and he must have sent the men this way. I just don't know why."

Branwen looked towards the trees again as they walked, peering through the gloom. "Well, let's be cautious, for they may be planning to attack Cardhu tonight."

Donnell studied the forest's edge again for a moment. There was nothing to see, no movement. "Agreed, we need to be careful," he said finally. "But I think that we disrupted whatever plans they had. Whatever those two were up to, it's probably not a full-scale attack. I mean, that wouldn't make sense, not with such a small force. They could be planning mischief – another fire perhaps… but no, it seems to me more likely that they must be going into or even through Holm's Wood. I can only guess why."

"Look, if there are really only two, then let's follow them," said Branwen. "You can get a bow from the tower."

They were nearly at the third tower, and he stopped again. "Didn't you say I was unwise to be travelling out at this time?"

She shrugged. "With a druidess to keep safe, it was unwise. The two of us know how to defend ourselves."

He paused and looked round with a smile. "You are very courageous," he said. "But it really is too late to be setting out, even if we were both to go together. We have no supplies. I know these forest paths as well as anyone, Branwen, but not in total darkness. And who knows how far our foes are travelling tonight?"

She peered at him for a moment, and then at last she nodded. "Very well."

He wasn't sure if she sounded relieved. "We can at least take a look from the nearer tower," he said, pointing.

They walked on in silence until they reached the third of the watchtowers and ascended, briefly greeting a skinny teenage lad who was standing atop the structure with a bow, looking scared and out of place.

From the platform, Donnell looked around; he could see for miles in every direction, but not through the cover of the trees, and he was still unable to make out the young Norse warriors. He looked again from side to side, and paused as he looked to the north across the top of the trees. Was that simply a bird of prey, far to the north, or something larger? He leaned forward against the platform balustrade, peering in that direction as the shape circled, then dived out of sight at an indeterminate distance.

Scanning the nearby forest's edge again, there was still nothing visible. "Surely they cannot stay in Holm's Wood the whole night," he muttered to himself.

"We know where they are, and they can't get into Cardhu without passing these watchtowers," said Branwen, who had also ascended. "Donnell, you're tired. Why don't you get back to the village – we'll keep a close watch on the forest, I promise."

Donnell nodded slowly for a moment before responding. "You're right. I could do with some rest," he said. He looked around at her, and put one hand on her arm. "I'll see you at training tomorrow, Branwen."

Mysterious Powers

Returning to the village square in the dead of night, the moonlight glittered on damp rocks and illuminated the clouds that were drifting briskly across the sky in the breeze. There were very few other sources of light except for a warm glow coming from the doorway of the Greathouse. Donnell stepped inside to check on Sahar's condition one more time.

Fenella was standing over Sahar, hair tied back and sleeves rolled up. He walked closer. "Sahar…" The young woman was lying still, in the deep sleep of the gravely injured or ill. The bloodstain at her arm was dry, but her whole body showed signs of poison, or worse. Her eyes were sunken, her face coated in sweat.

"It's not good at all," Fenella continued. "But yet she holds on."

"Is there anything I can do?"

"Possibly." Fenella's face was unusually drawn, exhausted beyond what he would have expected even despite the late hour. "If it comes to that…I may need you. For now, I have stabilised her."

"Stabilised? What do you mean?"

She sighed. "I had to stop her from slipping away. I used this." At this, the druidess touched the bracelet at her wrist. "An enchantment. And now she won't deteriorate further, I am fairly certain. But unless I find a new means of treatment, she won't improve either."

Donnell touched the unconscious young woman's cheek; her complexion looked washed out, with a bluish tinge around her brow. "You mentioned something else we could try – that I could help with."

"I am not certain…but as a last resort, yes." She looked at him and nodded a few times.

While Sahar slept, Fenella and Donnell stood at the entrance to the Greathouse, looking down towards the coast and the sea beyond.

"Well, Iohric escaped from us at Eas Mòr," said Fenella. "And I expect he went back towards Weir. That makes him safe, for now."

"What do you think he is up to?"

"I really don't know."

"Meanwhile those two men went to Holm's Wood and haven't been seen since. I wonder if he could be mustering troops in the forest. We need to find out what they were doing near the East Wall."

"Iohric is the priority," she said, and sighed, looking weary at having to state the case again. "And the white druid stone."

"I agree," Donnell replied, "but we know that those Norse warriors were his men. He must be involved with whatever they are doing. But…" As thoughts raced through his head, he tailed off, walking away from the druidess slightly, and then returning. "Yes. It might be quicker to go down to Weir first. That has the advantage that our enemies will at least be easy to find."

"You will pursue Iohric to the new keep? Niamh is against that approach."

He winced, and looked towards the covered door. "I think it's the only option right now," he said. "Just to scout, though. We need to find out where he is. But I have training tomorrow, and I am due to take watch at the road in the early evening, too." He sighed, and looked at the druidess. "It's frustrating – the time it takes just to establish where our enemy is."

"You can only do what you can. One step at a time. Anything you can find out might help. And perhaps the evening will be the best moment to make your way down to Weir without being observed."

"All right. So, we first investigate the Norseman at the keep, and investigate the woods when the others have returned. I'll set out later tomorrow, and see what I can find."

"I would come too, but I think I should stay with Sahar," said Fenella, glancing back inside as she spoke.

"No need. I can go myself, Fenella."

"Alone?"

Donnell briefly thought again of Branwen; the young woman was a fine archer, competent, and they had an intuitive understanding from their months of training together in the forest as youths. But he dismissed the thought. "It's a dangerous mission, and requires stealth. One person has more chance of success."

"Then be careful. Whatever you do, don't engage anyone in a fight. We can't risk losing you."

He smiled and placed his hand on her shoulder, noticing the concern on her face. "Of course." He glanced back towards where Sahar still lay in a poisoned sleep. "No more reckless attacks."

Fenella turned away from the door and stepped back into the main area of the Greathouse. "Can you go and fetch that object we discussed?" she said, gazing at Sahar as she spoke. "The brooch – the druid stone. I think the time has come for you to learn how to use its powers."

He hesitated; Fenella had told him not to wear it. But there it was – if Sahar's life could yet depend on it, the time for secrecy was over. He reached inside his tunic and touched the gold brooch, grasping it in his hand for a moment, then unclipped it and pulled it out.

"I am sorry, Fenella. I know you said not to wear it, but I had it with me, and haven't been back to my lodgings since…" He tailed off.

She flashed him a baleful look. "Never mind." She squinted towards the door, and then walked over. "There won't be many people around at this hour, but still, just in case – I'd rather keep this to ourselves." She pushed the great double doors shut, and secured them with two cut sections of log.

"Sit," she said, returning, and Donnell took his place in the centre of the Greathouse floor as indicated. "Hold it up."

He lifted the amber brooch in his hand, and she mirrored the movement, removing her bracelet and placing it on the palm of her own hand just a foot away from his. As she did so, the two gems glowed gently as if responding to each other's presence. With a clearer view of the red gem, he could see that both stones were identical but for their colour. The amber gem in his brooch and the red one in her bracelet were twins.

"Can you see?" she asked, with a slight nod towards her own hand. He peered downwards; sure enough, something was moving there. Tiny specks of gold light were travelling in a circle from one druid stone to the other, entering the glowing red stone and then coming out again, arcing towards the amber.

He watched it for a moment. It didn't speed up or slow; the two gems appeared to be in perfect balance. And then, as he focused on them, the glowing specks started to get slightly larger.

Were they responding to him? As he looked at them, concentrating, he realised that he could manipulate the tiny glowing shapes slightly through willpower alone. Make them larger, yes. Widen the circle. Change it to an ellipse...

"Well done," she said, gently lifting her hand and causing the circle to stretch and the lights to spin around faster, closer to their faces. "You are better balanced than I expected. You have an instinctive understanding of the druid stones." She smiled.

But Donnell still didn't feel that he understood the stones at all.

Still holding the brooch in his palm, he looked up at her face. "You mentioned enchantments, druidess. What exactly are the powers of the stones?"

She didn't answer straight away, but when she did, she looked up at him, the tiny golden glowing lights reflected in her green eyes. "Each one adds to the power of the others," she said, "and they can be connected by physical touch, but only if the users' minds are focused. And the stones are also more potent – more responsive to our commands – in certain locations."

"Like where? Here?"

She put her head on one side slightly. "Not this building specifically, but Cardhu, yes. And especially the Celtic Rock. As I told you, it is a sacred place."

He gazed at the circling lights again. "Did you say that every druid has a stone like this?"

"No. Only the Mor-druids. Donnell, these are ancient artefacts. There are only five, although the great tales say that we had more of them in the past. When the world was young. Yours is the amber stone, dedicated to Étaín, the sun goddess. It's likely that the Dark Shadow will inherit it when we free him, for he was Gabrán's brother."

Donnell nodded slightly. He felt a pang at the thought of giving up the amber brooch, and at the same moment, the circling golden specks began to dance up and down slightly, as if they had been knocked.

"Mine, as you can see, is the red stone of Brighid, the healing goddess. My companion the druid Loarn has the green stone, which is now safely concealed inside a wand. It is dedicated to Lir, god of the sea, but it has a connection with the forest, too."

Donnell nodded, curiosity coming to the fore again. "That makes four, together with the white stone on the ring which Iohric has stolen. What about the fifth? Another of the Mor-druids?" He tried to remember the membership of the druid circle from Samhain.

"My good friend the druidess Méabh has a violet stone, which is set in a silver pendant," said Fenella, helping him out. "It is dedicated to

Cailleach Bheur, the lady of winter."

"Cailleach Bheur," he said with surprise. "But we in the village see her as…"

"Evil?" Fenella caught his eye again, and he nodded. "I know what people say. The winter mother is veiled from us. She is the master of cold, of frost, of cyclical death, but not evil, no. And there is no sweeter person than Méabh. She is able to generate some cold from the pendant whenever she requires, but she does not use it to cause harm to other people. Far from it."

Donnell glanced down at the brooch in his hand. "Do any of the other stones have particular powers like that?"

"Mine, of course, assists my healing, and it can warm things just as Méabh can produce cold. Besides that, I don't know as much as perhaps I should. Loarn is able to transform the shapes of some things. I have even seen him transform an object to water."

"That's…incredible." Donnell's mind immediately flitted to the potential harm that Iohric could do with the white stone – or with any of them. "Why wouldn't Iohric want *all* of the stones?" he asked.

Fenella inclined her head slightly. "We return full circle to our previous conversation. Why indeed? Using more than one could be dangerous for him – putting them close together without training in the lore can lead to unpredictable releases of energy. But I doubt he even understands that. Given the man's obvious lust for power, my guess is that he simply doesn't know what they are capable of as a group, and has just chosen to focus on the one which is associated with a warrior god."

"We must ensure that the white ring it is not lost to the druids forever," said Donnell.

"Yes." She nodded slowly. "Now, talking of which – I need you to concentrate. Make the circle complete."

Donnell looked back at the lights.

"Join them," Fenella called out softly.

He focused again on growing the golden specks of light. He had already managed to move and grow them – could he expand them enough so that they merged, forming a single glowing ring of light between the two druid stones? He began to try, and slowly the circle began to speed up, each speck of light lengthening, reaching towards the ones before it and behind.

At just that moment there was a moaning sound from Sahar's direction, and Fenella looked around and began to move. As she did so, the druidess closed her hand over the bracelet, and the tiny glowing gold lights faded and vanished. She stood and hurried over to Sahar, and Donnell felt a snap, a shock in his hand as the ring of glowing energy broke contact.

Wincing, he clasped the brooch in his hand, and followed the druidess over to Sahar's side.

Fenella was wiping sweat from the young woman's brow. "Apologies, Donnell – I shouldn't have stopped so suddenly. Did I hurt you?"

"No," he lied. "But what's wrong with Sahar?"

The druidess took a moment to reply, checking the young woman's wound and also feeling for her pulse and her temperature. "Actually, there is no real change," she replied at last. "As I said – she is stable. I am tired, and feeling a bit on edge."

"You should get some rest, Fenella."

"I'll try. And you should as well. I will call if I need you."

As he walked from the Greathouse, he thought again about the power coursing through his body when they had linked hands, and found his hand sliding in to touch the brooch again. How much damage could the druid stones do to their enemies?

The Norse Dungeon

The following evening, a light shone out across the road from inside each of the two low stone watchtowers that now guarded the main road into Cardhu, but nobody called out as Donnell walked past in the shadows. The cloak appeared to be helping him again. The path he knew well, whether in light or dark. His hunting blade was already in his hand. Sneak, scout, gain information on Iohric and the white stone: he knew the plan. But of late, plans hadn't been turning out quite as intended.

He had risen early that morning, as the first glimmering of sunlight was appearing over the Eastern hills. And when he had checked back at the Greathouse, Sahar was still unchanged, neither better or worse. "The girl sleeps. Donnell," Fenella had said. "You need to get on."

The task of pursuing Iohric, however, had had to wait until after his village duties. He had checked on the guards at the East Wall both before and after his training session with the mounted troops. The night had, apparently, been quiet – there had been no more sightings of Norse, or of forest folk either. Since then, his own guard and scouting duties had kept him away from his planned mission to Weir for longer than he would have liked but now, at least, he had the cover of darkness.

The road flattened out as it hit the junction with the main coastal route of the Laird's Road, which ran along the top of the shore, long, wide and flat. Donnell looked in both directions, but there were no signs of any warriors or patrols.

Keeping his hood up – hoping, but also doubting, that its apparent power of concealment would be maintained now that he was out of the tree cover and in the full moonlight – he hurried across the road. Beyond, the familiar route down to Weir village and Longfort Keep was formed of a rocky path, and he moved lightly, keeping the noise of his footsteps almost to nothing.

The wood-and-stone-built fortress itself was clearly occupied, light blazing out from several of its higher-up windows, suggesting that fires were lit in its hearths. Donnell walked slowly, glancing around for guards, and made his way to the right of the building, past the main entrance and circling round behind it. So far, he had not seen any Norse guards, but he covered his knife, holding it beneath the cloak to avoid its blade glinting in the moonlight.

He could make out the low houses of the fishing village up ahead. A couple of new dwellings had been added, in addition to the keep itself; there was a new open-fronted stable nearby, and a large round barn with a turf roof had been constructed near the water's edge.

As he continued to circle the keep, he heard a voice, and froze, crouching low. No – two voices, in fact, and they were coming closer. He turned around fractionally, so that he was able to look in the direction of the speakers.

Sure enough, two guards were approaching, each lightly armoured and wearing helmets without visors. They were speaking in low voices, but seemed relaxed; Donnell was fairly sure that they hadn't seen him. Could he stay still enough to keep it that way, he wondered? He tried to make his breathing softer, as he had learned to do when stalking deer.

The pair had come around from the far side of the keep, where he could make out vertical bars on the lower, stone section of its foundation wall, and they were now circling in the opposite direction to him. He knew that he was almost perfectly still, drawing on years of experience from the forests. The knife, a weapon that had been passed on to him by his father but not one that he ever used to make a hunting kill, was starting to feel slippery and uncomfortable in his hand.

He didn't understand enough of the men's tongue to know what they were saying, but he thought he could make out the words *'Iohric'* and *'Völundr'*, and perhaps also *'schiff'*, the Norse word for a ship. He wasn't quite sure why, but he had a feeling that there was an unspoken disagreement between them. The two were now so close that he could have taken a single stride to reach them. He squeezed the knife's handle slightly. He did not want to have to stab the two men in the dark.

The pair paused suddenly, looked around, and Donnell felt a chill run through his body. One of the guards, heavier set than his companion, pointed up towards the moon and grunted *"gothr"*, meaning 'fine'. The companion nodded, looked for a moment, and then resumed his walk along their original route. The heavier-set guard followed on, just behind him.

Donnell slowly exhaled as they walked away, realising that he had not been breathing at all during the moments when they were just a pace away from him. He took the softest of steps in the other direction, and then another.

Soon, the danger had passed, as the men skirted the front corner of Longfort Keep itself, moving out of sight. He fervently hoped that they would stop at the main entrance, or even go inside entirely after their patrol.

Hurrying but ensuring that his footsteps were as soft as possible, Donnell approached the rear of the keep, looking down at the base of the structure. This area was mainly constructed of very weathered stone blocks that had been present in the previous ruin, but two openings were newly protected with gleaming vertical iron bars. Bars could mean keeping people out, he thought, but could also mean…

He looked closer. The barred openings were just above the ground, suggesting a dwelling level below the ground itself – perhaps for slaves or prisoners. Donnell crouched and peered in, trying to make out what was inside, and urgently aware of how easy his silhouette would be for anyone within to see. But even with his exceptional vision, it was hard to make out more than a few irregular shapes in the gloom within.

"Hello?" he whispered.

"Who's there?" said a croaking voice from deep within the chamber.

"Shh!" whispered Donnell, glancing from side to side. "Speak softly – there are guards around. Who are you?"

"I am Güntar Schmidt," said a different voice, a gruffer one this time, and he was able to make out a figure approaching the bars.

"And what about the other one?"

"Who I am," came the other voice, "depends on who I am speaking to."

Donnell shrugged. "That sounds like the sort of thing a druid would say." He crouched down a little closer, placing his hand on one of the bars. "Are you by any chance the one they call the Dark Shadow?"

There was a movement within as if someone was standing up, and Donnell was able to make out a round, pale face with a fulsome dark beard and hair, but little else of the man's features. "Yes. I'm a brother of Gabrán, and a druid myself. A great one, or was once," said the man, his voice wavering as he spoke, and lending the impression that he was very ill or utterly exhausted. "Are you... a man of Weir?"

"No. I am of Cardhu. I met Gabrán once, a few months ago, but he is dead now. I am sorry to pass on that news." As he spoke, Donnell glanced to both sides once again, watchful for danger.

"I already knew this, man of Cardhu." There was a slight grunting noise. "Ah...I'm in so much pain," the druid continued in his wavering tones, and he sat down again in the shadows.

"Did they torture you?"

"No. At least, not yet. But I am not in good health these days. Do you have any food or wine?"

Donnell shook his head slightly in the dark. "I'm sorry. We want to help you get out of here, though. I'll return with the druid Fenella. When she finds out that you are here…"

"Ah, lovely Fen. She trusts me, even if I have not fully earned it."

Güntar Schmidt took another step closer to the bars. "But can't you get us out now? I am unfairly imprisoned here. I was taken as a rowing slave, and locked in here as a punishment for attempting an escape."

"I will help, Güntar, but not tonight. I came here to find the druid, and I must go for help before I can do more – I can't break into this place by myself. But I'll do it as soon as I can."

Donnell stood and took a moment to walk to each corner of the keep and look around the edge, but there were no signs of any further patrols, and so he returned and crouched back down. "Listen, do either of you know where Iohric is, or what he is planning?"

There was another low groan from the back of the cell. The druid sounded as if he could expire at any moment, and Donnell silently cursed himself for not bringing any food or water.

"What about you, Güntar?"

The man looked up at the bars, and Donnell could just make out a blotchy face with thin scraggly whiskers. "Listen, stranger," he said, "Iohric is in charge of some of the Norsemen. He wants enough prisoners and slaves to fill his ships. Big man, very unpleasant, and dangerous. I don't think you should face him."

"Thanks," said Donnell, "I know who he is. But I need to know *where* he is now."

The man spread his hands in a shrug, and then moved away from the bars slightly. "Hey, Fáelán," he said from inside the cell, "get up. You know more about this than I do."

A feeling like cold ice flowed through Donnell's body at the sound of the name. "Wait – are you Fáelán?"

There was silence, but for a low groan, and Donnell heard someone from within the cell spitting. He paused, looking around, and considering walking away. But then there was a shuffling noise, and he knew he had been heard. "Well? Are you? The renegade druid?"

"Yes I'm Fáelán", said the thin voice at last, though the man still did not approach the bars. "I already told you who I was."

"I didn't think…" Donnell stopped. What had he been thinking, exactly? That Fáelán was long dead? Probably, yes – as he himself had put a spear in the shapeshifter years ago. And as for his being Gabrán's brother, well…it had been wrong, clearly, to assume that the druid had other brothers.

"You attacked me," said Donnell through gritted teeth. "You're a shapeshifter, and you transformed and gored me!"

"That's your imagination, young man…" muttered the druid.

"It's a fact. You're a disgrace to your people, a thief, and a murderous wretch."

"Not really," said the man, and then coughed dreadfully.

"Don't lie to me! Eochaid told me all about you. I know that it was you in the forest that day." Still slumped at the back of the dungeon cell, the man cleared his throat in a way that was both noisy and painful-sounding, but did not reply.

"Fáelán!" Donnell whispered sharply. "Get over here, or I leave right now. I'm not going to help while you lie there feeling sorry for yourself."

Again there was no response, and Donnell risked raising his voice a little. "Last chance. Get over here if you ever want to get out."

"Don't walk away, man. I can tell you more," said the gruffer voice.

"Be quiet, Güntar. You've already admitted to me that you know nothing."

There was a moment's silence, and then another rustling sound followed by a groan. At last, Donnell was able to see Fáelán slowly approaching the bars.

"I know you work for Eochaid," said the druid, more life and conviction coming into his voice, "and he's as much of a renegade as I am. Perhaps I should just take my chances with the Norse."

"Eochaid? No, I don't work for him. It's true that he warned me about you. But not until after you'd upended my friend Malcolm in the forest on our bonding day. You transformed into a huge boar with silver stripes, and chased us through Holm's Wood almost to the edge of Cardhu."

There was a long pause. "Well," said the druid at last, "you were young lads, and memories can play tricks on you. Are you sure it wasn't something else that you saw? A large rabbit, perhaps?"

Donnell clenched his fists. "Look, a part of me wonders why I am even talking to you. You nearly killed me, and I was little more than a child. But if you want my help, the least you can do is give me the information I need."

For the first time, Fáelán came close to the bars, and Donnell was able to see the man's bushy dark beard, streaked with silver, and though his face looked much thinner and more tired that he was expecting, he was a handsome man with a thoughtful expression.

"Very well. I'm sorry, lad. I never meant to gore you, or hurt your friend. Your story is new to me in a sense, but I don't deny the truth of what you are saying. A mist comes over my thoughts and vision when I change form, and I only half remember it."

Donnell licked his lips and nodded slightly as he considered this. "Fenella doesn't know that you can change shape, does she?"

"That I used to be able to. If I still could, do you think I'd be here? It was no special talent of mine, in any case. No gift of Étaín." He shrugged and looked off to the side.

"Malcolm thought that you were a messenger of Brighid. But that's not right, is it? It was the belt."

He nodded fractionally, coughed again, and then stared up at Donnell, bringing a single finger up to his lips. "Most people don't know – even the Mor-druids. Please, keep it that way, if you don't want your enemies finding the thing and using it to cause great harm."

Donnell thought for a moment about the trouble that had already been caused by Iohric's pursuit of the white druid stone, and nodded. "Very well. But you'll need to tell me everything you know about Iohric. Your brother conspired with him, you know, and murdered one of his fellow Mor-druids. If you won't tell me everything, we're finished here, and I'll leave you to enjoy the cell."

There was another pause and he began to rise, but then Fáelán spoke again in the same rough-sounding voice.

"Iohric, he was paid to come here by the Laird's brother in the north. But now…" – the man coughed – "… now he has broken that agreement."

"Continue," said Donnell coldly.

"I'm tired," the man said in a slow, croaking voice. "But I will tell you what I can. He's not here, first of all."

"What do you mean?"

"I have heard the guards say that Völundr is in charge here now. He has made a deal with the Laird, and promised peace, although most of his men don't agree. And Iohric has turned coat against his own people, and has taken a band of men up to the forest."

"Dung. In that case, he must be mustering troops there, as we thought." Donnell's mind raced. It was as he had half-suspected – they were planning something in Holm's Wood. And that may mean that the East Wall and the handful of guards there were in imminent danger.

It appeared that even Sahar's suspicions underestimated how untrustworthy the huge Norseman was – if the druid was right, Iohric had first conspired with the northern Laird to cheat and betray his own brother, and was now backstabbing that partner, too.

"One more thing – did the Norsemen bring a big group of people from Eas Mòr, to sell as slaves?"

"No," said Fáelán. "These Norse scum are notorious slavers and villains, believe me – I know all about it. But there have been no slaves here recently. Not a large group, anyway. I would have heard."

"Are you sure?"

"Aye. Sure enough. Though I suppose you could check the other buildings…" He coughed some more. "The new one especially."

"All right." Donnell stood. "I will return when I can. Try to stay alive until then." On an impulse, Donnell reached out and passed his long hunting knife to the man through the bars. "Here. Take this and keep it concealed – perhaps it will come in useful until we can rescue you."

The man took hold of the blade and grunted, and then muttered, "It's all coming back to me now." He moved away from the bars, and Donnell could see enough to make out that he had sat or lain down further away.

With that he rose, and hurried away from the keep. He knew exactly where to go – other than the stable, the only new structure at Weir village itself was the large, round building with a turf roof near the water's edge, which he had at first taken for some kind of barn. Were the Norsemen using it for a different type of livestock?

He crept that way now, walking bent over to avoid being silhouetted against the moonlight which was now behind him.

The building stood apart from the main village, making it easier for him to approach stealthily. He saw a pair of guards close to the shore line – possibly the same ones that he had seen before, making a larger circuit of the area – and he paused. They were standing still, looking out to sea, but after a short time they began walking again, moving along the edge of the rocks above the sea itself. They were far enough away that he was able to evade their notice without difficulty, and in short order Donnell reached the building itself.

It looked larger, close up – bigger than any of the roundhouses in Cardhu. Its walls were smooth, clay over stone, and they were also high, no doubt making it difficult or impossible to reach the roof from within. He could see no windows.

He walked almost right round the building, and as he came to the section that faced towards Weir village, there was a single narrow entrance, blocked by a heavy, wooden, reinforced door. And it was unlocked.

Donnell reached out and pushed tentatively, and the door swung open with a squeak – iron hinges. He winced and looked around, but could not see any foes approaching. The village itself was quiet at this hour, though firelight shone from many of the doorways. He peered in the direction of the Norse guardsmen, but they were now out of sight – circling back towards Longfort Keep by going around the back of the village? He couldn't be sure, and it would be best to stay cautious.

He walked in.

The building smelled foul, like stale urine. The floor was rough and damp, with a modicum of straw spread over some mud. It was unoccupied, and almost completely unfurnished. It didn't look clean enough to be a storeroom for anything but livestock, and with its sturdy door and walls, could easily house slaves. But one thing was certainly clear – there were no animals here now, and no human-chattel either.

Donnell crouched down and peered closely at the ground, making use of what little light was coming in through the entrance. There didn't seem to be any recent footprints, discarded items, or other signs that prisoners might have left behind.

If the unfortunate people of Eas Mòr had ever been held here, they were gone.

* * *

It had begun to rain by the time Donnell hurried up the steep, tree-lined road that led from the coast back up towards Cardhu. As he did so, thoughts raced through his head. He thought of Iohric mustering his men in the forest. Of the Norsemen launching an attack on the East Wall, burning the towers, slaughtering the guards. Facing off against a few brave but hopelessly outnumbered defenders in the village itself. Taking the people of Cardhu as captives – the likes of Fenella, Branwen, and Niamh's children included – and holding them like cattle in the round building at the shore before shipping them off to the slave market across the sea at Dubh-Linn.

They might just be images in his head for now, but as a sequence of events, it could well be what the future held for all of them. And there was nothing one man could do to stop any of those things from happening.

It wouldn't be long before he would reach the guard towers again, and he slowed his pace. If he identified himself they would, of course, let him pass, but he'd rather slip past undetected again – any alternative would simply take up extra time.

The road curved to the left and then to the right again before the towers appeared up ahead. When they did, he saw that there was a light only in one – what had happened to the guard in the other?

He approached slowly, cautiously. As he did so, he saw a figure, half-hidden behind a tree a couple of dozen paces from the nearest stone tower, and he stopped dead, pulling the cloak around him again. He cursed himself for giving away his hunting knife; he still had his smaller blade concealed in his boot, but it was difficult to access, and he would be at a significant disadvantage against a well-armed foe.

The figure hadn't moved; they were short, and he could see the tip of a bow. Enemy or local? Could it be a Cardhu guard who, for reasons unknown, had decided to leave the tower and stand on the road instead?

There was very little light to see by under the thick tree cover, and he decided to creep a little closer. When he did, he saw that it was indeed a single lone figure, standing on the road in between the two stone towers. Donnell took another step, ready to duck down and hide if necessary. But the figure was very small, slim…and familiar. He knew that face – it was Niamh's daughter Kit. The girl had a short bow in hand and a quiver of arrows at her hip. She looked frightened but determined, peering into the darkness – but clearly had not spotted him yet.

"Kit," he whispered urgently as he approached, and then hurried on and stopped a few feet from her. "Don't shoot. It's Donnell," he added.

"There you are!" she said, lowering the bow. "The druidess sent me."

"About Sahar?"

Kit nodded.

"And…is everything all right back there?" He glanced around as they spoke, but there was no further movement from the direction of the watchtowers.

"I don't know," the girl said quietly, almost whispering, looking around at the trees as she spoke. "But she wants you to go to the Greathouse."

"Very well. Thank you," he said, and began to run in that direction. Kit ran alongside, her bow across her shoulder.

"I notice that we are a guard down," he called to her, pointing back at the unlit tower. "Is someone coming?"

"I think so."

He nodded, and increased his pace, rain lashing his face as he reached the village centre at full speed, Kit sprinting along behind. It was quiet on the approach to the village square; a couple of villagers could be seen hurrying towards their roundhouses, but most were abed. As he ran, the news about Fáelán that Donnell had been intending to share with the druidess was momentarily forgotten as he began to picture the scene he would find back at the Greathouse. Had Sahar awoken? Or worse?

When he reached the Greathouse itself and hurried inside, Fenella was standing over Sahar. She looked up as Donnell entered, and nodded grimly. The areas beneath the druidess's eyes were dark and lined, and he realised that unlike him, she had not slept at all since the night before last.

"We're losing her," she said.

Departing and Returning

"There must be something we can do," said Donnell, stepping closer and wiping the rain from his face and brow with his sleeve. Sahar's wound looked much the same as before, but her face was paler still, her lips grey from loss of blood.

"Why do you think I sent for you?" Fenella replied, taking hold of his arm and pulling him towards the injured woman. "Here – take both of my hands. Hold them firmly. We need to make a circle directly around her head. Remember – just the way I taught you."

They stood on either side of the bed where Sahar was murmuring and twitching, semi-conscious in the depths of her suffering. Fenella didn't stop to explain her plan in detail, instead issuing Donnell with a sequence of instructions.

Before long the pair were each upon their knees with their hands joined, ringing Sahar's upper body and head with their arms in a circle, fingers enmeshed. With the brooch and Fenella's red gem each between their joined palms, no golden light was visible from the gems; Donnell briefly wondered to himself whether this power was still flowing in some other way.

Fenella had begun to chant words that were so low as to be hardly audible, but what Donnell could hear sounded to him like a mixture of the old Celtic language which was now only used in some of their elders' fireside songs, and of Roman words that he had heard Malcolm reading from books in Eochaid's abode during their childhood.

"Concentrate!" shouted the druidess, and he tried to focus his mind, picturing the glowing energy that he had seen emanating from the two druid stones the night before, even though he couldn't see it. Fenella's red stone was in contact with his left hand and he felt a pulsing sensation, powerful and regular, like a heartbeat or a horse's hoofbeats, strong but controlled. His right hand, which was touching the yellow gem of his own brooch, sensed something very different. Something wild, untameable, but at the same time friendly and familiar; he was briefly put in mind of the child-like and chaotic Caelia of the forest folk.

The gems were clearly glowing strongly now; although both were covered, he could see light shooting out from the cracks between their interleaved fingers. It was bright enough to glow slightly even through the flesh of their hands, and the Greathouse as a whole looked brighter as golden light mixed with red. He glanced around the room in wonder.

Suddenly there was a fizzing noise, and everything returned to the dim, candlelit conditions of before.

A deep silence followed, and Donnell heard his own quick breaths, and felt his heart pounding.

"Is it finished?"

Fenella didn't respond, but she unclenched their hands, and then slowly, deliberately, returned the bracelet with its red gem to her wrist, breathing heavily. Donnell restored his own brooch under his tunic.

He leaned in, his hands on the edge of the bed staring down at Sahar's face. "And? Did it work?"

"It felt like…," the druidess began, also looking at the young woman. "Yes," she said more decisively, with an exhausted smile. "It worked. She will wake soon." The druidess exhaled deeply and then walked towards the centre of the Greathouse, closing her eyes for a few moments, and then she turned on her heel and returned to them.

"It was incredible," said Donnell in a low voice, taking a step back from the bed. "Your power...can you tell me, how did you know what to do? How do you make the stones work together?"

"By the will of the gods, my friend," she smiled. "And years of practice."

She pointed towards her wrist, with its mystical bracelet. "Each stone somehow gives us a greater connection to our patron god. Alone, the gems can help us do small things, but more is possible when we link together. There is power inside them, and linking allows it to flow, and build up. You saw what we were able to do all five together, cloaking the village when it was under attack. But combining them in any way requires caution."

"I don't understand it," said Donnell. "But I felt it."

"As did I."

He nodded, glancing off to one side, and thinking about the mysterious feeling which had occurred when they had linked hands the previous day. Walking over towards the doorway, he looked out into the night. The square was silent, but the rain had stopped falling.

Just at that moment Sahar stirred, and opened her eyes, peering at them with an ill-tempered look. "Ouch," she said, grimacing and wriggling up onto her elbows while looking up at the pair of them, and then glancing around the room. "How long was I out for?"

* * *

Donnell gave a shout of relief and hurried over, grasping hold of his friend's hand. Fenella beamed and put an arm around Sahar's shoulders. "How do you feel?" asked the druidess.

"Oh – uh. I don't know exactly." The young woman shuffled back a bit further and sat up, leaning against the exterior wall of the roundhouse. "My arm is very tender," she replied, stretching it and then circling it right round as if it were merely stiff rather than having been stabbed just a day before.

"You took a serious wound," said Fenella. "Poisoned, too. It has been a close thing, in truth. But now, gods willing, you are back with us."

Sahar nodded to herself for a few moments, and then quietly thanked the druidess.

"It was Iohric that did it, you know," said Donnell. "Do you remember our battle? You bested him. But he had a poisoned blade."

Sahar blew out air from between her lips and shook her head slightly at this.

"I know," Donnell said.

"To think that he called my crossbow an unworthy weapon," she said. "His ancestors will rot in Helheim for this."

Fenella stood back, smiling as she watched the two friends resume their easy manner with one another.

Donnell, likewise, took a moment to breathe fully, feeling some of the tension that had gripped his body over the past day or more gradually dissipate. At last, not quite sure how to express his relief and gratitude, he said, "Fenella, I can't thank you enough for what you have done…the way you have been at Sahar's side day and night. It's overwhelming."

"In the end, it wasn't me that saved her," she replied.

He smiled. "It was mainly you. But I'm happy to have helped."

He walked over to the door once again and peered out. With the immediate threat to Sahar's life having passed, the recent revelations from the Norse Dungeon were now forcing their way back into his consciousness, and he turned, looking back at the pair of them. "Fenella, I managed to speak to Gabrán's brother. You were right – he still lives, and is being held captive by the Norse."

She looked at him eagerly. "Donnell, well done. It won't be easy to free him, but that's wonderful news all the same."

"There was a man called Güntar Schmidt there, too," he added.

She shook her head. "No idea who that is."

"Right. Well, anyway, there's more – he thinks that the Norse are mustering under Iohric at Holm's Wood. Fenella, I'm going to need to go there now to alert the guards. We could come under attack at any moment."

She frowned. "Well, if you must, then you must."

Sahar sat up further and swung her legs around to the edge of the bed, stretching her arms towards the roof and yawning. "Well, since I'm feeling better," she began, starting to rise. "I think I will join you."

"No, no!" said Fenella, putting her hand on the younger woman's shoulder, forcing her gently but firmly back onto the bed. "It's great that you are recovering – eternal thanks to my goddess Brighid – but I need to re-dress that wound, and you still need a lot more rest. A lot more. I absolutely insist, dear girl. Lie back now. Donnell, please, wait just one minute."

Sahar rolled her eyes, but lay back as she was told. Fenella spent a short while administering some potions and binding up the wound with herbs, as Donnell hovered impatiently by the doorway and watched on. From what he could see, there was no longer any bleeding at all from the stab wound. Soon their young friend had dropped off again into a calm, healing sleep.

"Get some rest, Fenella," said Donnell as he moved towards the door. "Please. It's unbelievable what you have done, but you have to take a break."

"Very well," she smiled. "Thank you, Donnell. As should you."

"I will – if all is quiet. But first I need to establish what Iohric and his men are doing in the forest."

She looked up at him, alarmed. "No – you can't risk going in yourself by night!"

"I must. How else will we find out what they are planning?"

Fenella frowned and shook her head, momentarily unsure of herself.

"It will be all right," he added. "I'm just going to scout nearby. Fenella – really. If the Norse at the keep didn't see me, well… neither will these. I don't think their forest skills will be a match for mine."

She walked towards him, and picked up his spear. "At least take someone with you. Some back up. What about Branwen? She's a fine archer."

He paused, looking out towards the dark of the village square – all was still, and the moonlight still shone down. "Very well," he said, taking the spear from her. "I will go and wake Branwen. Now – please do rest."

She nodded, moving away. "I will."

* * *

As Donnell left the village, he mumbled an apology to Cernunnos for his lie to the druidess. He wasn't willing to risk Branwen on a dangerous night mission into the woods, even though she had already declared her willingness to go. The young woman meant the world to Niamh and the children.

He also had no intention of rousing the other Cardhu guards. They would slow him down, and couldn't keep hidden in the forest the way he could. Indeed, if he could get past the East Wall without having to speak to them at all, so much the better. Further discussions would just waste time – and potentially alert enemies.

Pulling his travelling cloak close around him, he made his way on foot through the outfield. Reaching the East Wall, he leaned on it for a moment, looking and listening. There were no sounds from the forest, but a Cardhu guard, bow strung across his back, a clutch of arrows thrust into his belt, had begun to patrol up and down the outside of the East Wall, between the watchfires. Donnell crouched back into the shadows and waited until the man turned and complete his circuit, returning to the watchtower. When the way ahead was clear, he vaulted the wall and hurried to the forest's edge.

Donnell had walked through forests by night before, but not often; paths were easy to lose in the gloom, and the surroundings looked very different without the colours of day to navigate by. However, his newfound visual acuity seemed to be helping. It was dark, yes, but more of a pale grey than real black, and he could make out the path easily enough.

Any hope of immediately finding and disturbing a Norse gathering quickly faded, however. After having walked for a few hundred paces he hadn't seen or heard anybody at all, and there were certainly no glimmers of firelight or anything of that sort, as he had been half expecting. He stopped, and looked around in every direction. Could their foes be that much deeper in the forest? And if so, why?

The cloak, at least, was keeping him warm. He stood and tried to think of what the Norsemen might be doing, or where he would have gone if he was in their boots. There was an image in his mind that he couldn't let go of: one of the wood folk speaking to the Norsemen the previous day. He had seen it. And unless his vision was now playing tricks on him as well as being more acute, that meant that the little forest people had formed some kind of understanding with their enemy. An alliance, even.

"Caelia!" he called out softly, and then repeated it a little louder. The wood folk were small but alert, and had the sharpest hearing of any forest dweller. If she was within half a mile, she would hear him.

The thought occurred to him that perhaps she could see him, but was not coming to him. Or perhaps she was unable to come? Caelia was in many ways his oldest friend, the person who had taught him the ways of the forest long before Macswain had trained him as an apprentice woodsman, and even though he had rarely spoken to her in recent years, the thought of anything harming the little woman brought a sensation of physical pain.

He called her name one more time, and then turned, at last he realising that he would have to give up, and try returning with support and supplies by daylight. Fenella had been right.

He started down the path, returning the way he had come.

Disquiet

The summer nights were short, but this one seemed eternal. Donnell sat hunched up, the cloak around him, far enough back in the outfield that his presence was unlikely to alarm the watchers in the towers. He was warm enough in his cloak, but every so often his head nodded; when he found himself slumping forward he caught himself, rose, and walked a few paces around in a circle before settling again.

As the first light of morning began to glimmer over the trees and hills to the east, he stood and stretched, a heavy feeling of foreboding in his heart. He had failed to find Iohric's men. While it was a relief that no attack had come, he now felt no further forward in terms of uncovering the Norse plot, and defending the village. For now, though, there was nothing for it but return home and take his rest.

As he began to cross the outfield towards Cardhu village, he saw the first two dawn watch guards arrive – both of them elderly men, but doughty enough to hold a spear with confidence.

"Be extra watchful today," he called out, waving towards them.

"More boggles?" said one, looking in his direction.

"Boggles, certainly. But there are also Norsemen unaccounted for. Some have gone into Holm's Wood – they have yet to come back out."

One of them, an elderly crofter, growled as he eyed the forest. "I might be a greybeard," he said, "but I can hold a bow. Trust me."

"Good luck, then," replied Donnell, and then walked off with a nod.

His head was beginning to ache from fatigue as he reached the village square and he knew he needed sleep, but as he passed the Celtic Rock something caused him to pause. The cool light of morning was now much more fulsome now, illuminating the village square, but there were, as yet, few people around.

He looked down, and noticed that the cup markings – where the druids traditionally set their staves while performing the protection rituals at Samhain – were again full of murky water and dead leaves. He stooped and began to scoop the nearest out with his hand, but as he did so, he felt the druid stone burning at his chest. He pulled it out, and saw that it was glowing faintly.

He closed his fingers over it, and as he did so, an image came in to his head of the Greathouse, and the golden lights that flowed from one of the druid stones to the other. He looked up at the Celtic Rock. Did it have a similar power? Could it connect to the amber stone?

Walking closer to the huge Rock, he held the stone up to its dark, carved surface, and felt it warming still further within his hand. The glow it was emitting was not as bright as on the occasion of Sahar's healing – of course, only one druid stone was active now – but it was a comforting, homely glow all the same. He moved his hand closer still and felt a clear sensation in his hand and through his whole body. Although he was unable to see any moving lights, he felt sure that they were there.

Turning away, he glanced down again at the cup markings, and saw that they were clear – dry and empty, the triskelion markings around each one gleaming slightly in the morning light. For a moment, it felt to him as if the whole area was ready, expectant. Waiting for something to happen.

Clearly there was much about the druid stones that he had yet to learn.

Shaking his head slightly, he walked away from the Celtic Rock, and made his way back to his lodgings.

* * *

When Donnell woke a few hours later, he sat up with a start, and straight away hurried off to check on his injured friend. He was almost at the Greathouse by the time he remembered about the healing that he and Fenella had achieved, and Sahar's apparent recovery.

The druidess smiled at him as he entered. "She is a lot better," said Fenella, following his gaze, "Remarkably normal. But she certainly needs a day or two at least to be fully herself. What news from the wall?"

"Quiet. I stayed for many hours. Whatever the Norse are planning, it hasn't begun yet."

"And today?" she asked.

Donnell again placed his spear just inside the Greathouse door, and he rubbed the palms of his hands together for a moment, frowning. "Today, we find out what is happening in the forest." He paused and looked at her. "I did walk into Holm's Wood a short way last night. And I have to confess – I went in alone."

"That was rash! What did you see?" she replied. She was frowning in annoyance, but her voice betrayed her curiosity.

"That's just it – nothing. I couldn't see any sign of the Norse warriors that we saw, or any kind of camp or gathering. No sounds, no firelight – nothing. But then, I did not go deep enough to be sure."

"Very well, then," she said. "At least we know that they are not mustering an army just inside the forest's edge."

"Not one that I have found yet, anyway," he replied.

Donnell turned at the entrance and stepped outside, but Fenella followed close behind him. "And there is time to free my friend," she said.

He turned around to face her just outside the double doors. "Of course we will run the mission to the keep at Weir," he said, "and rescue your friend. But I will go by night again. I don't need to take on Völundr or his men directly – I just need to get past them and free the prisoners."

She caught his eye. "Tonight?"

He glanced down to the ground, tapping his foot. "Possibly. Or tomorrow. We can decide when I return from the forest." He spun to the left and began to walk up towards the roundhouses that nestled into the area on the northern side of the village square.

"But Donnell, why?" Fenella replied, hurrying to keep up with him. "We are close now to reuniting the druids. As I keep saying, rebuilding the circle will help with all of our problems. The Dark Shadow can certainly help us to regain the white druid stone."

Donnell nodded as he walked. "Yes, I know. And I will go there, certainly. But only when Sahar has recovered her strength. There is nobody I'd rather have beside me for a stealth attack than her. I suppose that another day or two won't make any difference to the man at this stage – they have been holding him for weeks, and although he sounded terrible, he can surely last a bit longer."

"So, what are you planning to do now?"

"I am returning to Holm's Wood with more people – if the Norse are mustering there, I need to know about it. Yes, I didn't find anything last night, but it seems a good bet that Iohric has a camp much further in. If so, there will be noise, fires, preparation. We will see them long before they see us." He stopped outside the nearest roundhouse, and turned and looked at the druidess. "I'm going to scout them out, and there is no time to lose," he added.

"I will go with you, then. To Holm's Wood. You could use my help – I know the forest almost as well as you do, and I know more about the white stone. And if it turns out that Iohric is there and has learned to use its powers, well…"

"… then we will need your expertise," he finished. "Very well. But first, I want to ensure that there are enough people guarding Cardhu. If you are sure you can spare the time to help, then please call on some of these houses. Ideally, I'd like another ten people at the East Wall." He pointed towards the houses on the other side of the square.

Fenella looked around briefly and then nodded once. "Very well, then. But how do you know that the Norse won't attack from both sides at once?" she asked quietly. "From the forest, and the shore?"

"I don't – not for certain. But your friend mentioned the Ganger having 'turned coat'. I get the impression that there are factions within the Norse. We can only hope that they are not working together on this. It may well be the case that Völundr calls the shots at the keep, now, and is feigning loyalty to the Laird."

"That makes a certain sense. If Iohric is has been trying to learn how to use the ring…it's not a power that can be easily shared with his captains."

"Let's hope it's not something he ever gets to use himself, either."

* * *

Donnell strode towards one of the closer roundhouses, but found it unoccupied. Passing the building and its neighbour, he walked to a small croft set back from the village square, and found Rian pulling weeds while sharing a joke with a much older man.

"Rian! Are you due for guard duty today?" called out Donnell as he approached.

"Yes," said the younger man nervously. "But not until later."

"I need you there now. As soon as possible. Get your spear."

Without waiting for a response, Donnell returned to the square, and continued to make his way around the village.

Meanwhile, Fenella had crossed to the other side and was calling on the dwellings which stood closer to the path that wound downhill out of the village and towards the coast. Donnell looked over, and saw the druidess speaking to Branwen. The pair glanced briefly in his direction, and then continued talking.

He himself hurried on towards the houses to the East side of the village, closer to Tarin's farm. A few minutes later, after calling on several homes, he met Fenella again on the main track that led back to the square, not far from the Celtic Rock.

"How many so far?" he asked.

"I spoke to four, though I am not certain they are actually going to go," she replied.

He nodded. "All the same. With mine, that makes nine in total. Even if only some of them proceed to the wall, it could make all the difference – a couple in each watchtower, we can hope. And perhaps a few capable warriors among them. Did Branwen say she would come?"

"I spoke to her," said Fenella, looking downhill in the direction of the small roundhouse where Niamh's family lived. "She had the children with her, but she understood the need. I think so, anyway."

"She will help when she can – I'm sure of that," Donnell replied.

"Good."

"And now we had best go and prepare ourselves for the journey into the woods."

Together they made their way back towards the village square. The route was busy with crofters, and a few children were playing outside their homes despite the gloomy weather.

"There's something I didn't get a chance to speak to you about last night," he said as they hurried on.

"What is it?"

"This prisoner. The 'dark shadow'. I know him from my youth. He is the man known as Fáelán, is he not?"

The druidess nodded her head. "That's right. That is his birth name."

"The younger brother of Gabrán? The one who refused to take up his place in the circle of Mor-druids?"

She looked at him, raising her eyebrows, but nodded again.

"Fenella, I know this man of old. From my days training under Macswain in the ways of the forest. We crossed paths in Wherrycross when I was only a young lad."

The pair paused, not a dozen yards from the brooding mass of the Celtic Rock, and looked at each other.

"Go on," she said.

"The man is a notorious renegade. A criminal. And I am sure that he's the shapeshifter that attacked me and almost killed me. He transformed into a boar, and charged and gored me."

Fenella narrowed her eyes. "No, druids are not shapeshifters. That is a myth, a tale that village folk tell each other. Have you ever seen me transform myself into a wolf, or a beetle, or a bird?"

He shook his head. "I know, I know. But this is different. I am sure he did it. I challenged him, and he didn't deny it. Well, not with any conviction, anyhow."

"I don't know, Donnell…"

"He had something that allowed him to transform. A magical item of some kind. I can't remember what it was called, but Eochaid would know. It gives Fáelán those powers."

"Did you actually see this happen?"

"Well, no, but Eochaid showed me the object. The man was wearing a belt when we saw him in Wherrycross."

"A belt. Well, what of it?"

"It was a silver belt. A magical one – the last of its kind. I swear, it allowed him to assume the form of a boar. Perhaps other creatures, too."

She shook her head, her green eyes scrutinising Donnell. "There are no such objects. It's a fable."

"Well, what about this?" He pointed to his chest, at the spot where the druid stone in its brooch was pinned to his undershirt. "Are they not also objects of legend? Perhaps if there was only one, and Fáelán had stolen it, nobody would believe it was real."

Fenella took a few steps closer to the Celtic Rock and leaned her hand against the monolith, but said nothing.

"Anyhow," Donnell continued, "the man is dangerous, corrupt. He turned his back on the druids. His own brother hated him, I am sure of it. And he was planning to take druid artefacts away and sell them to the Norse."

"Donnell, these are… simple rumours. Gossip."

There was a long pause, and then Donnell said again, "Fenella, he attacked me. I mean, it really was him. It was no normal animal. The boar's stripes of silver were just like those of his hair."

She sighed. "I can see that this is going to be difficult, Donnell. You know what you saw, and I am not doubting your honesty. But you also know me – and I think you trust me."

He looked at her. "I do."

"I've never asked for much, Donnell, from you or from anyone. And I don't ask for any repayment for healing, or anything like that. But I want to ask you for a favour now, please. If you will offer me this kindness."

He sighed slightly and looked at her as she leaned back against the Rock, knowing where the discussion was heading. "Mmm?"

"Listen to me." She put her hands on his shoulders and looked him in the eyes. "You must give Fáelán a chance. He is not the person you think he is."

"I just…"

"I know. If what you say is true – and I am not doubting that you got attacked. I treated the wound! But you can't be entirely certain that it was him. Can you?"

"Well…"

"And even if it was," she continued, "then…" She winced and looked around as she tried to find the right words. "I know that man. I've known him for a long time – since he was a child, in fact. He is a good person, with a good heart. One of the finest, kindest people I've met, on the whole. A rule breaker, yes, and a rogue, I admit. But not a cold-hearted killer, not someone who would intentionally attack and maim a youth, and certainly none of it just to make money out of selling an artefact. That is just not him."

"But Eochaid…"

"Eochaid is a brilliant man, Donnell, very wise, very learned. But he is not a druid. He doesn't know Fáelán as I do. And even clever people can be mistaken."

"I suppose you are right."

"So, I think you know the favour I am going to ask. Will you trust me? At least, Donnell, if nothing else, just until such time as we free him? After that, you don't need to do anything for the man."

They hurried on, and Donnell was silent as he considered the druidess's words. Ahead, down towards the shore, above a silvery strip of sea the great mountains of Arran were clear despite the cloudy conditions, every rock and gully on its eastern side picked out by the morning light. He could easily recollect the agony that he had felt in when he was gored by the shapeshifter. If the man would do that do a young apprentice, little more than a boy, then what wouldn't he stoop to…?

"Very well, then," he said at last, trying to sound positive and open minded – though it was a struggle to do so. "I will listen to your guidance."

Fenella nodded. "Thank you, Donnell," she said. "And if I turn out to be mistaken, well…"

He raised his eyebrows. "You might end up having to heal my leg again."

She grimaced slightly.

They hurried on, passing the centre of the square again, and approaching the entrance to the Greathouse. And at just that moment, Donnell heard the sound of horses' hooves and wagon wheels approaching from the west.

The trading party had returned from Wherrycross.

* * *

Donnell hurried over as the wagon emerged from among the houses and drew to a halt in the centre of the square. Niamh had indeed returned with the wagon and their two riders, but she had not come alone; Macswain, the Laird's chief hunter, sat beside the Luftenand upon the wagon along with a man of roughly his own age, a freckled and lean man whose long reddish hair was tied back with a strip of leather, and who was dressed in the dark colours typical of his trade. Donnell recognised him as Luguwalos, one of the Laird's team of hunters – a harmless enough man, but an infamous know-it-all.

They were also flanked by three of the Laird's armoured knights. Their own pair of horsemen, even the broad-shouldered Erik, looked very underwhelming in comparison to this group, each of whom was clad in full ringmail, wore iron helmets, carried greatswords and tournament shields, and had battle-axes strapped across their backs. Their horses were enormous, and were also equipped with light ringmail protection which hung across their front quarters. Looking at the knights, Donnell was reminded of Mac Rath, who had travelled through to check on their defences just a few days before. Like him, these men looked magnificent, as if warriors had stepped out of the old tales.

As Donnell walked out and greeted the group, he realised with a start that Malcolm was absent. Macswain spoke to him as she stepped out of the wagon. "Greetings, young Donnell," she said. "Can you see to these horses in the new stable? Oh, and you may not know the Laird's Marischal, Toirdelbach. He will take charge of our relations with the Norse, while I supervise the defences against the threats from the woods."

One of the three mounted knights had moved closer – Toirdelbach, he presumed. Donnell noticed that this man had more elaborate armour than the others, and he carried a richly decorated shield with an image of a griffon which had something white coming out of its mouth – it looked to Donnell like milk, or possibly vomit. The man dismounted and removed his helmet, revealing long straight light-brown hair cut to the length of his jawline, and a neatly trimmed beard of a slightly darker colour. Without a word of greeting he handed his mount's reins to Donnell, and then turned his back to face out into the square, where a small number of locals had now gathered.

Relations was an interesting way to put it, thought Donnell, as he took charge of the warhorse.

Toirdelbach then cleared his throat and spoke. "Your master, the Laird of Wherrycross and Cunninghame, has mustered his troops against the Norse insult. For it appears that all the while the Norse at the shore have proclaimed peace and promised to accept your Laird as their master, they have been plotting against him." The man's voice was surprisingly high and whining for one so tall. "And so, your Laird and his warriors will ride out here equipped for battle, just as soon as our Irish and Wessexman mercenary warriors arrive in port. The Norsemen will bow to the Laird and to the authority of the King, or else they will be driven to the shore and slaughtered."

Donnell looked around. There were a few people nodding and one or two people clapped half-heartedly, perhaps confused at the sudden change in policy from Wherrycross. He supposed he should also be pleased – their message about the treachery of Tudorr ab Owain had been heard – but it sounded very much as if there was about to be a battle on their doorstep. And that could drive Iohric away, and the druid stone with him. If he was to locate the Norseman and also free Fáelán, he was going to have to move quickly.

To the Forest

Macswain was already walking away from the square, the younger hunter beside her, and Donnell hurried after the pair, leading the warhorse. He called out: "A quick word, huntsmaster!"

She glanced round. "Young Donnell." She paused and reached towards her hips with both hands, and patted the handles of a pair of long hunting knives. "I gather you have a boggle infestation. Seems like it's time to think about something bigger than this village, and do what you do best. The forest doesn't look after itself."

"I know," he said, and pointed at his leg. "The first time a boggle has shot an arrow into me in my life! You think you've seen boggles, but these ones are acting differently. Really cunning. I mean, you wouldn't believe they are just boggles. And then there are other things that come in the night, too." He realised he must sound to them like he was raving, and calmed his voice a little. "And can I ask about Malcolm? Is he all right, and did he have any sort of message for me?"

"Your blacksmith friend? Yes, he is fine, I think. He said something… he had another errand to attend to, I believe."

Macswain remained where she had stopped, looking around at the village. Her fellow hunter stood expectantly a few paces away, failing to acknowledge Donnell. "And I really think we need to post guards at all of the new towers today," she added. "We can't risk the Norse flanking us and occupying the village."

Donnell nodded, with a slight frown. "Of course, Master Macswain. There are plans afoot to tackle the threats." He sniffed. "I'd say we should double the current numbers of guards, and increase the supply of arrows. We have been working hard, believe me. Sahar has been incredible – training the youngsters to shoot, developing fixed bows that can shoot two arrows at once harder than a grown man can shoot. They can even shoot spears. You would hardly believe it."

The woman thought about this, and then glanced over at the red-haired hunter beside her.

"Those sound like standard fixed bows," he said, "but thank you for the suggestion."

Macswain chuckled slightly, and the young man blushed. "Luguwa-los here doesn't know what he doesn't know. But he's right about one thing – we need to draw on the local knowledge that you and your friends have. It makes our role simpler." She nodded in greeting, turned and began to walk away again.

"But we've realised that there is more to it," Donnell continued, hurrying along beside her. "There appear to be Norsemen using the forest as a base. In fact, I think their leader is mustering his most trusted men there. You know, perhaps you have head of Iohric the Ganger? He led the assault back in the springtime."

"All right..." she replied slowly.

"So, perhaps the Laird's Marischal should focus his attentions there?" he finished, looking around at her.

She frowned, and looked in the direction of Holm's Wood, holding her herself totally still for a moment as if listening. "Well, things do appear to be out of balance. Creatures don't start attacking villages for no reason. So, what do we know?"

"Not much," he admitted. "But I do know that Norse have made contact with the forest folk. Perhaps... perhaps it could be that some creatures are being controlled, and forced to attack," – he looked for conformation – "or else they are being pushed out, and have nowhere to go."

She nodded. "And what else has changed?"

"Uncertain. The druids, I suppose, have had less influence on Holm's Wood since the recent deaths of two of their number. But like I say, the Norse..."

"The Norse are people of the water. But you are correct, we need to consider the original source of any disturbance."

"And Toirdelbach? Do you think he will be willing to send his men into Holm's Wood?"

"There is not a chance that he will ride in there, Donnell. But if any evidence of this emerges from our work, we may persuade him to put troops at the wall."

"Very well. I am ready to go as soon as I've stabled these horses."

"Go where, exactly?"

"To find Iohric."

She gave her former apprentice a long, cold look. "The Marischal has been sent to treat with the Norse. You can't get involved, old friend, especially when it comes to their leaders. I forbid it."

She walked off without looking back again, Luguwalos trailing in her wake.

* * *

Donnell caught up with Erik at the new stables.

"This shouldn't be your job, chief," said Erik, as he led in the other two visiting warriors' steeds. "Bondsman work, no? I can tie up these stupid animals."

"It's all right," said Donnell with a shrug, as he patted Toirdelbach's mount. "I enjoy spending time with the creatures. More so than dealing with people, at times. And please, don't speak of horses that way. They may not share our language, but they have souls, and can understand you."

Erik made a noncommittal noise.

"I trained in the ways of the forest and in hunting with Macswain as a bonded youth," Donnell continued. "She taught me to respect all animals, even your quarry. As a hunter you take only what you need, and you help animals that are hurt or wounded if you can. They are all part of the wildness, the gift and the realm of the hunter-god, Cernunnos."

Erik lifted a small half barrel, and poured water from it into the drinking trough, his muscles bulging as he did so. "We have different stories of gods and hunts. Our bards say that the forest needs to be tamed. Killing the beasts that reside there is for the good of all, if you don't want them to come sneaking into villages and homes by night."

"Mmm," murmured Donnell, thinking of the boggle threat again.

With the new horses settled and watered, they returned to collect the two Cardhu horses from the Wherrycross expedition, as well as the mules that had drawn the wagon. Donnell turned to his companion again as they re-entered the stable. "Do you know anything more about where Malcolm has gone?" he asked. "Did he meet with the old sorcerer, Eochaid, by any chance?"

"Hmm. I know that he spoke to that little goblin creature," said Erik, "That much I know. And after that I didn't see him at all."

Donnell nodded, but said nothing more. For a moment he felt sorry that he could not ask Malcolm's advice about Fáelán, but he quickly dismissed the thought from his mind.

The two men then ensured that all of the animals were secured and had plenty of food and bedding after their journey. Donnell felt impatient to get going, but was also careful to do the work well – he knew that the animals' comfort depended on it. They removed the armour from the knights' horses, and hung it upon the stable walls.

When Erik asked about their training session later in the day, Donnell paused, thinking through his options, and checking on his own steed, Beira, as he did so. Despite Macswain's orders, he was in a hurry to prepare for his expedition with Fenella, and to continue their search for Iohric. They could certainly use another fighter for this journey, and he liked Erik. On the one hand, the others didn't appear to entirely trust Erik, because he was one of the men who had arrived at Cardhu as part of the Norse invasion.

"There's a change of plan, today," he said at last. "We need to make a short journey into Holm's Wood. It shouldn't take too long, if you want to come along? But please, don't tell Niamh or the huntsmaster."

Erik nodded thoughtfully, and then laughed at this comment. "It's about time we hunted down the source of all the trouble," he said. "Afternoon?"

"No. If you're coming, then get something to eat quickly and then meet us near the East Wall straight after. If I don't see you on your way, make sure you are there by noon. Come armed."

When the two men emerged, however, thoughts of their own plans quickly faded from their minds. A confrontation had developed near the main square, with the Laird's Marischal, Toirdelbach, pointing his sword directly at Sahar, who was standing in front of the Greathouse. "That foreign girl has to go", he called in a hoarse voice. "We don't want her kind here."

Donnell hurried over, but Niamh had already barged in and confronted the man, stepping between the point of his sword blade and the young woman. Fenella also closed in on the scene, placing both of her arms firmly around Sahar's shoulders, and beginning to pull her clear from the threat.

"Absolutely not," said Niamh. "This young woman is like a daughter to me, and a sister to my children. She's one of us now. I can assure you that she poses no more threat to Cardhu than I do."

Donnell came to stand beside Niamh, admiring, as ever, her indomitable spirit. Toirdelbach, however, did not seem to be as impressed. "She goes!" he said in a lower voice, eyes narrowing to slits. He was very nasal, as if he had been suffering from a pox of some kind. "You heard the Laird's command."

"I am still in charge in the village," said Niamh. "And the Laird said you should work with me. This has nothing to do with Norsemen or wars. I'm still the Luftenand, and the villagers follow my command."

The man kept his sword up towards her, his face was reddening as he spoke. "As I am in charge of *protection* of the village, I can banish whoever I like. She is an outsider, and a threat to our people. I tell you; she must go."

Donnell noticed that some of the other villagers nodded at this sentiment, but Niamh stood her ground. "It's not going to happen. We trust Sahar, and she has also helped us with the defences of the town. In multiple ways," she replied calmly. "If you wish her to stop helping with the defence then she will. That is your domain now. But you have no right to send her away from her home and family."

Several others had gathered around, with Macswain and the other new arrivals from the south standing not far away. Donnell looked back to see how Sahar herself was reacting, knowing all too well her tendency to rush into a fight. He was pleased to see that Fenella had now drawn her back into the entranceway of the Greathouse and away from the confrontation. Branwen, meanwhile, had appeared at the door of Niamh's house, holding the two younger children close to her.

Niamh and Toirdelbach stood staring at each other for another few moments, Toirdelbach's sword blade wavering as he held it up, until at last he dropped its point and sheathed the weapon, and then spat on the ground. "She has two days," he said. With that, he turned his back on Niamh and walked towards the other soldiers.

* * *

Donnell was swift in gathering his weapons, and quick to leave his dwelling and make his way towards the outfield, too. And before he reached the East Wall, he saw his companions gathered there – Fenella and Erik…and Sahar. They peered over at him with concern as he approached, and again, he realised that he could make them out clearly before they could identify him. He gave a friendly wave, and hurried on.

While back at the square, he had taken a few minutes to ascertain that his young friend was unharmed – and she had seemed relatively unfazed by the threat. It wasn't the first time she had been threatened by a powerful warrior, he supposed, and while Toirdelbach was intimidating, he couldn't come close to the menace of the enormous Norseman Iohric – who Sahar had now fought twice. After agreeing to see them at the East Wall forthwith, he had then picked up his spear and hurried off to prepare for the trip. He had assumed that Fenella would settle the young woman back at the Greathouse to rest in the interim – it appeared he was wrong.

"What are you doing here, Sahar?" asked Donnell as he approached, smiling and patting the young warrior across the back. "It's good to see you, but…"

"But what?" asked Sahar, narrowing her eyes, and Donnell smiled.

"She says she's ready," said Fenella with a shrug. "And in truth, there is nothing physically wrong with her. The wound is healed. And then, well…" She gave a slight nod back towards the village, and Donnell picked up her meaning instantly. With Toirdelbach and his men effectively in charge of Cardhu, the druidess had clearly decided that Sahar would be safer with them.

"In that case, 'but' nothing. It's wonderful to have you back," he said.

She nodded. "It's good to be setting out alongside comrades, weapons in our hands," she said. "I'm feeling strong again."

"So, what's all this about?" Erik asked. The tall warrior was wearing a stout leather armour jerkin and a helmet, and he carried both a spear in his hands and an axe at his belt. There was a short bow and quiver of arrows across his shoulder, a knife strapped to one of his legs and a billy-club to the other. He certainly hadn't ignored Donnell's instruction about arming himself.

"We have reason to think that Iohric is in Holm's Wood," said Fenella. "Or if he is not there himself, his troops may be mustering there under the command of one of those black cloaks."

"In which case, would it not be better to work on the East Wall defences, and be prepared to ambush them when they attack?" asked Erik.

"Perhaps," said Donnell. "But we need a scouting mission to see what we are dealing with. We don't know where they are, or how many. Once we have established those facts, then perhaps we can think about leading them into a trap."

The Norseman nodded, and they set out without another word. Glancing around, Donnell saw that Sahar had retrieved her crossbow at some point, and was loading it. Fenella had her pouch with healing materials, as well as a staff and a knife. However, it didn't look like the others had brought any supplies with them. His own satchel contained just a day's trail rations. He wondered how far into the woods the Norse were, and how hard it would be to find them.

They crossed the wall, and then the small cleared area between the wall and the forest itself. Donnell looked up at the central tower, and made out two figures there. He narrowed his eyes. One was Luguwalos, Macswain's red-haired underling, the other a teenage lad who seemed to be getting some tips on using a bow. Donnell shrugged. If the newcomers were going to be here, then good, at least, that they were making themselves useful. Worryingly, there was no sign yet of the extra guards that he and Fenella had earlier called on.

He turned and walked towards the edge of the forest. "The arm?" he asked Sahar, as they passed the stumpy oaks that marked the beginnings of Holm's Wood, both of them following Fenella's lead. Sahar shrugged and patted the area where she had been stabbed, then looked up at him with a slight wince. "It's all right," she said. "Better. I can feel the wound, but that is all." She looked at him. "Thank you," she added.

Fenella fell back to walk closer to him. "I should thank you too, Donnell – or perhaps apologise. I kept telling you to be wary of using the brooch, and then, well… it was the only way in the end. Each additional stone increases their combined power, but only if a different person wields it. I couldn't have done it by myself."

Once again, Donnell instinctively touched at the spot in his tunic that covered the brooch on his chest. "That just shows that you were right. I don't have the first idea how this thing works, and it isn't right for me to keep it. It will be a relief when the circle of druids is restored."

Sahar glanced from one of them to the other, looking puzzled, but didn't ask for an explanation.

As they continued deeper into the trees, Donnell took the lead, walking steadily but cautiously, and crouching periodically to check for tracks. Erik came alongside him.

"Any signs of Iohric's men yet?" asked the Norseman, hefting his spear in his hands as he spoke.

"Yes and no," Donnell replied. "I saw two of his men enter here after nightfall the other day, and there's a good chance that they took the path we are taking, as it's by far the most obvious route into the heart of the forest. Many feet have gone both in and out. But I can't tell yet if they are still in here, or how many others might have come. Have you any idea where they might be headed to?"

Erik narrowed his eyes. "Not really, chief. I'm guessing that if Iohric saw Cardhu as a target, it wouldn't make sense to go too far in."

"Right," Donnell replied. "Although it's strange. There were a group of six of your former comrades at Eas Mòr, and only two came this way. That doesn't suggest a war party."

The tall Norseman nodded slightly, pursing his lips.

"Erik," began Donnell, pondering over how to phrase a delicate question. "Back in your, um…raiding days, did you hear anything about Iohric's plans? Long term, I mean. Any alliances that he might have formed on the mainland? What his end goal might have been?"

Erik thought for a moment, and then shrugged. "Not really. Loot, and slaves for the markets – those were always the goals. Of course, there are always disputes between the lords. Ímar is the great King, the most powerful man of the western seas. He rules from Dubh-Linn together with his close kinsman Olaf the White. They have conquered every last island, and defeated one Irish king after another. But while he wages war in Ireland, other Jarls are constantly struggling for control. Iohric is one of those men."

Donnell nodded. Fenella had come close up behind him, and touched him gently on the arm as he spoke. "Even if we only find his henchmen, we can question them."

They continued along the path. The trees here were very tall, meaning that the leafy canopy was far up above them. The ground underneath was relatively dry. Donnell scanned the branches for signs of boggles or their traps, but thus far everything looked normal.

As they continued, the path dipped until it ran along a small burn, and then rose again to wind between two enormous rocks. The stones between the rocks formed something close to a natural stairway, and they proceeded single file, with Donnell in the lead once more. Beyond the rocks, the path narrowed and wound through a stand of yew trees with their thick dark foliage, and then opened out into a clearing. There, near the centre, stood a familiar figure, bow and arrow in hand. She nodded at Donnell and his heavily-armed companions.

"Mushroom picking, are you, or just out for a walk?" asked Macswain.

Macswain

"As you heard this morning, I am in charge of the East Wall and the defence against creatures from the wood," said Macswain. "And I told you not to go looking for Norsemen or challenging their leaders. This is insubordination."

They had been arguing for several minutes. Donnell, having quickly abandoned any pretence of an innocent ranging mission, had shifted tack, and was now instead trying to talk Macswain into joining them.

"I understand, huntsmaster. It's just that we are sure Iohric and other Norsemen are hiding out inside the forest, waiting to attack the village – perhaps at the very time that the Laird moves on Longfort Keep. We need to scout them out…"

"I decide what scouting gets done. Not you."

Donnell nodded. "With respect huntsmaster, I have been in charge of scouting for the past season…"

He didn't finish his sentence before they all began to look around, clutching their weapons. A deep growling noise was coming from somewhere just outside of the clearing. They all looked around, bows and spears at the ready, peering into the gloom of the undergrowth.

In the tense silence that followed, the bitter argument was forgotten and the group were as one, forming an outward-facing circle against the unseen menace. And then it plunged through a stand of thorn bushes and emerged into the clearing.

The creature lunged towards the group and stopped just short of Donnell and Sahar, snarling. It was hunched down, but unmistakably walking on two legs. This was no ordinary forest animal. It was a wulver – perhaps the same one as Donnell had seen before, though he couldn't be sure. Inside the forest it looked larger than ever – only slightly taller than a man perhaps, but hugely broad across the chest, and with the head and fur of a wolf, grizzled black and grey. Its long yellow teeth were bared.

Sahar raised her crossbow but Donnell stayed her arm and began to back away. "Wait," he hissed. "It's an intelligent creature, but confused. I don't think it will attack unless we do."

The five of them stood in suspense, now arranged in a semi-circle ahead of the creature as it snarled and looked from one to the other. Donnell took another slow step back and then another, holding up one hand towards the wulver, and saying "Easy, now…"

Just then, Erik lurched towards it, and it took Donnell a moment to realise that his companion had hurled his spear full force at the beast. The wulver staggered back, hunched over, and began clawing at the spear which was now protruding from its lower side.

"No, no!" cried out Fenella, but Erik followed up his attack, freeing his axe from his belt. He rushed in, and swung the weapon down upon the creature's upper back. It collapsed in a heap, twitching, and then fell still.

Fenella rushed over and crouched down beside the fallen beast. She reached out and tentatively touched the fur of its neck. It was now quite still. "No, Erik, just…this is not right," she said. "These are peaceful animals."

"That one wasn't," said Erik, standing back and pulling out a rag with which to wipe his blade. "It's gone bad. We have many stories about wolf-men back home. They often times steal children and take them into the forest to devour."

She shook her head, but said nothing. Donnell and Macswain looked at each other. "You see what we are saying," he said cautiously. "Something is disturbing the forest creatures, and everything has been shifted away from its natural pattern. It could be because of the incursion of the Norse warriors. The forest folk could tell us more, I am sure."

As Erik retrieved his spear, Macswain walked once around the clearing, peering out at the trees, and then stopped to look at the fallen wulver. Fenella had now risen up and was standing nearby the fallen creature, looking miserable. Macswain crouched down, taking her place, and pulled out her hunting knife. She placed two fingers under the animal's throat for a moment, then, using the blade, lifted its upper jaw to look inside its mouth. Finally, she turned the huge body over onto its back, and stood up. At last she nodded. "Very well. We will see what is causing this, if indeed there is a single cause. But if we don't find anything, then I absolutely insist that you do not take on any more independent scouting trips. If you do, there will be harsh consequences for all of you."

* * *

The group began to move on through the woods, taking another small path that led away from the clearing. Donnell led with Macswain alongside him; both experienced foresters were intimately familiar with all of the major paths.

Sahar followed the pair, with Erik next, polishing his blades. Fenella hung back, still visibly shocked at the brutality of the slaying of the wulver. "There's something not right in Holm's Wood," Donnell was repeating to Macswain. "The wulver, the attacks on our village, the Norse – it's all connected."

"If the Norse truly are mustering an army here," she replied, "then it's possible that their actions could be throwing things out of balance. Creatures will have had to react, perhaps been forced out of their territories, lost their food supplies, or even been attacked directly." She gave a pointed look over her shoulder at Erik.

"Yes, I'm sure they have," Erik replied calmly.

"The wood folk are somehow involved, too, I believe," said Donnell. "I just hope that they have not allied with the Norse – or else we're in deep trouble."

As the path dipped down and the surroundings darkened, Fenella walked up closer to the two foresters. "Take your thinking one step further back. The five druids who met in Cardhu every Samhain each channel the power of one of the greater gods. Until all five are once again in harmony, things are going to be out of balance. The forest is vulnerable, and more easily corrupted."

Macswain looked at her. "Tell me more about your five," she said.

"The Mor-druids? I am the youngest of the group. But as you know, I have been away, bringing the healing of the goddess Brighid to the villagers who have been harmed in the recent fighting. Each of us have work to do through the year, and we converge on the Celtic Rock come Samhain. But now the druids of Étaín the sun god, and of Lugh, the great crafter, have been slain."

The others were listening.

"And?" prompted Sahar.

"Well, this means that other gods, less peaceful ones, are stronger in this place than they should be."

"Well, that fits," said Donnell. "The forest folk worship Cernunnos especially, though they call him the Huntsman, and they imagine him like a stag who walks upright," he said. "He is the wild god of the forest."

"We also revere him," added Macswain. "For he is the lord of the forest, and we walk its paths by his mercy."

Fenella moved closer. "Perhaps you remember my companion,

Loarn," she said. "People see him as the druid of Lir, the sea god, and that is correct. But for a long time, the druid in his position has also revered Cernunnos. For we druids also reside in the forest much of the time."

"Then would Loarn be able to exert control over the forest folk?" asked Macswain, "if it does turn out that they are a threat to us?"

The druidess frowned. "It's possible. But… well. It's not easy to control their kind. He always had more influence over the small people than did any of the rest of us, but they are also wild… chaotic."

"And what about the boggles?" asked Sahar.

"What about them?"

"They worship the same god?"

"Not exactly. They have their own ideas of gods, though we druids consider boggles to be children of Cailleach Bheur."

"Boggles could be gathered into an attack force, I suppose, if someone pretended to represent their gods?" Macswain asked the druid.

"Not really. They are mischievous, certainly, but not usually warlike, nor organised enough to wage war. I was surprised to hear that they had even been using bows."

The companions walked on in silence. As they progressed it got darker still under the thick forest canopy, although Donnell knew it was still the middle afternoon.

Soon they reached another path which crossed theirs to the left and right. It had been recently widened – trees had been felled, with most of the fallen trunks left lying by the side. Donnell was fairly certain that the right-hand branch of the path would lead towards Druid's Hame – a place he had visited earlier in the year – and he could see Fenella looking in that direction, her green eyes narrowed. "If we go that way," she said, "We might seek the assistance of my fellow druids, Loarn and Méabh."

"From what you are saying, it's unlikely the Norse will be anywhere close to them," said Macswain. "Especially as Iohric recently attacked your brethren, and would fear retaliation. As we are here to scout, let's go the other way."

Not wanting to further antagonise the huntsmaster, Donnell agreed, and he took the left-hand branch of the wide path along with Sahar and Erik. Fenella hesitated, then followed.

Every so often a tree had been felled to clear the route, which gradually widened as they continued. The sun broke through the canopy up ahead, sending a blinding shaft of light downwards, and Donnell found himself half-covering his eyes as he continued. As the path twisted round and back several times to avoid larger trees, they entered a diamond-shaped rocky glade, which was also bedecked with fallen trees. Donnell spied a small gathering up ahead, and he dropped his arm, waving to those behind him while stopping and crouching low. He made out three figures around an enormous tree stump, on which a small iron chest had been placed. Two of the figures were clearly not human – both were boggles, cloaked, grinning. The final figure was an unusually large human, a hulking figure with bone-white hair. Iohric.

* * *

The Norse warleader was not armoured; he wore only the body of a tunic which left his muscular arms entirely bare, the multiple scars from his recent knife fight with Sahar clearly visible. There was a huge, ornate battle axe at his waist – the one that Sahar had described, perhaps? – and the bronze key for the keep's dungeon was hanging from a leather band around his neck.

Ignoring his silent hand signals, the others caught up with Donnell before he could react, and Iohric, a score of paces further up the track, looked up with a grin. "Ah – welcome. I see that you have brought me another druid," he said. Donnell noticed that he was openly wearing the ring with the white druid stone upon his finger. "She will bring a fine price. Erik – seize her."

Donnell's head whipped round, only to see that their companion Erik had grabbed Fenella, the warrior's huge hands holding her upper arms behind her back so that she couldn't turn or run. The man's eyes were downcast.

At the same moment, two other warriors, dirty-looking Norsemen who had clearly spent some time in the forest, emerged from behind them onto the path and grabbed Sahar and Macswain from behind, holding knives to their throats. Both women lowered their weapons.

Unable to help his companions, Donnell stepped towards the Norseman, spear raised, but Iohric simply laughed, and the two boggles at his side raised bows and hissed, their red eyes gleaming. "Come. You see what we have here. You're outnumbered, spearman. Time to drop your weapon, or I will order the others killed."

Donnell hesitated, then looked around. They were surrounded. Fenella struggling against the traitor Erik, had a look of shock across her face.

Donnell dropped his spear. One of the boggles hurried over and picked it up, then took the weapons from the others, including Fenella's staff and the knife at her belt. They then produced a length of thick dark cord, seemingly from nowhere, bound Donnell's arms behind his back, and then moved over to secure Fenella, too. "You..." began Donnell, looking back at Erik. "I...I can't believe it. You would betray us? And all this time I trusted you when others would have told me not to."

"Sorry, chief," said Erik, failing to meet his gaze. "Believe me, I don't like the dishonour of this act, but I have to do the Jarl's bidding."

"This warrior is loyal to the true King, not the local fool that passes for a chieftain around here," said Iohric, his voice rough and deep. "He has been following my orders since you sent him to the waterfall town."

Iohric then walked over to where Sahar had been disarmed; she was still struggling hard against the Norse soldier who was holding her. "Four good slaves, but this one – no. She will just be for sport. I will take pleasure in killing her slowly." He lifted his huge axe and cracked the side of it across Sahar's temple, and the young woman slumped into her captor's arms, stunned. The boggles moved over and tied her too, allowing the Norseman to let her limp body fall to the ground. The boggles then dragged her towards the centre of the clearing, and led the others to this area too, tying a single cord between all of their wrists, which one of the Norsemen took and held.

"How could you do this?" Donnell said to Erik, who this time did not respond. And then, "so, did you kill Óengus yourself?"

This time Erik looked him in the eye, his face reddening. "No – it was as I said. The scoundrel Völundr slew him."

Donnell shook his head, and flexed his muscles against the bonds. As he did so, he felt the outline of the small knife that was still concealed in his left boot. He didn't even want to look at it, but he could feel it – if there was just some way of getting his hands free…

As he looked around at the others, three new figures emerged into the glade, and he recognised the slight but muscular forms of forest folk. A surge of hope raced through him, remembering how his childhood friend Caelia, herself of the forest folk, had rescued him from boggles just a few months before.

This time, however, the visitors were strangers to him, and didn't appear primed to leap to his defence. They eyed Donnell and the others suspiciously, then began to speak rapidly to Iohric in his own Norse language, pointing around with their long skinny hands – mainly in the direction of the small iron chest on the tree stump. Donnell sensed the conversation getting heated, but then the huge Norseman held up his hand that had the ring upon it, and the forest folk fell silent, looking up at him. After a moment they turned and walked into the trees, then returned, leading a man that Donnell recognised as Loarn .

The druid was a shadow of his former self, however. He didn't look like he had washed in the months since Donnell had last seen him, and while it was nothing new for him to have twigs and leaves in his mass of grey curly hair and beard, his face was unusually sallow, his eyes drooping slightly and underscored by dark patches.

"Loarn?" called out Fenella. Concern etched across her face; she tried to move, but she was held fast by the cord at her wrists.

"You druids must stay away from each other," said Iohric, looking round and eyeing them suspiciously. Then he turned back to the forest folk, and gestured. They bowed slightly, and one lifted the chest from the tree stump. It appeared they were getting their payment.

"And now – to the forge," said Iohric.

The Fire Pit

They walked for what felt like at least a couple of miles, with the unconscious Sahar being carried by the boggles. The other three companions had long ropes attached to them from the front and back, meaning they had enemy warriors both in front of them and behind, and no choice but to keep up the pace. Clearly the Norsemen were not new to force-marching bound-up prisoners.

Iohric was at the very front of the group alongside the druid Loarn, the boggles next, and then the first of the Norse troops. Erik was among the group behind the captives. What was he thinking, Donnell wondered? Did he feel guilt? Or was he smiling, gloating at them over his successful deception – and the victory of his people?

The path away from the diamond-shaped glade resembled the one towards it: wide, and with occasional tree stumps and cleared areas. The footing was even, but Donnell nevertheless found it difficult to keep up the pace without his arms for balance, and stumbled numerous times, as did the others. He could tell, though, that they were going northwards – closer to Eas Mòr.

As they walked, he considered the healing power that he had shared with Fenella. Perhaps something could be achieved if they linked hands again – the *féth fíada*, or something similar. However, their hands were bound, and Macswain was in between the two of them. The huntsmaster – so used to the freedom of the forest – had remained almost totally silent since their capture, wary and watchful. Donnell could only guess at what she must be thinking and feeling; he sorely hoped that she had come up with an idea about how to escape.

Eventually the party reached another clearing, this one much larger and with a long narrow building at the centre, its walls made of entire horizontal logs. Clearly it was newly constructed, as the exposed areas of wood showed no signs of weathering at all. Its roofing was made of branches and turf, and overall the place looked much like a typical family dwelling in Cardhu but for being rectangular rather than rounded. Alongside it stood a single cart of the type that could be drawn by a lone horse or mule.

In front of the place was a large smouldering fire, and at the edge of this, an anvil – Donnell was sure that it was the same one that he had recently seen standing in the burned-out forge at Eas Mòr – sitting on top of a long, low rock. Beside it was a water bucket, bellows, and other tools and apparatus typically found in a smithy.

Everyone stopped walking. Iohric called out some directions, and the boggles dumped Sahar down on the ground near the firepit and then stepped back. She had begun to stir slightly, Donnell noticed, and he tried to shuffle closer to her.

From within the building, two more Norse soldiers emerged – he was fairly sure it was the pair of young men who had passed them and whom they had followed to the edge of the forest. In between the young soldiers, being held firmly by his upper arms, was a man who Donnell recognised as Ambarsan, the smith of Eas Mòr. Just behind him walked another figure that Donnell recognised – it was the wizened old man that he had seen down at the village of Weir, still dressed in his goatskin cape.

Chanting softly in the Norse language, the old man took the huge battle axe from Iohric and placed it onto the forge, and then waited while Iohric removed the ring with the white gem from his finger. This was placed carefully on top of the axe head. Close up, Donnell was able to see the intricate gold carvings that Sahar had described – the warrior's head, with multiple knotted decorations around the great iron blade. It was a magnificent and no doubt fear-inducing weapon.

The old man then retreated to the shadow of the wooden building, and Iohric began speaking quickly in Norse and gesturing to both Ambarsan and to the druid, Loarn.

And then Donnell realised what had been meant by creating a weapon. Iohric sought to forge the ring into this axe, combining the two. It seemed likely – probable, even – that the ornate axe was indeed the legendary weapon of Harald Wartooth, used by Iohric to rally supporters to his cause. What powers might come from combining the relic with a druid stone, he could only guess.

Ambarsan walked forward and poured more coals into the fire pit. He nimbly removed the axe's blade from its shaft, placing it upon the coals, and began to work the bellows. All the while, Loarn was mumbling his own enchantments under his breath, holding a smooth, dark wooden wand above the furnace. Fenella was gazing at him intently; her fellow Mor-druid had the face of a defeated man.

With all eyes on the forge, Donnell tried to lean forward to reach the knife at his boot, but he was bound too tightly. He thought he saw Erik glance in his direction, and quickly stopped moving.

The axe head was beginning to glow now, and Iohric stood over it, grinning, the gleam reflecting off his brutish scarred face. Loarn chanted and wove his wand in intricate patterns. Donnell noticed that the wand itself had carvings on it which appeared to glow, and recalled that it, too, had a druid stone concealed within it, according to what Fenella had previously told him.

As the chanting continued, the clearing seemed to narrow and the surroundings to dim, and Donnell thought he felt – or perhaps simply imagined – the druid somehow channelling the natural power of the forest on this particular spot. Iohric held out the white ring towards the blacksmith, and the man held out one huge hand ready to take it.

"It is time for me to take up my weapon," said Iohric. "And the kingdom."

Just then, Donnell noticed a movement near his feet, and he glanced down. Sahar had regained her senses, and with all other eyes upon the ceremony, had lifted her hand towards his boot. Deftly she reached for and unsheathed the knife, and cupped it in her hand, and then – still moving in a way that was barely perceptible – began to slice through her bonds.

*　*　*

Leaping to her feet, Sahar deftly split Donnell's bonds with a single upward slash of the knife. The follow-through of the blade seemed to pass close enough to his chin to nick a few hairs off his beard.

With his movement restored, Donnell grabbed hold of the druid brooch at his chest with one hand, and lunged towards Loarn with the other, grasping the man's forearm. He felt a surge of dark, mysterious power as he did so, and the druid looked at him in shock as a sparkling circle of golden light sprang up around them. Iohric, standing nearby, lunged towards Donnell as if to wrestle him to the ground, but he deflected off the glowing light, and staggered backwards, shielding his face.

Sahar was freeing Fenella. Across from them, the guards finally realised what was happening and began to close in on them – all but one. Erik pulled the club from his belt, and swung it not at the captives but with crunching force into the face of a fellow Norseman. He then loosed his spear into the back of a second who fell to the ground with a strangled scream, and turned to face off against a third of his one-time compatriots. Donnell gaped for a moment to see their turncoat companion suddenly taking their side again, but was still clinging to Loarn, and there was no time yet to ask questions of the deceitful warrior.

Freed from her bonds, Fenella sped over towards Donnell. With one hand, she snatched the white ring from the hand of the blacksmith and held it up, while grabbing hold of Loarn's arm with her other hand. Donnell reached out and took hold of the druidess's hand, and for a fraction of a second the three of them formed a circle, all three druid stones in contact.

There was an explosive noise, like a tree being hit by a lightning bolt, and a blast of crackling light shot outwards in all directions. Iohric was flung backwards against a tree and slumped down, while Erik, Sahar, and the other remaining warriors and boggles were likewise bowled over. The blacksmith Ambarsan had been flung right across the clearing and had thumped hard against the front of the building; he was no longer moving, his neck at a strange angle. Only the three completing the circle were untouched.

Donnell released Loarn and there was a further short blast; this time he felt himself being thrown backwards. The white ring shot up and away from Fenella's hand and far through the trees into the depths of the forest, while Loarn slumped towards the fire pit.

As Fenella tried to help her fellow druid up before he was seriously burned, Donnell turned to look for Sahar, but his young friend was already back on her feet. Unarmed, the knife having been flung from her hand and into the undergrowth by the first blast from the druid stones, she ran over to the unconscious Iohric, checking around him for weapons with which to finish the kill, but there was nothing to be seen. She looked over her shoulder and shouted "knife, quickly!", then turned and grasped the key which was upon a thin leather cord around the huge warrior's neck. She pulled it loose, and tucked it into her belt.

Then, apparently having second thoughts, she yanked the cord apart, pocketed the key, and began to circle Iohric's neck with the cord, twisting it, tightening it until it was digging in deeply.

However, the boggles were now rising and drawing weapons, as were two of the surviving Norse warriors. "There's no time," yelled Donnell, and pulled his young friend away. "Come on!"

He sped out of the clearing in the opposite direction to the main path. Macswain kicked a dagger from the hand of one of the boggles, and then followed Donnell. Fenella was dragging Loarn's hand, leading him along behind them and urging him to hurry. She had picked up her staff, but otherwise the group were unarmed.

The forest was dark as they sped away from the fire pit, and in their hurry it was difficult to stick to a path. Nevertheless, Donnell instinctively knew his direction, and he called out brief instructions as he ran. "Left here...duck that branch...now to the right!" He dearly hoped that they would establish some distance before armed Norsemen could get organised enough to chase after them.

"That was incredibly dangerous," said Fenella, who had caught up and was running alongside him. "You could have lost an arm."

"I had to do something."

"Did you see where the ring went?" she asked.

"No – but it went really far. Nobody is finding that any time soon." As he said it, though, he thought of the resourcefulness of both boggles and forest folk, and doubted his own words. But for now, they needed to escape with their lives.

"If it is lost, then we failed," she replied.

"Not entirely," said Sahar, panting as she ran. "At least Iohric no longer has it. He won't be using that axe again, either. And also," she said, holding up a clenched fist, "I have his key."

There was dried blood at the young woman's temple, and Donnell peered at her as they hurried on. "How's your head?"

She screwed up her face. "Fine," she said. "My revenge upon him will be all the sweeter for each hurt that he causes."

* * *

His fall onto the fire pit had left Loarn burned up his side and arm, and the druid was struggling to keep up with the rest of the companions. With no immediate sign of pursuit, the group slowed their pace, Donnell falling back to watch the path behind them.

Fenella took a moment to look at the key that Sahar was holding. "Yes, I'm sure of it – that's the one that I saw Iohric with at the battle," she said, "the one that Gabrán wanted." She held it out to Donnell.

"If so, we can use it to free the Dark Shadow," said Donnell, taking the item from Fenella and peering at it. "And what's more, we know that Iohric is not at the keep right now. We need to get moving quickly…"

He left the statement unfinished. They were still a long way from home. There would be time to make plans after they got back to Cardhu, and not before. And he knew also that there were many other Norsemen at Longfort Keep, under Völundr. Nevertheless, it seemed like time had come to attempt the rescue.

They crossed another path, and Donnell recognised a narrow deer run that led towards Eas Mòr – again, it had been widened, and there were cut trees and cart tracks upon the ground. "This could well be the way that Iohric used to reach here from the village at the waterfall," he said. "They had to get that cart in here somehow – presumably with the anvil on it."

"Where now?" asked Sahar.

"Not this way, anyway – I expect it leads right back to that building in the forest." He glanced around again. "This way," he said, pointing. He led the way down a smaller diagonal branch from the same path that led in the direction of Cardhu; the others followed in single file, now walking, but still making haste.

A mile or so along the narrower path the trees were thinning, and Donnell realised that they were approaching the forest's edge. Just then, he spied a small figure up ahead, looking in their direction. It was Caelia, his friend from among the forest folk. But he hardly recognised her, for her posture showed none of its usual mirth and buoyancy. Instead her shoulders were slumped, her face anguished.

"I'm sorry," she said, walking closer. But Donnell realised that she was speaking not to him, but to Loarn. The druid, however, didn't answer, appearing to have entered a world inside his mind.

"Caelia, what happened? And what have your people done to the druid?" said Donnell.

She looked around at him, and smiled sadly.

"Not my people. These are of a different tribe – the Vortigern. They are beholden to the druid, and have been arming boggles at his instruction."

"Then they are helping Iohric?"

"In a sense, yes. Forest folk will always follow the will of Cernunnos, and so they listen to the druid of the green and follow his instructions. I have tried to tell them that the Norsemen were somehow controlling him, but they don't seem to listen."

"And now?"

She looked at him. "I can't say for sure. Our two main tribes of this area are now hopelessly divided. It's a cruel time for the forest folk."

"Come with us, Caelia, back to Cardhu. If we share the same enemies, then we have to work together."

"I wish I could help. But it is… complicated. I cannot fight against my own kind, and nor will they harm me." Suddenly Caelia swung round, pulling her bow free, and firing three arrows in quick succession into the woods behind them. "Boggles on the other hand…" she muttered.

Boggles had started to appear by the trees further back along the narrow path, and as Donnell looked on, an arrow thumped into Loarn's back a few inches above his waist. The druid made a groaning noise, and then slumped to his knees.

"Loarn!" shouted Fenella, lunging towards him.

As the druidess attempted to treat Loarn's wound, two further enemy arrows whistled harmlessly past the companions. Caelia shot several arrows back in quick succession, and as she did so, two more of her kind arrived behind her, also holding bows. Between them, the three downed a pair of nearby boggles, and the remaining attackers drew back out of sight.

"You really need to hurry – you'll be badly outnumbered before long," said Caelia, as her fellows took hold of the druid's arms. He was kneeling on the ground, groaning, and they raised him to his feet. "Leave him to us, now, mistress Fenella. Run!" She shot another boggle out of a tree, and then nocked another arrow, moving up a tiny side path with her fellows at her shoulder.

Without needing any further prompting, Donnell, Sahar, Fenella and Macswain ran, ducking and weaving to avoid the stones and occasional arrows which were now starting to hit the path.

* * *

They were still running as they reached the edge of the trees, Sahar just out in front, and the boggles close at their heels. As they saw the great structure of the East Wall up ahead, Donnell stopped and looked around. Around twenty boggles, many with bows, had emerged from the forest behind them and were closing in. Fenella kept running towards the central tower, while Macswain turned and kicked out at the nearest attacker, and then retreated a few more steps. As she did so she took an arrow to the leg, and sank to one knee.

As Donnell looked back, a tall red-headed figure emerged from the trees just behind the boggles – Luguwalos – and he realised that the man must have been waiting at the forest's edge for their return. The young hunter flung his spear, catching a boggle full in the back, and causing several of them to turn and surround him, firing. Luguwalos strung an arrow and shot a further one of the little creatures, but then he, too, was hit by an arrow to the leg, and another to the side. He staggered slightly, lunged forward, then wrestled a short sword from the hands of the nearest oncoming boggle, stabbed its owner with the same weapon, only to take two more arrows in close succession, causing him to fall to the ground. In a flash, a boggle was standing over him, its rusty sword coming down towards the man's neck.

Then, all at once, Sahar was there. She parried the boggle's blow, dodged a riposte, and faced off against the creature as others approached.

As Donnell pulled his knife and began to close in on the scene to help his friends, he heard a twang and felt the swoosh of something flying past his head, and moments later the nearest attacker fell with a long shaft through its chest. Recognising the spear-like weapon, Donnell briefly turned and looked up towards the walls.

Small figures were on the towers, firing bows. And just as he thought they were finished, led into a trap, he realised that they were not boggles, but children. Sahar's proteges were at the wall, firing arrows and javelins, Niamh's girls Kit and Rana among them. The attacking boggles began to fall to the ground, one after another in quick succession. Finally, the last three fled for the cover of the trees.

Soldiers

Sheathing his knife, Donnell hurried over to Macswain, who sat a few feet away, clutching her wounded leg, her face looking drained of blood. However, it was to her companion that she looked, rather than to her own injuries. Luguwalos, the red-haired hunter who had accompanied her to Cardhu, was collapsed on the ground, his body punctured with several arrows, and his limbs at an unnatural angle. Sahar had blocked the killer blow on the man, but the ultimate outcome – it appeared – would be the same. Sahar herself stood nearby, her head bowed.

Rian and three other guards from the East Wall appeared on the scene, and together they lifted and carried the young man's body up to the wall. Over in the outfield, some of the child archers gathered round looking concerned, though none had known Luguwalos well, as he had rarely been seen in Cardhu. Donnell realised that despite their long-time acquaintance, he didn't even know whether Luguwalos had any family. He should really have found out more about the young hunter.

Donnell turned and crouched down by his former mentor. Both looked at their fallen companion while Fenella checked the man's badly-wounded body for signs of life. She looked up. "There's nothing that I can do for him," she confirmed.

Macswain leaned forward and covered the man's face with his own cloak.

As the shock wore off, Donnell realised that he, too, was bleeding – one of his arms was clammy and stained dark red, although he didn't know from what injury. Taking a deep breath and patting gently at his own body to ascertain the damage, he decided that it wasn't immediately life threatening – but he did have a new gash that ran down the back of his upper left arm from near the shoulder, as well as a few minor scrapes and cuts.

Fenella noticed the wound to his arm, and stepped over. "Let me see to that," she said, and before long was applying a small bundle of dried heather and mistletoe to stem the bleeding. The druidess then bound it firmly. "Is that fine?" she asked. "Can you still move it well enough?"

As Fenella worked, Donnell saw a mounted scout cantering unsteadily across the outfield towards the wooden towers, and recognised his recent recruit, Calin. "The Laird's army are down at the shore," shouted the lad, pulling at the horse's bridle as he closed on the wall. "They are marching on the Norse Keep!"

Donnell and Fenella looked at each other. "Then it has begun," he said.

"Yes. And the Dark Shadow is still a prisoner inside."

* * *

By the time Donnell, Sahar and Fenella had made their way back to the village square, there was pandemonium. Some of the locals had looked out weapons of various kinds, but many more were acting as if an unexpected festival had been announced. Many – children and adults alike – were setting off for the bluff to look down upon the road, hoping to catch a glimpse of the Laird's soldiers and of the impending battle from a safe distance.

The three companions, in contrast, had agreed to pursue their plan to head for the keep, regardless of the approaching army. They stopped briefly at the entrance to the Greathouse.

"These events could help us to slip into the keep undetected," said Donnell. "But we need to gather some weapons. Get whatever you can. And we may need a rope too."

"Are you sure you are up to this?" asked Fenella. "You're wounded, and Sahar is still recovering, too."

Sahar gave a single nod, and Donnell patted at his wounded arm. "The bandage will hold up, Fen," he said. "And my leg feels strong enough. We'll see this through."

Donnell quickly changed his bloodied undershirt, and left with the intention of calling at the blacksmith's for new weapons. However, as he reached back to the square, he spied the familiar tall figure of Erik running towards him from the direction of the fields, a bag slung at his belt. The Norseman slowed and approached with an apologetic air, arms raised to his sides and palms lifted upwards. As he came closer, he paused and pulled a spear – Donnell's spear – from where it had been slung diagonally across his back, and then held it out handle first towards his erstwhile companion.

Donnell marched towards him, and the men stopped, inches apart and staring at each other, close to the centre of the village square.

"You as good as handed us over to Iohric, man," growled Donnell. "Why?"

"I had no choice. I'm sorry I couldn't warn you before – I didn't know they were there. So, I made a fast, perhaps not very clever choice."

Eyes narrowed, Donnell reached out and took the spear from Erik. "We could have fought them off if you had defended us," Donnell said. "Don't think that helping us later is enough to make up for it."

"If I had fought at the start, I think we would all have been defeated, and then all of us would be, you know…" – he gestured around his waist in a circle – "tied up."

Just then, Sahar and Fenella emerged from the Greathouse. Sahar lunged towards Erik, but Fenella stayed calm, and held onto her younger friend. Seeing them, Erik took hold of a bag that was slung over his belt, and opened it up. "I'm so sorry for it. Look, I brought back your weapons. I know I've been a coward, but I had a plan of sorts, and I was following the Luftenand's instructions."

"Niamh knew about this?"

He nodded. "The Norsemen caught up with me after Óengus was slain. I was knocked from my horse, and they beat me senseless. When I woke, Iohric had a sword to my throat, and made me swear to him."

"So, you swore," said Sahar, still scowling. However, she reached out and took the bag from Erik, and clipped the crossbow back to her belt.

"It was that or die," he said. "I know – it was cowardly. But my loyalties lie here, now. I knew that I could play the part of a spy, and later use it against him."

"Easy to say that," Sahar said, folding her arms.

"I told Niamh – she can confirm it for you. She knew that Iohric thought that he had won me back to his side, and wanted to find out what she could about possible attacks from the keep. She has twice sent me to exchange information with him."

"So, all this time, you knew where he was?" Donnell said sharply.

"No. The exchanges happened by night, at the far edge of the East Wall when I was on watch. I tried to find out where his men were based, if he had a second camp, but I honestly did not know. But I did find out about Iohric's dealings with the Laird, and I passed that on to Niamh."

"What dealings?"

"He somehow learned that the Laird knew of the alliance between the Norse and his brother. Perhaps he has a spy in the Laird's camp."

"The traitor Ogledd, most likely," said Donnell, looking at the others. Erik nodded. "Anyway, he has been working to ensure that Völundr gets the blame for this conspiracy – and to clear his own name."

"Devious," said Fenella.

"I can't see that working," said Donnell. "I think we've gone too far for the Laird to trust Iohric now. And in any case, we would only need to tell him of what Erik knows – and what we witnessed today and at Eas Mòr."

Sahar was shaking her head, eyes narrowed, but Fenella nodded slightly. "It seems that Erik did what had to be done, Sahar, and then helped us to escape. It was a horrible shock at the time, but here we are. We escaped – it worked out."

"No," said the younger woman. "How do we know he isn't still playing a game, working for the other side? Perhaps they are waiting for us down by the road, did you think of that? He didn't start helping us until things went wrong for them in the forest. I had already cut myself free."

She shook her head and took a few paces away. "I don't think we can trust him anymore."

There was a moment of silence as they all thought this over.

"I think we might have to," said Fenella at last. "At least until we can speak to Niamh for confirmation of his account. For my part, I can say that his story fits with the injuries that he had. The bruising."

"It does fit with the tracks we saw at Eas Mòr, too," said Donnell slowly. He was still peering at Erik, studying the man's face. He had always *wanted* to trust the young warrior – but had he been a fool to do so?

"I promise," said Erik, "I think of you all as friends, and I would have told you everything sooner if Niamh had not instructed me to keep quiet. There's a lot that you don't know, but she knows it all. I had to pretend to work for them. She wanted them to believe that I was still their man."

"Maybe," said Sahar. "But where's Niamh now? Conveniently absent."

They glanced over in the direction of the Luftenand's house, but there was, indeed, no sign of Niamh or her family members. Kit and Rana had not returned from the East Wall, and none of them had seen Branwen since their return from the forest, either.

"How did you get past the boggles?" asked Donnell.

"They chased after you, but I took a different path," the big Norseman replied. "I ended up on the route that leads to the waterfall, and then I ran along the edge of the forest back in this direction until I reached the East Wall. I suppose I got there a bit later than you."

"And Iohric?" asked Donnell, looking to Erik.

The man shook his head. "As far as I know, he lives, as does the little witch-man. The blacksmith is dead, as are three of Iohric's warriors. I can't say for sure what happened to the druid."

"Nor can we," said Fenella, her brow furrowed, looking back towards the forest.

"For now, we can but hope that the forest folk took him to safety," said Donnell, "and we have another druid to rescue. Are you with me?" He raised the brass key in his hand.

They all nodded.

* * *

When they reached the road, they heard the noise of hundreds of soldiers before they had even left the cover of the trees, and soon the gathering came into view. Two clear army camps were present, covering most of the coastal route itself – not that any locals or merchants were trying to pass.

Men of Ystrad Clud were immediately ahead of them and to their left, their line of troops beginning near the foot of the Cardhu path where the companions stood, and stretching some distance back along the Laird's Road towards Wherrycross in the south. Most were foot soldiers, though there were around two dozen horsemen near the front of the army. A line of Irish archers stood nearby amid the Laird's foot soldiers, while further back they could see mercenaries from Wessex, recognisable by their blueish plate-iron armour and the ornate visors upon their helms.

Opposing this force, and not far to the right of the companions on the northern stretch of road, a horde of Norsemen could be seen as well, partially silhouetted by the afternoon sun. Although they were rugged and well-armed, they were greatly outnumbered, and would surely soon be soundly defeated unless they rapidly retreated to their keep.

However, everything looked peaceful at present. At the meeting point between the two armies – just to the right as the companions looked on – a parley seemed to be in progress, with the principal leaders of each group standing in a circle in the centre of the crossroads, deep in conversation. The Laird himself was visible, and Niamh and Toird-elbach were also present, along with half a dozen Norsemen, mostly cloaked in black. The Laird's bastard son Mac Rath, recognisable from his braided dark hair, was off to one side, sitting upon his enormous black horse. The knight was in full dark-burnished plate iron armour rather than the ringmail that Donnell had seen him wear before, with his familiar black helmet resting on the pommel of his saddle.

"This looks less like a battle than I was expecting," murmured Donnell as they began to make their way along the edge of the road, alongside the Laird's men. It wasn't going to be easy to get *through* the massed soldiers towards the keep, he realised, and nor could they skirt around the back of the Norse horde without being seen.

Just then, he saw a familiar face. Ahead of them, near the edge of the Laird's mounted warriors, was one who was sitting unsteadily upon a white mare – Malcolm. He soon caught Donnell's eye and rode over with a slight grin.

"Well met, my friends," he said as he pulled up. He winked at Donnell. "How do you like my horsemanship now?" The huge war hammer was hanging from his belt as he held the reins.

Donnell patted the white horse that Malcolm was sitting upon. "This seems like a fine beast, and you are riding well."

"It's Eochaid's mount, of course," added Malcolm, dismounting a little unsteadily. "I've never ridden a horse like it. It seems – strangely wise."

Donnell smiled slightly, then glanced back towards the Laird and his advisors whose parley was ongoing. "But what is happening here? We heard that the Laird had gathered troops to assault the Norse Keep. Has a peace been reached?"

Malcolm nodded towards the leaders of the two forces. "It looked like battle. The Norse leader Völundr was wounded in single combat, and their army retreated close to their keep and took the man inside. But now they have sent out a group to negotiate, and the Laird is hoping to strike a deal and avoid further bloodshed. They are drinking mead and talking peace right now." He nodded in that direction, and indeed, they could make out the Laird deep in conversation with one of the black-cloaked men. At first Donnell had assumed that it was Völundr, but he now realised it was just another black-bearded Norseman, a tall man who rather resembled Iohric.

At that moment, Donnell realised that Sahar had split off from them and begun to sprint directly towards the parleying group. The Laird turned towards her, and two of his nearest men drew their swords. "You must not treat with these men!" called the young woman in a shrill voice as she reached the Laird. "They are dishonest. We have heard it from one of Iohric's own servants – they plan to attack Cardhu and sell the people as slaves. They have already massacred many of the people of Eas Mòr!"

Cursing, Donnell ran after her, hoping to interrupt before the hot-headed young woman could say something that would get herself killed. Most of the warriors nearby were looking at Sahar with a mixture of perplexity and amusement, although a number of the Norsemen were now clenching their weapons more tightly.

Fenella, Erik and Malcolm had followed him, the latter leading the white horse. However it was Niamh who reached Sahar first. Stepping out from among the Laird's group of representatives, she put an arm on her young charge's shoulder, while turning to apologise to the Laird for the interruption. Toirdelbach tried to push past her, but she shoved him back disdainfully, and resumed speaking.

Just as Donnell reached the group and looked to see the Laird's reaction, he saw a strange look come across Niamh's face. And all of a sudden, his old friend was sinking to her knees, clutching at a spreading red mark on her torso.

Turning, Donnell saw blood on Toirdelbach's sword, and it took him a moment to register what had happened. Niamh was still holding her hands cupped to her body as if holding something small and precious, a look of total shock on her face.

"This woman was a peasant, and disobedient!" cried Toirdelbach. "She has failed your people, my Laird, and allowed this" – he gestured towards the arriving companions – "*outsider* into our midst."

The man's blade had gone through Niamh's back and punctured her through her chest; blood was now pumping out and pouring down her clothing. Her eyes flicked to the side, looking at Donnell, and then became unfocused. She fell forward to the ground, twitching. Sahar gasped and flung herself down, taking Niamh's shoulders and gently turning the wounded woman over and onto her lap.

Donnell leapt forward and hammered the haft of his spear against Toirdelbach's hands, and the man screamed in pain and dropped his sword. Two of the Laird's nearest guards raised their spears and approached Donnell, and he backed off, his own spear raised, while

Erik rushed in to stand side-by-side with Donnell, axe in hand. Just behind them, Malcolm and Fenella hurried over and helped Sahar to gently carry Niamh's body to the edge of the road, where they lay her down carefully on her back. Fenella crouched down to assess the wound, and then shook her head sadly.

Several of the nearer Norseman had now pulled their weapons, unsure of who was fighting whom, and the scene looked set to descend into warfare until the Laird forcefully shouted for calm, and most of his own men stopped moving and lowered their weapons.

Just then the assembled Norsemen started speaking excitedly in their own tongue, and Donnell looked up to see a new figure emerging from behind their assembled ranks, having approached from further up the Laird's Road to the north.

Iohric had returned.

An Escape

The huge Norseman entered the circle of leaders, and sweeping his cloak behind him, knelt briefly in front of the Laird with a bow of his head.

"Bring me the traitor Völundr," Iohric croaked as he stood up again, his stone-like voice as calm as ever.

Perfectly on cue, the doors of the keep burst open, and Völundr appeared. He was limping, and nearly doubled over. A Norse warrior on either side of him half-supported, half-dragged him to the scene.

"This man," shouted Iohric, "has harmed my people, and spread hatred and lies. His deceit has threatened the peace that we have worked for together."

The Laird nodded. "What the Norseman says is correct," he called out for all to hear. "I struck an agreement with him, whereby his men would live peacefully with the folk of Weir, and would use their ships to help protect us from enemies across the water. The man Völundr mutinied and tried to break this agreement."

"Fool," called out Sahar from the side of the road. "Iohric lies."

"Kill the traitor," shouted the Laird, and Iohric stepped forward, taking a sword from one of his followers. With a swift, precise blow he lopped Völundr's head from his shoulders, and the man's body went limp and fell to the ground, bleeding.

"Behold," announced the Laird loudly, stepping back from the gruesome scene to stand beside his guards and Toirdelbach. "What a show of strength can accomplish! The traitor lies dead, at my instruction and by the hand of this warrior. From this day forward, Iohric will be the newest Luftenand of my realm."

The Laird held out his hand, and Iohric knelt again and kissed his ring, whereupon the Laird clapped the Norseman in the shoulder. Iohric stood and acknowledged some of his nearby countrymen with handshakes.

Donnell glanced over towards Mac Rath, and noticed that the warrior was still on horseback, and was keeping his distance from both the Laird and Iohric's men, a wary look upon his face.

"This is no longer to be called the village of Weir," continued the Laird, looking around at his assembled captains. "Weir is no more! Iohric the Ganger and his men have pledged allegiance to me, and have committed to ruling this area for the good of all our people. Any Norsemen who deny their command will be seen as traitors to the King and will be executed – something that they will see to directly. As will any local folk.

"With the traitor dead, Iohric will again take control of this mighty keep, and all who are based here," the Laird continued. "From now, the settlement here shall be called Longfort, and its Luftenand will have command of Cardhu, Eas Mòr, and all the surrounding farms, in my name."

There was some muted cheering from the Laird's ranks, and a roar and clanking of weapons from the Norse.

"And now," continued the Laird after the men had stilled, "with the power of Norse-built ships from this port, as well as our newly strengthened army, we are ready to take command of the coast and the islands, and drive all enemies far from our shores. We will bring might and strength back to Ystrad Clud like the days of old!

"For too long have we waited while enemies on all sides raid us and take our land from us island by island, farm by farm. And the King, of course, sits in his castle at Dumbarton, or goes hunting by the Loch. No more! Now, it is time to take command of the seas, before the whole kingdom falls to invaders."

There were greater cheers now from some of the assembled soldiers, though Donnell noted that many of the men local to Wherrycross looked doubtful, and some urgent muttering could be heard.

"My knight Toirdelbach will continue in his role as Marischal of Cardhu," the Laird continued, "and Iohric will appoint his own Marischal at the new settlement of Longfort. The first tasks of my new Luftenand will be to rebuild the village and forge at Eas Mòr, and to supervise logging to strengthen my fleet." Toirdelbach had just picked up his sword, and the man managed a short, awkward bow at the mention of his name.

Donnell stepped forward. "With the greatest of respect, my Laird, these Norsemen are killers and slavers. They will not strengthen the kingdom. My young friend spoke truly – I have personally witnessed the massacre of your own people at Eas Mòr. They were slaughtered and burned, and their cattle and possessions stolen."

"He lies, my lord and master," shouted Iohric in his gravelly tones, face red and sneering. "They witnessed no such thing. The killing was done by the turncoat Völundr, and my men were simply trying to find survivors when this man attacked us and killed three of my men." He turned to Donnell. "You didn't see me do any such thing. Admit it."

The Laird looked at Donnell. "Did you witness this massacre with your own eyes, huntsman?"

"Well…" said Donnell. He hesitated.

"You see!" crowed Iohric. "He cannot even say the words, because he knows it to be untrue, and he would be cursed by the gods for his lies."

Donnell glared back at the murderous Norseman. "If that was the case, then what about the slaves that you have brought here to sell, long before Völundr was in command?" However, as he spoke, he knew that he had a problem – the only witnesses to back up his assertion were currently in the Norse dungeon.

Iohric shook his head. "The truth is that Völundr killed and burned the villagers," he replied loudly, "while my men tried to protect them. We alone represent peace and freedom." The assembled warriors muttered among themselves, with clear uneasiness among the Norse contingent. "This liar should be punished for his falsehoods," he added, pointing at Donnell.

"Luftenand, what would you have me do?" asked the Laird, moving over to stand beside Iohric, and looking at the five companions.

Iohric folded his arms. "Give them all to me. They can be handed over to my kinsmen as the spoils of war."

The Laird thought for a moment. "No. Nobody will be handed over as property, for that is no better than slavery. Instead, I hereby say that the woodsman and his companions are banished from the kingdom." The Laird waved vaguely in the direction of Donnell, Erik and Malcolm, as well as Fenella and Sahar who were still beside Niamh's limp body.

Fenella stared at him. "You cannot banish a druid," she called out.

But the Laird only shrugged. "I can do what I see fit, for the good of the realm."

Donnell stepped forward again. "You are making a mistake to trust this man. Iohric works only for himself. He will use this alliance to gain a foothold, and then turn on our people after he has strengthened."

"Silence," hissed the Laird.

"This man Donnell has tried to kill me more than once," said Iohric to the Laird, glaring in Donnell's direction. "He is too dangerous to be allowed to go free."

"Perhaps you are right," said the Laird quietly, stroking his chin.

"Don't be a fool," called out Donnell, thumping the shaft of his spear on the road.

There was a moment of total silence, and then angry shouting began on all sides.

The Laird held up one armoured gauntlet, and in a few moments there was silence once again. "Now we can all see what kind of man stands before us," he said in a commanding voice. "One who disrespects his betters. Let it be widely proclaimed that the man Donnell of Cardhu has attacked one of my Luftenands with intent to murder..."

"He was no Luftenand at the time, my Laird, but a Norseman and a threat to my village!" said Donnell urgently, taking a step forward.

The Laird gave Donnell a steely glare, and continued. "He is therefore a criminal against the King's law, and will be executed forthwith."

Donnell winced in pain as two of the Laird's warriors grabbed hold of his arms, and forced him to his knees, causing him to drop his spear. Toirdelbach unsheathed his sword once again, took a step towards him, and raised the blade above his neck.

* * *

At this moment, the black-haired knight Mac Rath nudged his horse, and entered the circle. "My Laird, if I may speak," he said, and then continued without waiting for permission. "The woodsman and his friends have proven themselves to be valiant and resourceful this year. The new defences around Cardhu are remarkable, and some of the local crofters have been developed into an adequate defence force. I would suggest that these people simply need closer guidance. Let me take this group into employ in my personal household, to deal with..." – he looked from side to side – "*the issue we discussed earlier,*" he finished darkly.

The Laird held up his hand as he took a moment to consider this. After a short pause, he nodded, and then gestured to Toirdelbach to stand down.

"Very well. You will take them with you to your household at Castlecraik, and keep them out of trouble. My judgement is not nullified, but it is suspended for as long as these individuals are under your protection." Toirdelbach sheathed his sword with a scowl, while Iohric just stood and stared coolly at the companions.

The Laird now turned and faced his troops. "Now, come! A better kingdom can wait while we feast. Toirdelbach, men of Wherrycross! We will now feast at the new Luftenand's invitation. Stable the horses and bring the ale. Today we fill our stomachs, and tomorrow we will move upon my treacherous brother in Inverkip."

* * *

As the Laird and other leaders began to billet their horses and make ready for feasting, the companions hurried over to the side of the road where Niamh was lying. Donnell knelt down by the woman, but it didn't take him long to see that there was no hope of another miraculous reprieve, even with the healer's skill or the power of the stones.

He looked up at Fenella.

"The blow pierced her right through the heart," said the druidess grimly. "There was no way of saving her."

They all looked around at Sahar who was standing a few paces back. "I'm so sorry…" Donnell began, shaking his head as he approached her. The young woman's face was streaked with tears, but she looked more angry than upset. Fenella put an arm around her shoulders, but she shrugged the druidess off.

"That man Toirdelbach is a brute and a murderer," said Donnell, looking around at all of the companions. "He's little better than Iohric, in truth. I don't understand why the Laird would send someone like that here, never mind how he could expect him to lead the people.

Surely nobody in Cardhu will accept him after this?" As he glanced around the small group, he realised that he and Malcolm were the only ones to have grown up in Cardhu, and he himself was the only one to have spent a significant amount of time in Wherrycross. How much would the others even know about the Laird?

Perhaps he didn't either. "I trust that justice will eventually be done," he added quietly, and then looked around as the dark knight Mac Rath moved closer to the companions and dismounted.

"Thank you for your…" began Donnell, but the knight raised his hand for silence.

"I've no desire to see an injustice occur, Donnell, but there are bigger stakes in the game here. My father the Laird once hoped to ally himself with his brother Tudorr ab Owain in Inverkip against the Norse. Now, though, he has unfortunately developed greater ambitions. You will remember Ogledd, formerly the Luftenand of this place, and now one of my father's advisors? He has persuaded the Laird that with Iohric's ships, he can control the whole coast. But as you rightly said, it is foolish to trust the Norsemen."

"But what can we do to stop this?" asked Fenella.

Mac Rath nodded at the druidess. "There is time for talk and for planning later. For now, you all need to get moving before the Laird has a few cups of wine and changes his mind about your punishment. He has been known to execute troublemakers for sport if the mood takes him. Get what you need, then ride hard for the south until you get to my castle. You may use this horse, for there is no time to lose." He passed the reins of the huge black warhorse to Fenella.

The druidess glanced towards the keep, and then looked back at Mac Rath. "Thank you again. We will. But we will need to gather some things from the village, first – healing supplies and so forth. It should not take long."

"Move quickly as you do so, then," said Mac Rath. "My household is at Castlecraik, on the Laird's Road beyond Wherrycross. Or you can reach it by ship if it suits you better. When you get there, speak to my steward, Pherson, and he will find you lodgings." He patted the black stallion once more and stepped away. "I will meet you all there very soon on my return from the battle to come."

Loss

Donnell pushed open the door. It was a strange feeling, creeping into the Norse Keep which had sat there for these past months as a quiet, sullen challenge to everything that he knew: the kingdom, the village of Cardhu, their way of life.

Behind him, Sahar's hand was twitching slightly. He knew that she missed her crossbow and knives. But the only possible way to enter the keep had been in the guise of Norse troops – chainmail, helmets, cloaks and short swords – thanks to a pair of drunken Norse soldiers that they had easily overpowered. Meanwhile, Fenella and Malcolm had ridden the two horses – Mac Rath's stallion together with Eochaid's white mare – up to Cardhu to collect their belongings, and Donnell had agreed to meet his friends at the south end of the village. If he got away safely, that was. If they actually pulled off their audacious, foolish rescue mission, by the will of the gods.

As that thought came to him, he touched his hand to the amber brooch, moved forward through the door, and smiled slightly. Their hunch had been correct; the long passageway at the side of the keep had let to a storeroom, and now, in a tiny and otherwise bare chamber behind, there was a stairway leading down. To the dungeon, he presumed.

Just then he heard a voice behind them in the storage area, and he and Sahar looked at each other. His companion had taken a helmet with a visor which largely covered her face, but he could see her big dark eyes clearly enough, and a glimpse of her curly hair. There was focus and determination in those eyes.

There were sounds of movement from beyond the door – somebody was moving barrels or boxes around. More food for the feast? Slowly, Sahar drew the sword that hung at her hip, but Donnell raised his hand and put one finger to his lips. Nevertheless, he rested his own hand on the sword pommel at his side, and waited.

The noises from beyond receded. Had the person collected some supplies and then left? He fervently hoped so. With his eyes on the door that they had just come through, he took a quiet step towards the stairway, and began to make his way down. Sahar, however, moved to the side of the doorway itself, in a position that would make her hard to spot if the stranger entered.

Still keeping an eye out, Donnell took another step downwards, and then another. He was trapped now, he knew. At least in the entrance hall the pair could have made a break for it if they had been spotted. Now, it would surely mean the death of both of them if they were seen and identified.

The bronze key was clenched in his left hand, and he noticed how clammy and warm his palms had become. He glanced again upwards towards Sahar, who give the briefest of nods, crept across the room, and began to walk down the stairway after him.

* * *

Gabrán's brother Fáelán. His attacker – trusted by Fenella. The one they call Dark Shadow. As he descended towards the dungeon, Donnell pondered over the meaning of this name. A free spirit, hard to pin down? A rogue? Ruthless and dark-hearted like his brother? Gabrán's last act had been to stab one of his comrade Mor-druids in the back.

Perhaps the familiar name was more literal – he had a dark hair and beard, as Donnell recalled all too clearly. He certainly hoped so – but still his intuition told him that the man was a source of betrayal.

A single burning torch cast a flickering pool of light a few yards on from the foot of the stairs, reflecting on the bronze covering of a drain set in the stony floor. Donnell led the way towards and past it along a two-foot wide stony passageway. Shortly the passage ended at a pair of reinforced oak doors, one on each side. It was too dark here to see the key or make out much detail of the doors, but he felt in front of him carefully – sure enough, each door had a keyhole.

He tried the one to the right. The key rattled loudly as it twisted, but it did not open. He tried again, more firmly, but he couldn't make the thing turn. Looking back to Sahar, he handed the key to his friend, then went back to the torch and removed it from its sconce on the wall. More light was sure to help.

"Wrong lock," Sahar murmured after she had likewise tried the door on the right. Donnell nodded, trying to mentally picture the aspect from the outside of the keep. In a forest, his sense of direction was perfect, but in here he had somehow been turned around one more time than he had realised.

A voice came from behind the still-locked door on the right – it was hard to make out any words, but whoever was in the cell was shouting aggressively. "Dung – we need to hurry up," said Sahar softly, as she placed the key instead in the door on the left. It turned with a click.

Donnell put his hand on the door. Now, he would face the man who had attacked him – charged him down, nearly killed him – all those years ago. "Wait by the stairs, Sahar," he whispered. "Keep a lookout." The young woman walked slowly back up the corridor, sword held high.

As Donnell started to push the door, the torch to one side in front of his face, he was struck by a vision of his past. The forest. A boar charging towards him. The pain in his leg as it twisted its tusk and gored him.

He pulled his hand away. Yes, he trusted Fenella – but there was no need to be careless. He gently pulled the Norse short sword from its scabbard in the stolen belt, and held it in his right hand as he pushed at the door with his foot, causing it to swing back.

All was quiet. He walked in, two paces into the cell, the sword still held close to him in his right hand. He then raised the torch and looked around in confusion. Where were they? Was this the right chamber?

Sure enough, there was a high barred grate just below the ceiling of the cell, providing a modicum of afternoon light – this was where he had spoken to the inmates, there could be no doubt. And as he scanned the room, he saw a figure slumped against the wall. The druid, Fáelán? No – it was Güntar Schmidt, the bearded stranger. And the man was slumped against the wall behind the door, his chest covered in blood.

Donnell walked over and raised the torch towards the man's face, confirming his first impressions. The prisoner was dead. And a bloodstain showed that he had been slain by a weapon. Donnell's weapon.

Sheathing the short sword again, he stooped to pick up his father's knife, which had just made its first kill. It had been cleaned and set precisely on the ground, its blade pointing away from its victim and towards the window. Holding the weapon's handle with distaste, even though there were no vestiges of blood upon it, he tucked it inside the sword belt of the stolen guard outfit.

* * *

Sahar was crouching by the stairs and she rose as he approached. "Where is he?" she whispered.

"Gone."

"But the door was locked."

"I know." He looked back, as if peering into the shadows would make Fáelán appear. But he knew that his magically empowered eyesight had not missed anything.

He turned back to Sahar. "Let's move. There was another prisoner, but he's not going anywhere now."

"So he's…" she began.

"Dead, yes. Slain by the knife that I gave them to defend themselves. Fenella won't like to hear it, but…"

Sahar finished his sentence: "Her friend is a murderer."

Just then, a shout came from up above in the Norse language.

"Wait," whispered Sahar, "let me." She called back, and then engaged in a brief dialogue with the people up above using their own language.

Shortly, two Norse guards descended the stairs and paused at the bottom step, peering at Sahar and Donnell in the dim light. Sahar pointed towards the cell doors, and waved them onwards. With a slight nod, the pair passed them at the foot of the stairs, and began to walk along the narrow corridor towards the cells.

"Run," said Sahar.

The pair sprinted up the stairs, any pretence of innocence abandoned. Leaving the small chamber with the staircase, they entered the storeroom, and Donnell took a moment to block the door with several bulky sacks before turning and pursuing Sahar to the main corridor. Here they walked as swiftly as was tenable; they couldn't be seen to be fleeing, but they couldn't allow the guards to catch up with them either.

From the main banqueting hall to their right, the Laird's knights and their Norse hosts were easy to hear – feasting and yelling rowdily.

"Here," said Donnell, leading Sahar to the small ruined outhouse that he had noticed on his previous scouting mission to Weir. He pushed inside the abandoned building, and quickly divested himself of his armour, helmet and sword, keeping hold of only his own knife. Sahar hesitated. "Come on. We'll run home quicker without it," he said, and she followed his lead.

Peeking around the ruined building, Donnell saw that the same two guards were now at the main door of Longfort Keep; the pair called out towards several others who lined the pathway up to the main coast road, all of whom were drinking. Receiving little in the way of a response, they walked out to greet their comrades, and began shouting and pointing.

"If they are going that way, we will go the other," said Donnell quietly. He led on to the north, skirting the roundhouses of Weir village, and continued down towards the shore, moving low and stealthily.

* * *

It was a slow uphill walk back to Cardhu, cutting through the trees at the edge of the Laird's Road such that they would reach the main path at a point close to the village. The sun was descending over the sea behind them, and both Donnell and Sahar walked in silence, reflecting on what they had seen and experienced over the past couple of hours.

Niamh was dead, that much was clear. As was Luguwalos. And now a stranger lay in a bloody heap within the cell of Longfort Keep. As he walked, Donnell mulled over the events that had led to all three deaths.

Niamh had died standing up for Sahar – a woman that *he* brought to Cardhu. And she had only been a part of the parley with the Laird and his captains because he recommended the woman to Mac Rath as a potential Luftenand. It seemed all too likely that without his interventions, the woman would still be alive.

As for Luguwalos – a man he had never really taken the time to befriend – would he even still be in Macswain's service if Donnell had not cut short his own apprenticeship? And when he was struck down, it was by the arrows of boggles – creatures that *his* scouting mission had encountered and led back out towards Cardhu as they had fled. 'We need to scout them out', he had said to Macswain. And now her fellow hunter lay dead.

And for all he didn't really know Güntar Schmidt, he couldn't help but feel responsible for that death, too. More so, if anything. He mentally pictured the moment, in the dark by the back of the keep, when he had handed the knife to the renegade, sliding it in between the bars. *His* knife. *His* responsibility. He might as well have pushed it between Güntar's ribs himself.

Donnell realised that Sahar was looking at him. "Are you all right?" she asked. Her own cheeks were marked with tearstains.

"I'll be better when all of you are safe."

* * *

When they reached back to Cardhu, Donnell and Sahar first saw Fenella up ahead, looking for them. "I'm sorry," he called out as they approached, and shook his head. "We made it into the keep, but were too late. He was gone."

She looked aghast. "Killed, then?"

Donnell shook his head. "No. I mean, actually gone. Vanished. He must have somehow escaped."

"Or Iohric's men took him elsewhere," she mused, frowning.

Donnell hesitated. "It didn't look that way…" he began.

"Then there is hope. Thank you, Donnell – for trying. I'm relieved that you are both back safely."

Donnell considered explaining the scene that had greeted him in the Norse dungeon – the innocent man slain with the knife that he had handed to Fáelán – but decided that it was a discussion that could wait. For now, they needed to get out of Cardhu, and quickly.

Malcolm stood by the main village road not far beyond the druidess, holding the horses. He had saddled up Beira, and Donnell saw two bags of belongings slung behind his horse's saddle. Malcolm was also holding the white mare and Mac Rath's great black horse. Erik was there too, and had taken his usual horse from the stable.

"Trust me or not, it's your choice," said the big Norseman as Donnell and Sahar approached. "I can't stay here."

"I trust you," said Donnell, offering his hand to the tall warrior as he approached. And though he recognised a frosty glint in Sahar's eyes, she said nothing.

Together they hurried down the slight slope to the village square, which was unusually busy; many of the local people had witnessed the truce and had at first gathered to celebrate and feast, but the return of the body of Niamh had led to a great outpouring of sorrow. The companions paused a few dozen paces away, Malcolm still holding the horses' reins.

Just then Sahar sprinted across the remaining space. Kit and Rana were there, tears in their eyes, and she enfolded the two girls in a tight embrace. Branwen was just behind them; her face was dry, but she was clearly in shock at what had just happened. Leaving Sahar to her reunion, he took a few paces towards his old friend.

"Branwen. I'm so sorry. I can't believe that Niamh is gone." He paused. Branwen pressed her lips together tightly. Donnell cast his eyes to the ground to avoid her burning gaze and continued, "I feel terrible. I just wish I could somehow have stopped…" He was interrupted by her hand on his arm.

"You would have, I know you would. I heard you nearly got yourself killed." Her amber eyes were wide as he looked at her and he could see her distress, but a same calm determination was there as well. This was a woman who would take action when the time was right.

"I didn't do enough, in truth. I should have stopped when we saw the troops. We were trying…well. Trying to rescue someone."

She took a step towards him. "It can't be helped now," she said quietly. "People pass on, and we are left behind."

Donnell looked around. Sahar still had her arms around Niamh's teenage girls, and the toddler was clinging to her, too. This was a family that had experienced a lot of loss. Too much.

"Branwen, we need to leave now – all of us. Sahar and I have been banished, but the Laird's bastard son Mac Rath has offered us protection. Will you come too?" The suggestion somehow sounded less convincing when he said it out loud than it had done in his head.

"Did he offer me a role at his castle as well? And the same for the children?" She raised one eyebrow, gesturing towards the nearby girls.

"No," he admitted ruefully, "and I know we are not in much of a position to strike a bargain, but if…"

"Listen Donnell," she said, cutting him off, "I'd like nothing better than to saddle up and ride off with you. But this is the children's home. They've lost their mother, and this is their village – it's all that's familiar. I need to be here with them."

"I'm just not sure it's safe anymore," he replied.

She nodded. "Well, if not, then we will do something about it. Or we will leave, if there is no other way – find a new village. A safer one."

He nodded. "And as for Toirdelbach, his time will come. I promise."

"Yes. It will."

"Speak again soon, gods willing." He turned to leave, and then looked back. "Branwen – all those years ago. When I ran from the path, I was trying to help. To try to draw the boggles away from you."

She raised her eyebrows. "Do you think I've been cross with you all this time?"

He smiled slightly. "I suppose not. Well, I just wanted to let you know, I was sorry about how things worked out."

She nodded, and he turned to leave.

* * *

On horseback, five companions rode past the Celtic Rock – Donnell, Sahar, Erik, Fenella and Malcolm. They passed Tarin's farm and turned to skirt the abandoned crofts to the south of the village, following the same route that Donnell had used to ride south earlier in the year. But this time, he didn't attempt to lead them up the clifftops. They would follow the ancient path until they reached the road, and from there ride to safety at Mac Rath's castle.

"Well for now, we are fugitives," said Fenella, riding alongside Donnell as they left the village. It was now the early evening, and they were beginning to feel hungry, and in need of rest.

"Yes. For as long as the Laird lives," said Donnell. "And soon he will see that Iohric is not the ally that he expects."

Malcolm was just ahead of them, and he nodded and looked around. "I don't wish any harm to the Laird," he says. "But if that comes to pass, we will return." He looked to Fenella. "The druids too, of course."

"My people are splintered, lost," said Fenella. "But the way ahead is clear. There is still hope that we will find Fáelán, for he is the last of his clan. And the lost white druid stone must also be returned – my brethren will find a way – and a fifth member of the circle found to wield it."

"Fen," began Donnell, and hesitated. He looked over at Sahar and she nodded but did not speak.

He looked down at his reins for a moment as he formulated a response. "Fáelán is not going to join your circle," he said after a pause. "He knew I was coming back, remember, but he fled all the same. And he did not merely escape – he murdered his cellmate. I found the man lying dead in the dungeon. It can't have been the Norse that did it. Fenella, he used my knife to kill an innocent man. And I think, from the way he put the knife down – pointing towards the window and to the ocean – that he meant to send a message that he is gone, and has no intention of returning."

"You heart was long since turned against the Dark Shadow, Donnell," she replied quietly. "This can't be true."

"I saw what I saw."

As her horse continued to trot forward, Fenella was silent for a long while. At last she turned to look at him. "If what you say is true, then the last of another druid clan has turned from us," she said at last. "But I cannot believe it, even after all these years. If he is still out there somewhere, I must speak with him. I have to hear his side."

Donnell sighed, gazing out over the sea. "I think that is a mistake. It would put you at risk."

"It must be done."

He looked around at her. "Then the challenge is greater than ever. But you are not alone, Fenella. We will be beside you as you rebuild the circle. We won't rest until the work is done."

The others nodded, and Fenella was silent again for a moment, all four of them looking at her as they rode. She was silhouetted against the last embers of the evening sun as it sank over the island mountains.

"Thank you," she said. "Then let's get going."

* * *

Thank you for reading The Twisted Forest - I hope you enjoyed it. The story continues in <u>The Mythic Spear</u>, *the next book in the Druid Stones Saga. Keep reading now for an extract!*

Chapter 1 – Battling with Boggles

An arrow flew from the stand of willow trees ahead, and Donnell ducked down. Looking around, he signalled downward with his hand held flat – *keep low.* He saw Sahar hunker down further behind the tree stump where she had taken shelter.

They were outnumbered, pinned back, and if they tried to move they would both be shot for sure.

Since fleeing their home in the wake of banishment by the Laird of Wherrycross and Cunninghame, Cennaid ab Owain, Donnell and his companions had found themselves under the protection of Mac Rath, the Laird's bastard son. However, Mac Rath himself had travelled north with an army, ready to meet the Laird's rebellious brother in battle. In his absence, his Steward – a man named Pherson – had tasked Sahar and Donnell with tackling the increasing threat posed by large, well-armed groups of boggles around the road which connected Castlecraik to the town of Wherrycross.

Donnell looked ahead once again, and crawled a couple of feet forward. He was in a slight hollow within a clearing, with a fallen, half-rotten log immediately ahead of him. Glancing at it, he wondered whether the decaying wood was sound enough to stop an arrow. It seemed doubtful.

Raising his body a fraction, he saw the gang of boggles at the edge of the nearby cluster of trees – three attackers were on the ground, and a further two of the monstrous little creatures had climbed high among the yellowing birch branches. One of the standing ones was an especially large and vicious-looking brute. Partially armoured, it was holding a rusted curved sword of the type that Donnell had sometimes seen used by traders from the south. The others were wielding short bows.

He pulled his small throwing knife clear from its holster, and made a double click with his tongue. In response, he heard three taps of wood on metal from where Sahar was waiting. One of many signals the pair had developed over recent weeks, this signified a coordinated attack after covering fire.

Three. Two. One. Donnell sent the knife arcing towards the spot where the lead boggle had been standing, and at the same moment, he heard a ping as Sahar released a crossbow bolt. Then he rolled to the right, got up, and charged forward.

His knife clanged off the metal breastplate of his target just as he moved, while Sahar's bolt exploded into a branch and sent shards of broken wood flying across the scene. They had got lucky – a dead branch with fragile wood. Its disintegration was enough of a distraction to their assailants.

Donnell spun his spear in the air as he approached the boggles, hitting the two nearby archers simultaneously with its shaft, and sending them stunned to the ground. The pair in the trees shrieked and leaped away. Sahar, approaching from Donnell's right, gave chase to them, while Donnell faced off against the leader to his left.

The creature had a wicked grinning face, and was a head height taller than most boggles. It swung its curved sword towards Donnell's neck, and he took a step backwards to dodge the blow. Raising his spear to chest height, he jabbed twice at his foe, but the boggle leader dodged both times and then swung its sword at the spear itself, knocking it from Donnell's grasp.

Without stopping to retrieve his spear, Donnell stepped in. He pulled his dagger from his belt and slashed upwards at the creature; his blade raked across its hideous face and it shrieked and fled, clutching at the wound.

Meanwhile, the stunned pair of boggle archers had started to rise up. The nearest one shot at him again, but its arrow flew wide; Donnell picked up his spear and charged in, but as he did so it swiped at him using its bow as a club, catching him hard on the temple and dropping its bow in the process. In response he spun round, his spear tip slashing towards the pair of wicked creatures, but both managed to step out of its way. One dropped its bow and raised its hands in surrender, while the other pulled a knife and stabbed towards Donnell's stomach. He sidestepped, and then ran the boggle through with his spear. Its companion then fled.

Ignoring it, Donnell bent down to pick up both bows; he snapped them and dropped them to the ground, and then tucked his attacker's dropped dagger into his belt.

There was a rustling to his right and he raised his spear again, only to see Sahar step out. He smiled as he walked towards her, but her gaze was fixed on a spot just behind him. She raised her crossbow and fired, and Donnell could feel the bolt as it whistled past the beard on his cheek. Turning, he saw the look of surprise on the lead boggle as he sank to the ground, staring down at a crossbow bolt which was protruding from his chest.

"You still need to be more careful," said Sahar with a nod at the creature's collapsed form. "He had returned to cut your throat." She walked forward to lift the weapons from their fallen attacker, and, while Donnell found and picked up his throwing knife, she broke its bow, rendering it useless.

"Let's go," she said. "We can see if Fenella has returned to the castle yet."

* * *

Donnell continued to rub his temple as they walked, and his friend glanced up. "You're developing quite a bruise," she said, "right across that side of your face." Donnell noticed that she was bleeding slightly from a gash on her cheek, but knew better than to fuss.

"The other two?" he asked as they walked.

"Both down, both stripped of their weapons," she said, narrowing her eyes. "Wounded, but I think they'll live."

As agreed with their new master, their policy was to avoid killing the boggles where possible, but to disarm them at all costs. According to Pherson, Mac Rath's instructions were to keep the roads around his castle safe, but he had decided it would be best not to provoke retribution from the malicious small creatures that haunted the forest.

Now, as he and Sahar made their way back along an overgrown path towards the road, Donnell gazed across to the islands, and down the cliffs of the coast. It was a beautiful place – and would be a great location for hunting in better times. From the rocky cliffs that marked Wherrycross town along to Castlecraik itself on its hill, the land to the south sloped more and more gently towards the sea in the distance, and the forest receded eastwards. This left a swathe of flat, fertile farmland, which he knew stretched all the way south to the Riverlands of Ayr, a fertile grassy valley that made the Laird of that region famously wealthy through his vast herds of black cattle.

As they left the last stands of woodland, the paved road came into view up ahead. To their left it led back to Castlecraik, the home of Mac Rath, who was now their master and protector. To the right, the same road carried on northwards towards Wherrycross. They walked southwards for a few minutes, as the road ran very close to coastal cliffs on one side and an outcropping of the forest on the other, marked by majestic oak trees.

"Wait," whispered Donnell, holding up his hand to signal to Sahar, who immediately stopped. He peered southwards down the road for a moment longer. A cluster of people stood in the distance, partially hidden by thorn bushes; from here, most people would just assume that it was a regular group of merchants or small farmers. Yet since he had begun wearing the mysterious druid's brooch with its amber gemstone, Donnell's vision had been enhanced far beyond normal capabilities.

"What is it?" Sahar said quietly, shading her eyes and coming closer to stand at his shoulder.

"An ambush, is what it is," he replied. "Merchants at first glance, but there is armour beneath their cloaks, and I spy iron helmets with visors, too."

"Strange. How many can you make out?"

"Six on the road. Another ten at least concealed behind the bramble bushes."

"Mac Rath is going to want to know about this. So, what do you think? Can we skirt around the back of them? Take a couple out with crossbow bolts?"

"We're not going to risk attacking them, Sahar. There's only two of us, and we've no need to engage."

"You think they'll let us past?"

"I'm sure that they won't." He licked his lips, and looked in both directions. "We could take a long circular route through the forest, but with the sun low in the sky, and the place still crawling with angry boggles, I don't think that would be wise."

"Then we'll need to go directly to the coast, and pick our way along the beach. It will be slow, but we'll get there."

"I have a better idea. What would you say to calling at the home of Eochaid? It's about time we caught up with Malcolm."

Sahar paused, and gazed northwards in the direction of the small town. It wasn't safe for them to travel there since the Laird had threatened Donnell with a death sentence, and then, after reprieving him, banished the entire group of companions. On the other hand, they were under Mac Rath's protection, and were in principle free while they remained that way. They were unlikely to be challenged as long as they didn't draw too much attention to themselves.

"It's possible that Fenella will have stopped there too, on her travels," he added. "And if we see any other travellers coming this way, we can warn them about the ambush."

She nodded. The druidess had become one of their closest companions over recent months, and had saved Sahar's life when she had been grievously injured by the Norse leader, Iohric. Now Fenella was determined to reunite her brethren and the powerful druid stones which they carried. As such, she had left Castlecraik shortly after their arrival to seek out her remaining companions and work with them to restore the Mor-druid circle, returning only occasionally and very briefly. Her other companions – including Erik, who had duties at the castle – had been anxiously waiting for news since she had set out on her most recent expedition a week ago.

"Very well," she replied, glaring at him, "but I want to avoid bumping into any of the Laird's troops. They may remember our faces." Sahar didn't say it, but she had been singled out and attacked due to her Moorish appearance by one of the Laird's knights, and the incident still troubled her deeply.

"I know, my friend. Don't worry. There is a hidden way into Eochaid's home that we can use to avoid any unwanted attention. And it's on this side of town."

With a shrug, Sahar walked out onto the road, and they began to retrace their steps, proceeding northwards towards the town. The weather had been dry, and the route became sandy and dusty as they walked northwards into the gathering gloom, with tall, dry grasses on either side.

The main town gates of Wherrycross, east facing, came into view up ahead before they saw another traveller on the road – a single merchant with a small cart loaded up with seafood, headed for Castlecraik. Donnell signalled him to halt, and relayed the information about the outlaws upon the road. "They're not far on from here. Please turn back, and see that a message reaches the Laird's Marischal, so that other travellers are warned not to set out tonight."

After this exchange, Donnell led Sahar off the road and onto a small, dusty, circular path that ran outside of the town wall towards the shore. They slowly rounded the settlement; at times the path skirted the wall itself, and at other points it weaved in between some small, poorly-tended crofts. Some crofters were occupied on their plots, but most were gathered near to the buildings, speaking to one another in hushed tones. Only the children appeared carefree, as they played noisily in the mild evening.

Before long, Donnell spied the distinctive cluster of rocks upon a hillock that he had been looking for. "Here," he said, as Sahar almost walked past.

"So that's it," she said. "I must have been in a daydream – I didn't see those rocks at all."

* * *

Leading the way, Donnell climbed up between the rocks and the town wall into a raised gap. There, it was apparent that this area had once been part of an older fortification, long-since disused; cut stone, corroded and weathered for what looked like many lifetimes, merged onto the larger rocks from the back. Some were marked with faded runes.

"This was a great city wall, or even part of a castle, I think," said Sahar softly, running her hands across one of the rocks. "It's badly degraded, but you can still see what fine workmanship there once was here. Much better than anything you can find in this area today."

"I didn't really notice, my friend."

"Pay attention, Donnell. It's useful to see what could be achieved if the right knowledge is in place."

But Donnell was now looking in a different direction. "I think it's up here, somewhere, but I…oh! Yes, this is it. That was lucky – last time I came the other way, and I didn't know how long it would take me to recognise it from this direction." Donnell reached down and pulled at a small brass ring, and then lifted what looked like an impossibly large rock, but was in fact just a thin layer of stone attached to a round iron trapdoor. The mechanism was silent and smooth as he lifted, and despite the size of the trapdoor, raising it was almost effortless.

"Down here," he said, nodding, and allowing himself to slide forward so that he was sitting on the edge of the entrance way with his legs dangling down. "Follow me."

"You think I'm going to climb into some dark, worm-infested hole just because you say so?" said Sahar, frowning. And then she smiled, and punched his shoulder. "Only joking. Hurry up, by the great god."

The pair clambered down, dropping just a couple of feet down onto smooth ground below, and Donnell reached up to reset the trapdoor. Whoever had constructed the tunnel had given some thought to light, as there were circular holes on both sides which somehow illuminated the path without having been visible from above, presumably making use of gaps between clusters of dark rocks. It was also nearly dry underfoot.

"This is – also nicely done," said Sahar, glancing around. "And we can get to Eochaid's place this way?"

"It's connected directly to his home. Runs all the way under the town wall. Let's go."

He led the way, Sahar following close behind and marvelling at the neat construction. Donnell, too, took more time to admire the workmanship than he had done before. For some reason, he hadn't asked Bib about this when he had used the route to escape from Wherrycross back in the springtime.

Ahead was an oak door, which again opened silently and with just the slightest effort. It revealed a set of stone stairs. This time Sahar took the lead, following the flight of the stairs as they wound upwards in a double spiral, before coming out into a large and wholesome-smelling cellar, exactly square, and with a large number of chests and barrels on display around its edge. A further flight of steps, wooden this time, led up from the opposite side. At the top of these steps, they could see a door – and it swung open as they looked on.

"Hello?" called Donnell.

Just then he heard the click of a crossbow being cocked.

Want to read on? Find out more at https://www.jfdanskin.com

THE DRUID STONES SAGA BOOK 3
THE MYTHIC SPEAR
J.F. DANSKIN

Join my mailing list

If you would like to read *The Bonding*, a novella which reveals more about about Donnell's back story and his first encounter with The Dark Shadow, why not sign up to my mailing list at https://bookhip.com/JKLSDR. You will also be one of the first to hear about my new books as they are launched and other promotions I share.

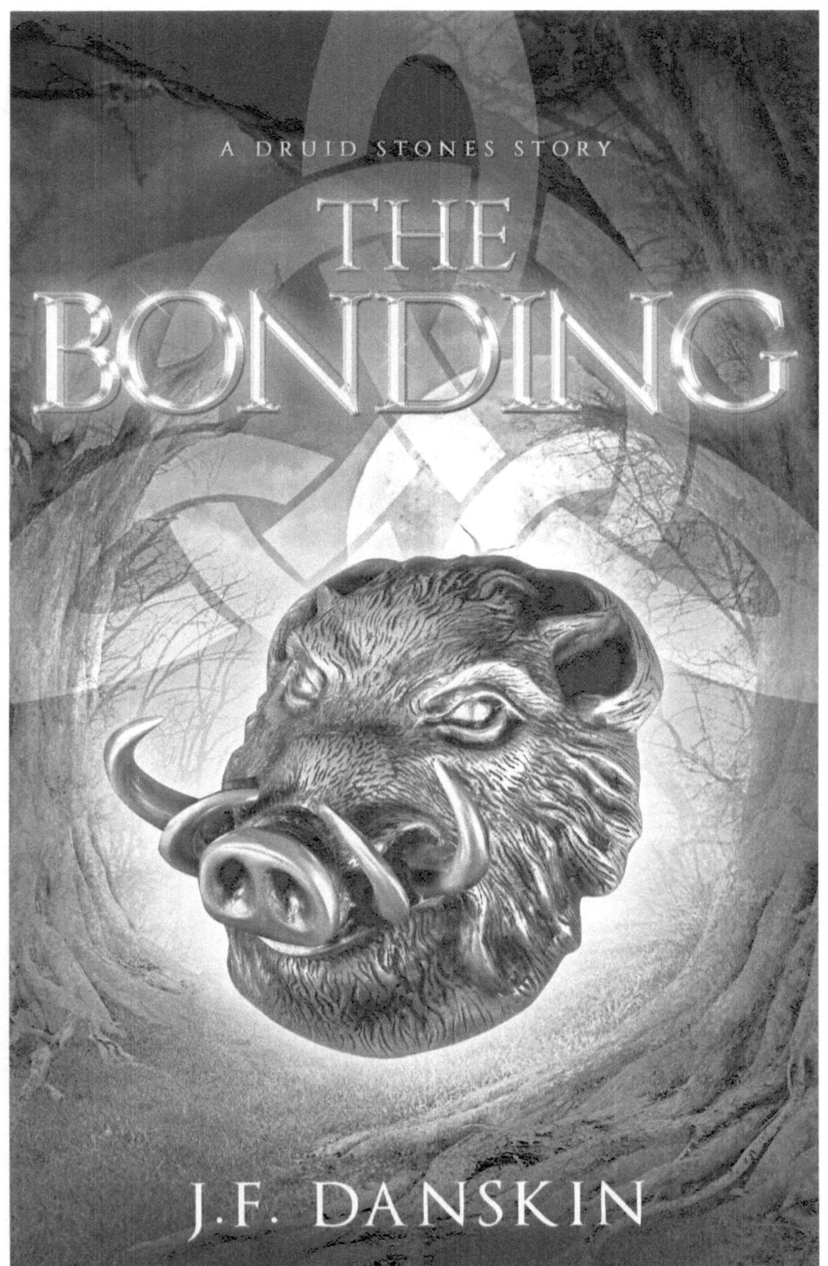
A DRUID STONES STORY
THE BONDING
J.F. DANSKIN

The Bonding (A prequel novella to Druid Stones Saga)

When you are chosen – what choice do you have?

Scotland: 9th century. Two friends await their traditional community bonding ceremony. Donnell thinks he knows his fate, while his friend Malcolm anticipates rejection. Haunted by a mystical encounter in the woods, both young men embark separately on their apprenticeships: Donnell with a mixture of excitement and guilt, and Malcolm with resignation – and a lasting bitterness. When fate brings them together again on a quest to find a renegade druid, Donnell's choices could affect the future of the realm – and directly threaten his own future too.

Scottish mythology and ancient Celtic lore meet historical fantasy in this prequel novella to the whole Druid Stones Saga.

https://bookhip.com/JKLSDR

Author Note

When I wrote this book, I was excited to explore more facets of life in Cardhu, as well as more about the nearby forest – including the creatures that live within it! I love trees and forests myself, and one of my aims was for each book in the series to introduce at least one new creature from Celtic myth. The wulver in this story is a good example.

I also began writing the first draft in the summer (having written *The Broken Circle* in the spring), so I was certainly inspired by my own surroundings – the hotter weather, the look of the land and plants (tall thistles, for example), and the way people act and speak when they are spending more time outdoors – not something that happens much in Scotland at other times of year!

<u>Notes on *The Twisted Forest*</u>

Some Scots words used during the books of this series:

Burn – a small stream or rivulet.

Drystane - a method of building walls with stone without mortar or cement.

Hame - the Scots word for home.

Laird - a Scots term for 'lord', referring to the local rulers who are subservient to the King.

Axe - we can assume that the axe used by Iohric in this story has been passed down through the generations. Historically, there was indeed a fabled axe used by Harald Wartooth, a great king of Denmark who was eventually slain at the Battle of Bråvalla, around a century before our saga is set. As he is both deadly with the axe and a great warrior despite his advanced age, Harald's story reminds me of the classic fantasy novel, *Druss the Legend*.

Eas Mòr - as Donnell says, "From these cliffs come the falls that gave the village its name". Eas Mòr simply means 'great falls', and there are several locations with that name around Scotland today.

Gift to the forest folk - there are many Scottish folk tales of forest people, fey spirits, sprites, boggles or elves receiving gifts in exchange for their magic.

Ímar and Olaf the White – these are real historical figures. Referred to by Erik as the great king who rules from Dublin (Dubh-Linn), Ímar was the founder of a dynasty of warlords known as the Uí Ímair, who went on to control the Irish Sea region for generations. It is unclear whether the historical figure is the same as *Ivar*, a major Viking ruler in England at around the same time. There is also dispute about the exact identity of Olaf the White – but the Tolkien-esque name was just too much to resist!

Keep - the Norse Keep in our story is built in a just a few weeks, which no doubt seems astonishingly fast. However, there is historical evidence of Norse invaders achieving this, particularly a century or two later. Often a wooden fortress would be built at first, and then this would be replaced with stone. There are also, of course, plenty of historical instances of conquerors using forced labour for building.

Norðreyjar - translating to 'north islands', this is the ancient Norse-British name for the northern Scottish islands, Orkney and Shetland. What we now call the Hebrides or Western Isles, as well as the Isle of Man, were referred to as *Suðreyjar* (*'south islands*).

Pacts with the Norse - although the specific deal made between the local Laird and the Norse in our story is not directly based on historical evidence, there are plenty of historical examples of local people making pacts with Norse leaders as the Vikings moved from purely raiding to colonisation at around the time of our story. One of the best-known examples is the Treaty of Saint-Clair-sur-Epte, signed between Charles the Simple, King of the Franks, and the Viking warlord Göngu-Hrólfr (meaning 'Hrólfr the Walker' – one of the inspirations behind Iohric in our story). According to the historical record, Hrólfr agreed to protect the area against other Vikings and to accept the Christian religion, and in exchange he was granted the Duchy of Normandy, which would later be the seat of the Norman conquests of England.

Thistles - thistles are a symbol of Scotland today, and are in fact the oldest national flower in the world. Their importance to the Scots dates back to the Battle of Largs in 1263, during which times Norse warriors invaded mainland Scotland. The story goes that sleeping Scots warriors were woken and alerted to the presence of the Norsemen because some of the invaders stood on the spiky plants, causing them to shout in pain. Although this took place in a later time period than the *Druid Stones Saga*, it is amusing to consider that the thistle gained its significance because it alerted Scots warriors to the presence of Norse invaders, while in this story, locals use the plant to hide quietly behind.

Wulver - the wulver features in Scots mythology, and that of other Celtic peoples. It is a creature with the head of a wold and the body of a man, but unlike werewolf myths, it was not thought to be a shapeshifter. And as Fenella states in the story, wulvers were not thought to be aggressive if left in peace.

About the Author

J. F. Danskin is a Scottish writer of fantasy novels. His work spans several sub-genres and he is currently writing and publishing the *Druid Stones Saga*, a historical fantasy series and the LitRPG *Shadow Kingdoms* series.

Published titles by J. F. Danskin
The Broken Circle https://books2read.com/DruidStones1
The Twisted Forest https://books2read.com/DruidStones2
The Mythic Spear https://books2read.com/DruidStones3
The Winter Tower http://books2read.com/DruidStones4

Connect with me:
https://www.jfdanskin.com
https://www.facebook.com/jfdanskin
https://bookhip.com/JKLSDR